D0825221

Restless Town

Restless Town

#10
thank you

★

Madison Scott-Clary

Also by Madison Scott-Clary

Arcana — A Tarot Anthology, ed.

Rum and Coke — Three Short Stories from a Furry Convention

All works © Madison Scott-Clary the year of their publication as stated in the afterword. These works are licensed under the Creative Commons Attribution 4.0 International License. To view a copy of this license, visit *creativecommons.org/licenses/by/4.0/* or send a letter to Creative Commons, PO Box 1866, Mountain View, CA 94042, USA.

All characters are fictional and any resemblance to actual people, living or dead, is unintentional. The town of Sawtooth, ID is, with apologies to the residents of the real town Sawtooth City, fictional as well, and not intended to represent any one particular place.

This book uses the fonts Gentium Book Basic, Tom's New Roman, and Ubuntu Mono and was typeset with X͙ǝʟᴬTᴇX.

ISBN: 978-1-948743-09-9

Restless Town

Cover © 2019 Julian Norwood
www.patreon.com/Cadmiumtea

First Edition, 2019.

10 9 8 7 6 5 4 3 2 1

Content warning: Many stories contain frank descriptions of sensuality and sexuality; *Centerpiece* contains explicit decription of a BDSM party and some shaky negotiation; *You're Gone* contains frank discussion of grief and death; *Every Angel is Terrifying* contains explicit description of depression, self-harm, and suicidality; *What Defines Us* contains mentions of abuse; *A Theory of Attachment* contains explicit description of mental health issues and a mention of abuse.

The Fool

The badger looms over a small table, the short sleeve of her smock tugged down by a glass candy thermometer. A deck of colorful cards rest neatly stacked on its surface.

Contrary to expectations, the room is bright and spacious. No hint of incense or dark velour drapes, just a simple living room in a simple home, a simple badger and some simple cards. She can't be older than fifty, and she's of a more motherly bent than a mystical one.

More motherly than my mother, at least, I think. *More earthy and far less mystical.*

"Tell me about your day, Avery," she begins, and as I speak, she shuffles a worn deck of cards, nodding along with me. She draws cards yan tan tethera, and lays them face up on the table with a casual slowness that does little to distract from my words. Still, my language is stilted, and I find myself tracing the edges of the table with my gaze or watching her paws rather than making eye contact.

"Now," she says when I trail off to an uneasy silence. The badger, the table and cards, a bright room with motes in afternoon sunbeams; an image more meaningful than I anticipated. And me—

1

dingy clothes draped over a broad frame I never wanted—out of place. "Here are three cards. Look, and tell me the first thing you notice."

"Notice?" I ask. I sound dubious even to myself.

"Notice," she confirms. "What do you see? When you look at the cards, what jumps out at you? Colors, motions, angles and lines. What do you see?"

I stare at the badger. She stares back, then lets out a disarming laugh and gestures down at the cards.

Three cards, laid out in a line. I move my stare to those, more bewildered than anything, trying to pick out singular things. "From each of them? One at a time?"

She shrugs, smiling not unkindly.

Odd, I think. *How such a small task could feel overwhelming.*

I puff out a breath of air, whiskers bristling, and tap at the first card. "Well, this one's upside down, for starters. The, uh...Page of Wands." Digging through memories, I try, "A page is like a squire or something, right? Someone who helps a knight?"

"Yes, a young person, someone in training." She grins and nods down to the remaining stack of cards. "There are knights in the deck, too, but that's for another time."

Whiskers still canted forward, I nod and hesitate for a moment. "So, what does it being upside down mean?"

"You tell me."

I roll my eyes. Still, she sounds kind rather than petulant or snide, so I think about upside-down cards. Upside-down figures, upside-down and tipped over, upset in the literal sense of the word. Upside-down meanings. Meanings inverted, reversed, turned over.

"I think I see." I intend it as the beginning of a sentence, but seeing the badger's smile widen, I leave it at that. I shut out the other cards, focus on the Page. "In training, hmm? They look like they're investigating or contemplating. The, uh...I guess the wand. The wand is the only thing growing, the only thing with green in the entire scene."

"Learning about life. Investigating growth." The badger nods, but neither confirming nor sage. Simply agreeing. "But reversed."

"Not learning?" At this, I sense her expression close down. It's not a visible thing; it's a sensation of her movement of thought being put on hold. "Not...not doing anything with learning, perhaps?"

The badger nods. I can see the clip on her thermometer holding it to the over-washed fabric, see beads of sugar still clinging to glass, bobbing with her movements. "Wands are for beginnings, for doing. Or perhaps activating is better." She sets a paw next to the card. "This Page—a bear, maybe? I've never figured that out—is learning, but not moving, not beginning. There is knowledge, but no decision."

"Activation energy!" I blurt, and, seeing questions in her eyes, continue. "Like in chemistry. It's dorky, but there has to be enough energy for an electron to jump from one sphere to the next; it just sits there otherwise. It needs the proper amount of activation energy to get going."

Questions turn to understanding, but her gaze stays locked on mine, waiting.

"I don't have the energy."

"Perhaps not. Or perhaps you do, but you're—you or something within you—is not letting it reach the activation. The energy may be there, but blocked."

I have to restrain myself from a snide smile. A reaction to my mom's mysticism, maybe. To crystals and blocked energy. In the badger, though, I sense only earnestness. "Energy as in will? Purpose?"

She shrugs. My choice, apparently.

"Everything's yellow in the card–"

"Energetic color, yellow."

"–yellow except for the black of the salamanders on their coat-thing."

She nods, murmurs down to the card, "His creations, perhaps. How many full ones do you see?"

I lean closer, nudging glasses further up my blunt snout. "Two, maybe three out of a dozen or so."

"If the card were upright, those other ones would be creations yet to happen." Her voice carries knowledge, and more authority than she's shown yet. "Reversed, that becomes flipped around. It could be creations abandoned, or it could be things you're afraid to start.

"These cards named after people or titles—the page, the knight, the king, the queen—they're sometimes about people. Maybe this card's about you. Or they all could be. Maybe–"

I smirk, nod my head toward the second card. "So I'm the fool?"

"Maybe they're just facets of yourself." She finishes, returning my smirk.

Thus chastened, I look at the second card. "Okay, well, there's a dog, one of those breeds with short fur, though it doesn't look like any of the dogs I've met. He's–" I catch myself, seeing androgyny in the dog's features and tamping down the yearning for my own. "They're stepping toward the edge of a cliff, with a little spirit thing dancing at their feet. They have one of those sticks with a bag tied to the end, but their tunic thing is what has me thinking. It's all growing things." I lean in closer and add, "And little splashes of water. Green and blue with flowers on navy."

We sit in silence for a moment while I think about the card more.

"There's a good balance of colors, come to think of it. More than the Page, at least. Blue and green and red and yellow." I hesitate, staring at the lean canine muzzle: the balance continues there, masculine and feminine, hard and soft, focused and uncaring. I say nothing, and wonder why.

The older woman nods slowly. "It's a fancy shirt, no denying. It'd look good on you."

I laugh, to which she looks up, smiling. "Seriously. It's a good mix. You're a good mix, too. But you wear all drab colors. Why's that?"

There's a sudden flush to my cheeks, at my appearance being so deliberately addressed. I lay my ears back. A blush along with the first hints of annoyance. These are soon replaced with simple embarrassment. "I don't want to– I mean, I don't think I'd look good in bright colors or fancy clothes."

"I think you would." She hastens to continue, speaking over my mounting disagreements, "I think you'd look good, if you dressed how you wanted. Don't you?"

I frown at her. She continues, "You didn't say you don't want to dress in bright colors and fancy clothes. You started to say you didn't want to do something else."

I held my breath. Anger is the wrong word for what I feel. Frustration? Humiliation, perhaps. Am I so transparent?

"I don't want to," I begin in a rush of pent-up breath, feeling that struggle blown out with it. My shoulders sag, and I complete the statement more slowly. "I don't want to be seen like that."

"The fool, here, they're everything. They're the beginning of all things, and they've already got all of the endings inside themselves. At the beginning of all journeys, there's the fool: taking that first step is a fool's gamble, after all." She pauses, looking at me earnestly, intently. "You caught yourself earlier, you said 'he' and then switched to 'they'."

I hunch down into my slouched shoulders, muzzle dipping as I struggle for words. "They looked– I mean, It's on my mind, I guess."

"I'll come clean," she admits after a pause, dark paws fiddling with the remainder of the deck, straightening cards. "Your mom told me you were coming, so I know that much. Even if she hadn't, though, it's written on your face. I mean this in the best possible way, Avery, but you don't make a very good man."

I close my eyes. I shut out the cards, the motherly badger. Motherly in the sense of speaking truths, in the sense of knowing children, in having seen them grow up. Motherly in lived experience. Experience lived in the moment, not in some dream world of crystals and chakras. *More motherly than my mom,* I think.

When I open my eyes, her gaze has softened.

"Why three cards?" I ask, deflecting.

"Past, present, and future." She laughs.

I nod, then sit up a little straighter, murmuring, "So it's more that past me that didn't have the activation energy?"

"Or didn't want to use it, yes."

"That makes more sense, then."

"How so?"

I shrug, continuing, "If I'm at the beginning of something now, it's because of how much time I spent fretting—and not starting—

before."

She nods. "And are you at the beginning of something now?"

"I think so." I sound dubious, even to myself.

"Why now?"

"College," I say.

"Away from home?"

"Mmhm."

She nods again. "It's a little freeing, isn't it? Being away from parents. So you, like the Page of Wands, have been investigating, leaving all that energy pent up inside. And now you're ready to...to what? Take that step?"

I catch myself fiddling with the hem of my shirt. It's an olive color, faded further into drabness by countless washings, no fancy tunic; even her washed-out smock is brighter than my shirt. It doesn't go with my fur. Nor do the well-worn khakis. A darker animal dressed in those would look rough and tumble, ready for a hike. A mountain lion looks like a mess of dirty laundry.

I look up from my dull self to the table once more, speaking to the cards. "I have an appointment to start talking about it—talking about gender—with a counselor."

"Congratulations," the badger says, smiling. And I realize she doesn't need to say anymore. I realize *that's* what I needed from my mom. I realize that's probably why my mom sent me here. I realize that there's probably more to my mom than I gave her credit for.

I realize I've stopped thinking of this—the tarot card reading—as something mystical.

I speak up, "The third card, then."

The badger returns her gaze to the table.

"It feels impenetrable to me."

She laughs and shakes her head. "It's not a book. You're not writing a report on its deeper meanings. You're picking up on some of those meanings, but you don't have to do it right away or all the time. Or at all, for that matter." Still grinning, guides my attention back down to the card with a gesture, badger and cougar looming over the table. "Just tell me what you see."

Abashed, I return her smile as best I can. "Alright. It's a...well, I want to say a woman and a child being ferried across a lake or something, but the boat they're in has six swords in it. They're upright, like they've been stabbed through the bottom of the boat."

"Stabbed? Like they're going through the wood?"

"Yeah."

"Is water coming up around them?"

I look harder. The bottom of the boat is pitch dark. "I can't tell, but no one seems in a rush to get them out, anyway."

This gets a chuckle. "No, no they don't. Maybe they're plugging the holes in the boat. Maybe it's best to leave them in."

Nodding, I keep looking at the card. There are lines to draw the attention. The swords, the boat, the pole of the oarsman, the horizon, the water...the water. "The front of the boat, where the swords are, isn't sinking. The people still weigh something, though. Look, the back of the boat's low in the water."

She nods, "Maybe they–"

"Like they don't weigh anything," I add hastily, cutting her short.

"–don't weigh anything, yes."

I lay my ears back and grin, "Sorry, didn't mean to trample."

She returns my grin, pats my tan paw in her black one. "You're excited. It's really nice to see."

"So why swords?"

"I don't know. What do swords do?"

I laugh. "Cut and stab. Kill people. Stuff like that."

"Fair enough," she chuckles. "Why would one do that?"

Her words stop me short. "To...to kill," I begin. "But that's what I just said. Are you asking me why people kill each other?"

She nods.

"To get something," I murmur, fumbling for words. "To gain something. To get what one wants, or needs."

"So, since this is the Tarot and there's bound to be a lot going on here, can we just say the swords are a tool?"

"Well, I'm not about to hack and slash my way to get what I want."

She leans in close to me, stage-whispering, "I'll let you in on a secret. None of the cards in the swords suit—in any suits—show blood. Death, yes. Change, definitely. But no blood. It's hardly hacking and slashing."

"But they're still–"

She holds up a paw, "They're still swords, but they're tools. Swords show work. Strife, sometimes, sure; striving toward a goal. But what they is show work. These swords aren't working right now, they're just standing there. So where is the striving?"

"Behind them?" I ask. "The figures are all facing away from something."

"Or toward something."

"So," I say hesitantly. "I'm going to go on a journey?"

She laughs, "Can you guess what my next question would be?"

I shake my head.

"My next question would be: are you? And then you sit and think about it for a moment."

"I sit and think a moment, then say: no, of course not, it's about the work of going through something. The journey is the work." I hesitate, then nod and continue, more sure of myself. "Because I'm here at the beginning. I'm the fool, ready to take the step, and then I just have to take the next and keep going."

She smiles and urges me on with a little gesture of her paw.

"So if I was stalling by investigating every possibility, never starting," I say, nodding back to the first card, the Page of Wands. "Then I guess what I'm focused on is taking that first step, and after that, taking the next."

"You're doing my job for me," the badger laughs.

My smile falters. "Fair enough, but what do I do?"

"That's advice, kid." That soft smile, again. She flips the cards over, one by one, and continues, "Advice comes from people, not from cards. And if I'm going to give you advice, you're going to need to tell me what's actually going on."

She leans forward, folding her arms on the table, and looks past the cards and to me.

So I tell her. I tell her all that stuff from childhood, all those stupid things—the dress-up, the questions, the uncomfortable guidance, the frustration at forced roles. I tell her all those things that meant nothing, may still mean nothing, and yet add up to a picture of a different me than who I am now. A different shape, a different body, different face and voice and name.

I speak more freely than at the beginning of the session.

I tell her about my mom, about telling her bits and pieces of my feelings, and her insistence at first that it was just a blockage of energies, and then her reluctant acceptance. I tell her about my dad, and how terrified I am of him and his iron grip on masculinity. I tell her about leaving for school and deciding that becoming my own self mattered more than their financial assistance and what belongingness they could offer.

"Your mom sent you to me," she states again, after a comfortable silence. "Did you tell her any of this?"

I shake my head. "She knows just that I'm, er–"

"That you're transgender?" she finishes for me. "Would that be fair to say?"

"I...yes, that's fair."

"But you don't want to say it?" she asks, kind eyes on my own. "You don't have to, can just say yes or no."

"No. I mean, I don't want to say it, but I should. Maybe that's part of the first step." I hesitate for a second, ears flat and eyes averted, before murmuring, "She just knows that I'm trans."

The badger nods, unclipping the thermometer from her smock and turning it over in her fingers. "Alright. And she sent you to me for advice? She told me to talk to you, mentioned vague facts."

"Yeah, she told me to go to you to work on things." I give a wry smile and add, "Her words, not mine."

She laughs and sits back in her chair, slouching and twirling that thermometer. "Your mom is nuts," she says. "I mean that in the kindest way, of course: I love her dearly. Have since school. I suspect she wishes the world worked differently for her. And for you, for that matter."

The unabashed laugh and words of affection are contagious and have me grinning. "Yeah, she's nuts," I echo. "Still, can't say I'm upset with what I got out of this."

"The cards, you mean?"

"Yeah. I was expecting fortunes, I got–"

"You got what you had when you came in the door," she asserts. "And a chance to talk it through. Now, you want my advice?"

"Yeah. I want to know what you think I should do next."

"About which bit?"

"Coming out, I suppose." I scuff at the back of my neck, paw feeling clumsy. "Maybe starting transition."

"Well, it sounds like you're on your way to both, right?" She clips the thermometer back to her smock and straightens the remainder of the tarot deck in deft paws. "You've told your mom, and you have that appointment, right?"

I nod, brushing fingertips over the overturned cards left on the table. It felt like we were both acknowledging their presence in our own ways. "But I still haven't told dad, and I'm still freaked out what the counselor will say."

"Anxiety, then?" she offers, waving a paw above the cards. "A bit of the Page of Wands still left over?"

I nod again, silent.

"Do you want to dig at that?"

"Mmhm. Do you have any thoughts on how to get past that?" She shuffles the cards and opens her mouth to speak, but I interrupt, "Wait, don't tell me. Now you'll ask if *I* have any thoughts on how to get past that."

Her laugh is kind and her fingers sure as she slips another card from the top of the deck, laying it flat on top of the first three.

The image shocks me enough to get me to sit up straight, as if by gaining some distance from the card itself I could escape it. "What the hell?"

"The ten of swords," she says, voice level, conversational.

I count the swords sticking out of the anonymous figure's back. Ten. A feline laid flat on his front, a dark sky, a calm shore, and ten swords buried in his back, each as high as the cat himself.

I clear my throat and manage, "I thought you said there wasn't any bloodshed in the swords."

"Do you see blood?"

Despite everything urging me not to do so, I lean in close and inspect the figure. "No," I admit. "Though his cloak is red."

"The color of passion. And yellow, the color of action."

"The dawn's yellow, too," I offer. I sound dubious, even to myself.

"Dawn, then?" The older woman looks down at the card curiously. "Dawn or sunset?"

I frown and shake my head. "Dawn, I think. It always feels like dawn chases the night, but sunset gives in to it."

"Poetic," she says, and her smile is earnest.

I count the swords again. "One in his ear, one in his neck. Three or four in his back." I stifle a giggle and murmur, "That's a lot of swords."

Her eyes brighten. "Isn't it? Overkill, in the truest sense of the word. Like an overreaction."

A thought occurs to me, and I lean in over the table. "Staring at the dawn, killed ten times over. Look, the water's even clear, like the–" I lift the last card up to peek, and continue, "Like the six. Like me staring at coming out and poking a billion holes in the idea without ever taking the step."

Her eyes stay bright. "Maybe it's an alternative to the six, then. Too much emotion, not enough action. Passion and action pinned down, rather than the work of the six. You could keep taking those steps, or you could keep killing yourself with indecision."

I nod eagerly and ask on a whim, "What's it like reversed?"

She gives a little shrug and turns the card over for me to see. "The swords fall out—that's a relief—but he's still dead, isn't he? Resigned to his place on the shore."

"Sure enough," I laugh. "Wait, 'he'?"

"You said it first," she says playfully. "Seriously, though, most of the figures are ambiguous. Or androgynous, I think. What you read into them can mean something if you let it."

"It could be nothing," I mumble. "Or it could be the old me. The 'he'."

She shrugs. My choice, apparently.

A chime interrupts us, me staring at the card and her smiling at me. A clock tolling slow hours. I check my watch to confirm it. Five.

"Oh jeez, I'm sorry. It's way later than I thought."

She laughs, "Conversations go where they will. There's no rush. I can pull together dinner for two if you want to stay." She taps at the thermometer with a grin, "I even made marshmallows, though they'll be sticky still."

"No, it's alright. Thank you. I'm getting pretty tired, as it is." I shrug, realizing just how true that statement is. "This took a lot out of me."

"It does that. It's a wonder we need exercise at all, when just thinking about things wears us out."

I laugh with her, nodding.

"Still," she continues. "You're in town, now. Don't be afraid to stop by, say hi. There's lots more we can talk about, cards or no. Don't wait for your mom to push you my way."

I lever myself up from the chair, swishing ropy tail once or twice to make sure it hasn't fallen asleep, and offer my paw to the badger. "I won't. I know she thinks we'll work on things, but I just want to talk. This was more than I expected. I didn't know I needed–"

She bypasses my offered hand and gives me a firm hug around the middle. Startled, I hold still. She smells of sweets. Sweets and baking.

I feel unfortunately tall. A rectangle. A lummox. A big, dumb cat.

I also feel understood, appreciated. Welcomed. I return the hug carefully. Then, with her farewell in my ears, take that first step out into the evening air.

And then the next.

Disappearance

"This is going to sting."

I nod.

"No, this is going to sting a lot."

That warrants a dry swallow and a second nod, more nervous this time.

The first thing they'd done at the mod parlor was shave my fur. A smooth line back from my muzzle toward my ears. They'd gotten all of both of my cheeks, down to the jawline and up toward my ears, though not quite all the way.

It's not a good look for a weasel, this awful grooming.

I'll have to live. I suppose it'll take a few months to go from stubbly to bristly and back toward soft, and then another few after that until I'm back to normal.

Well, not normal. New. Different.

"Alright, first bit," the rat begins, tugging over the lower part of a milk jug that's been cut in half. "Gonna get the bars super cold. You sure you want the straight lines?"

"Yes." I don't sound sure, even to myself.

The rat does that thing where he just sits still and silent, waiting on me. His ears have been tattooed black up along the backs, and the fluorescent lights shining through them cast blurred shadows, crenelated ideas of shapes.

I sit up straight in my chair and give a firm nod. "Yes. Straight lines. Three on each cheek, spreading out toward the back of my head."

The rat waits a moment longer, then cracks a goofy grin. "Good. Good choice. I'm gonna start the middle one a little further back. And I'll use tapered ones rather than rectangular. It'll make you look speedy."

We laugh at that, and I use the it to hide the terror. Not at the pain, mind, but at the sheer enormity of what I'm about to do.

"Alright, lady." The rat stands, pads across the room with claws clicking on linoleum. There's a hissing, gurgling sound, a sound of something more complex than water being poured, and then a soft curse. A single curse is more a matter of form, though, and the lack of follow-up keeps me from panicking outright.

The rat hurries back toward me, the half-jug in oven-mitt-clad paws billowing a sinking fog in his wake. This gets quickly set down on the steel table so he can shake the mitts off. The nitrogen fog continues its cascade, flowing over the table and onto the floor. From then, everything happens in quick succession.

I'm laid out on my side.

A thick petroleum jelly is smeared into the fur around my eyes, and a piece of aluminum foil massaged into that to create at least an attempt at a seal.

Footsteps.

A paw holds the foil in place. Another holds my muzzle down against a pillow in a sanitized paper pillowcase. A third, more spindly than the others, presses down on the side of my neck. Someone presses a rolled-up towel into my paws.

Murmuring.

A rush, a clatter, and then pain as something presses against my cheek. I grit my teeth, clench the terrycloth in my paws, and let out a sort of gurgled moan. Someone's counting down.

The pain leads with cold, then turns searing, and then is lost in a labyrinthine landscape: sere, white, a sun too bright to look at, and the smell of snow.

The countdown reaches zero, and the pressure against my face relaxes. That 'something' that was pressed against my cheek is lifted away, and someone murmurs dryly, "One down, five to go."

I spend the next half hour alternating between gasping for breath between each countdown and exploring that landscape. A tangled mess of chalk-white rocks, angular, thorny bushes with no leaves, lingering snow-scent, and a flute playing whistle-tones above it all.

I'd never known how intricate pain could be.

After the last countdown is finished and I am allowed to sit up once more, I finally allow myself a simple, "Fuck."

There's laughter as the foil is pried away from my gummed-up fur and I blink my eyes back into focus. There's the rat along with his accomplice, a weasel far taller than I, sitting on a stool with a kerchief keeping unkempt head-fur out of his eyes. On the table by him, a short copper bar clamped into a stainless steel handle is still oozing tendrils of too-heavy fog.

"Fuck," I say again.

"Stings, huh?" The weasel grins, and I recognize his voice from the countdown.

"Uh...I guess." I try to smile, feeling cold-burnt skin pull at my cheeks, and the smile turns into a wince. "Bit of an understatement. What does it look like?"

The rat reaches to snag a mirror and hold it up to my face. Shaved cheeks—that much I'd seen—cutting fine brown fur almost down to the skin, and three bars on each cheek, radiating away from my whiskers toward the back of my head. The bars show up as patches of matted, crispy, burnt fur.

"It'll turn white soon enough," the weasel says. He stretches out his arm and bunches up his sleeve, revealing simple coiling patterns of white fur amidst the brown of his fur. I'd seen it before in pictures (that being the reason I'd chosen this parlor), but seeing it in person made me all the more eager for the fur on my cheeks to grow back.

"Now you just need some piercings." The rat laughs as I shake my head.

I pay in cash. They accept cards, but I had more than enough on hand.

★

From the mod parlor, I head home to take care of the apartment. All the stuff I need is already in the car, packed into a backpack and a suitcase. Nothing from inside, of course. This all has to stay. Still, it's good to make sure.

Everything's neat. Not too neat, of course, as I can't keep up with Jarred's standards, and he can't keep up with the rate I make things messy. Stuff's on shelves, dust free. Clothes are put away, but the hamper's overflowing. The kitchen's wiped clean, but there's a stack of plates and glasses in the dirty half of the sink.

Poor Jarred. Ah well.

Once my account of the house is done, I begin to dismantle the life I'd built up for myself. I unwind it in slow, circular passes of the apartment, starting from the ground up. I carefully destroy what I was, slowly unticking a checklist, item by item, of the things that got me where I am, made me who I am.

Drawers are tugged open and clothing strewn haphazardly about the floor. The bed sheets are pulled free of the mattress and shredded with my claws to look as though it was all done in haste.

It's not. It's all careful. I have to be quiet for the neighbors, and I have to be deliberate for myself, even if it does feel like watching someone else work.

The mattress is thrown askew as though someone had been digging for cash beneath it. The bathroom is mostly left alone, but pill bottles are dumped in the sink, looking like someone was hunting for something more interesting than aspirin. The top shelf of the closet is ransacked, with shoes tossed on the floor and the contents of my jewelry box tucked away in a backpack, along with Jarred's nice watch. I didn't care for the stuff, but I knew a burglar would.

The living room is more difficult. We have a TV, which a burglar would latch onto immediately. I'd planned for this, though, and the TV is set neatly by my door while I see to the rest of the room.

I tip over the speakers on their poles and scratch carefully crazed claw marks around their bases, a show of trying to detach them. They stay on the floor.

The bookshelf is dismembered as quietly as I can manage. Books are pulled off in armloads and scattered around on the floor. One from every armful is bent and torn, my heart aching to do so. A yearbook tweaks memories and is discarded. Paintings are removed from their hooks and tossed on top of the books.

The couch is shredded and exposed just as the bed had been. Nothing there beneath those torn cushions.

The kitchen is next. I step quietly over the pile of books and head on in. There's a cursory pass of the fridge and cabinets: pushing glasses and food to the sides to expose the backs of them. My concession to looking hasty is to put a glass in a plastic bag and crush it under my foot, then scatter the shards over the counter and onto the floor. A very careful "whoops."

The garage had been my space, and is the last to get torn down. We'd rented half a duplex and paid extra for the side with the attached garage, which I'd claimed for all of my painting stuff, but which was under constant threat of being slowly consumed by junk.

I eviscerate my old camping gear. I trusted Jarred to never pull himself away from his computer long enough to even consider camping. So much time at the keyboard, so little to spend elsewhere; so much time spent on him, so little on anyone else.

My easel is easy to deal with: I just tip it over. The rickety thing clatters to pieces just shy of the front bumper of the car. A sketch of a painting, burgundy on black, tumbles askew. Boxes containing old clothes are turned out. A clock is broken most carefully.

Jarred and I, we'd never hidden anything together, but I have to look thorough.

On my own, though, I'd hidden cash. Just shy of twenty grand in a locking cash box disguised as a two-quart thermos tucked firmly into my old backpacking gear in the mess of our garage.

Or it had been. Now it was tucked into the car, just behind the driver's seat.

My life isn't completely unwound. Not yet. But I'm getting there.

I reach in the car and grab a bag of odds-and-ends fur sweepings.

Little bits snagged here and there from shedding coworkers. Some from a grooming place. Even a bit from the mod shop's bin before I was shaved. I make a quick circle around the apartment, scattering fur on the most torn up bits

I grab the TV on the way back to the garage—a flat screen thing that we only ever used for movies——and lay it down its back by the car. I give it a kick until it's squarely behind one of the front wheels.

Here we go.

I climb in the car and hit the button to open the garage.

When I reverse over the TV, there's a delightful crunch. I can't smile without my newly branded cheeks burning, so I breathe satisfaction out on a sigh.

⋆

My paws ache all the way to Oregon. I had thought it would be pretty easy to slash up the inside of my car before I abandoned it, but the seat cushions were tougher than I had imagined. I'd managed to come out of the experience without breaking any claws, at least.

Once the seats had been shredded, I carefully cut my finger along the side and smeared blood along the claw marks. The car was trashed as I rolled it into a ditch. There was a tiny forest there, with crumpled cans and paper wrappers mixed in with the fallen leaves. After thinking for a moment, I squeezed out a few more drops of blood onto that garbage and bound my wound.

The bus driver had greeted me with the tired acknowledgment of a fox who had seen much worse than a sloppily dressed weasel with newly branded cheeks.

I'd never been on a long-distance bus trip. Jarred and I had never been wealthy, never higher than lower-middle class, and this wasn't helped by me having pretended to make several hundred less than I actually did a month at work, all that extra cash making its way into my thermos. A cross-country bus trip is unthinkable when you can fly, when you have a car.

But you can buy bus tickets with cash.

The seat is cramped. About what I'd expected, to be honest, but I wasn't prepared for this quite as much as I thought. No one sits next to me, but I still felt hemmed in on every side. I tell myself to just enjoy myself, enjoy this new life. This non-life. This life without history.

Hard to do when you are bumping down the road at sixty-five and no faster.

I use the toilet as little as possible.

★

I have made a huge mistake.

If I were a smarter lady, I would've spent more energy figuring out what to do once I got here than what I spent on that hour of unwinding my previous life.

I can stay here, of course. There's a long-stay hotel that doesn't side-eye my cash too much, and there's a little kitchenette in the room with a two-burner stove that's plenty for cooking on the cheap for myself. Getting groceries with cash is as easy as expected.

But I can't get a job.

If I were a smarter lady, I'd've changed my name before leaving, keeping it a secret from Jarred as best as possible...but even that isn't smart. That would've tipped off investigators immediately. "Weasel changes name, weasels out of debt." I can only imagine the headlines once I was caught.

But I can't get a job.

I'm educated and all. I was a fantastic accountant, and it felt awesome to be one of the few who actually uses her college degree for what she does for a living and *enjoys it*. I worked for a few CPA offices and was on the short track to moving up at the last one. I'm fantastic with numbers, which is why I thought I had this all set.

But I just *can't get a job*.

No one is going to hire an accountant with no name. With no history, no verified skills, no bank account, no credit, no social security number. No one is going to hire even the smartest weasel to run numbers if that weasel doesn't legally exist—or is at least trying not to.

Fuck.

I can't get a job, I can't rent a place, I can't open another bank account. I can't even change my name, since that would mean engaging with my old identity, the one I'd tried to kill.

Fuck.

I can live here for a while. I ran the math on my recently-purchased calculator (cell phone was back in the car, of course—no more net for me, much as I can help it), and I can live here for maybe a year and a half. Longer, if I find a cheaper long-stay. At least I have time to try and fix this.

★

The proprietor, Adam, and I have been getting on surprisingly well.

He's a good guy, which I hadn't picked up on at first. I'd taken his silence while handing over my key as standoffishness. There was certainly an element of caution to it, but he's also just a quiet guy.

We exchanged nods daily for the first two weeks I lived here, then simple pleasantries for the next two. He came off as soft-spoken and content with where he was in life, and as far as I could tell, he was.

A week or so into my second month staying in that little studio, and he's invited me over to the patio behind the office (which I suppose is also his home) to discuss arrangements for the future.

"Discussing arrangements," however, has turned into sharing half a bottle of rum while sitting in deck chairs. The rum's fantastic, but comes out of a vodka bottle. The glasses are half-pint canning jars.

I can't decide if it's hipster or hippie, but the more I drink, the less it seems to matter.

"So." A pause to toss another cube of ice in his jar along with another inch of rum. "Why you out here?"

I hesitate and swirl my own glass around, letting the melting ice water down the rum. It's definitely overproof, and almost certainly homemade. "Needed out of where I was, I guess."

He does that thing—the thing that rat at the mod shop had done—where he simply waits in silence. There's no shared glances, and the silence is comfortable, but also expectant. Maybe that's a thing that people who are happy can do.

"I needed out of that life. I packed my stuff and left without a word."

"You seem like you ain't hurting for cash," he says.

"Well, no. I brought along enough to live out here for a while."

"Mm." He looks at me over the rim of his glass as he sips at his rum. Otter expressions, I'm discovering, are close to weasel ones, but use the whiskers more. The look isn't exactly crafty, but getting close, as he continues, "Problem with cash is no collateral. S'why I charge you up front."

I nod. It tallies.

"But you seem straight."

"Straight?" A smile tugs at the healing brands on my cheeks. They're starting to come in white.

He laughs, "I ain't making a pass at you, don't worry. Sex ain't a thing 'round here. Not for me, at least. Hell, maybe you like girls too. Not my business." He copies my swirl and we both enjoy the pleasant clinking of ice against glass. "No, I mean straight. You're a good lady. You're out here to get away, you say, and I trust that's all you're doing. No thieving, no running, you ain't in trouble."

I settle back into the deck chair and attempt to use that 'silence' technique I keep running into. He just grins.

"So what I'm asking is this. That number I said before?" He gestures behind himself, as though that's where the past is. "I'll cut it in half if you can do some work 'round here."

"Work?" I tilt my head, turning over ideas of what that'd entail.

"Sure. Work. What can you do to cut down your rent?"

"Uh, I can...I mean, I was an accountant. I can run your books, file taxes, that stuff."

The minute I say "taxes," Adam perks up and his whiskers bristle outward with his grin. "Deal. Sight unseen. I'm good at what I do, but that ain't taxes."

I laugh, I can't help it. "Half rent? For taxes?"

"Sure," he says, sounding content. "Run the books and handle taxes, and I'll halve your rent. You can take the desk some days if you want a bit more off."

I rub my paw over the short, bristly fur of my cheeks, a habit

I picked up as it grew back in. The crisped, branded patches had largely been replaced by normal, soft fur, now growing in white. All the shaved spots were taking a while to grow in.

"A secretary, hmm?"

"Well, sure. It ain't grand. Accountant like you ain't gonna find anything grand without being legit."

At that I fall silent.

He continues, "Jobs these days, you need to be legit. You couldn't offer me anything but cash, not even an ID to hold. You needed out of life so bad, you left behind your legitimacy."

My silence becomes darker, seems to close in around me. Ears pinned back, eyes burning, muscles tensed, I try not to visibly panic in front of Adam.

"It's okay, though." He settles back into the Adirondack chair with a sigh. "You can get by without that. You're just gonna have to let go of the idea that you'll ever be a part of that world again. You might, but it's best to expect you won't."

From then on, it's silence. I cry as quietly as I can. Adam pours me another inch of rum and leans across the table between us to tip another ice cube into my jar.

★

Adam is *set*.

He owns his property outright, and is up-to-date on all his licenses. Business is good. "Half rent," for me, covers twice the cost of maintaining my studio—utilities, that share of property tax, everything.

And he's happy.

⋆

With my stay here nearly doubled, I've started exploring further into town.

We're a ways out from Portland: I could take the regional bus there in about an hour and a half, but I never do. Instead, I stick to this little town I wound up in, a town picked because I got too anxious about Portland and got off the bus a few stops before. Probably my best idea yet.

I'd just gone to the dinky supermarket before, but now I started taking walks in town instead of the ceaseless hiking and doodling in a sketchbook. Originally, it had just been a "stretch the legs before shopping" exercise, but now I was even heading into town just to wander. There's a neat little cafe with huge single-pane windows and a rocket stove that I've taken a liking to. Something about the impracticality of the windows combined with that adobe stove behind the bar tickles me. And as long as I stick to drip coffee, it's not too much out of my budget.

I even ventured to the lone grooming stop in town to get my cheeks checked up on. I had been worried that they'd be weirded out by them, but I was greeted by a punky opossum with a bright pink streak of fur from the tip of her snout down to the nape of her neck. She said my cheeks were looking good, then talked me into buying a tube of dye. She suggested pink, but I went for the blue instead.

I don't know why I did that. Being an accountant wasn't just an occupation for me. It was a whole identity. I bought into the smart pantsuits and that sensible jewelry, the latter of which was still in my suitcase, to mark my position hard-core. The tight grooming and the calm speed of numbers, that's *who I was.*

Now, I don't know. I have three pairs of jeans, a frowzy canvas skirt, and a bunch of long- and short-sleeved button up shirts and tees—only some of which fit well—I grabbed from a thrift store before this whole excursion began.

Maybe I just figured I'd own it. I got the cheek brands, after all; might as well get the dye, too.

Tonight, I'm dyeing a diamond shape into the white down my front. It'll sit just above my breasts, with a tendril curling down beneath them, and another tendril curling up over my front to my neck. I can hide it with a scarf if I need, but otherwise, it'll peek up from above my shirt. Just a little tease. One that could go "sexy" when I want, or just "artsy" otherwise.

The thought's actually quite embarrassing, but it's been a long time since sex. Jarred and I were pretty into it at first, but then it became routine, and then scarce. We hadn't fucked for a month before I took off, and since then I'd been too busy hiding to worry about it.

With this new arrangement with Adam, though, I don't know.

Maybe being a little sexy will be okay.

⋆

Holy shit, I may actually be able to pull this off. It'll be crazy, but maybe I can do it.

I guess Adam did some talking after I'd asked about more possibilities, and now I've got the owner of Starry Night, the town's little cafe, as a "client" of sorts. He's having me do the taxes and help run the books. He even offered to let me run the till if things get busy. They haven't yet, but he's promised me it's still the off-season. Not cold enough to be winter, but not yet warm enough for holidays.

He's not paying me anything close to livable, but with the deal I'm getting on rent, I might just be able to do this.

It's such a small town. It looks bigger than it is, since so many of these kitschy stores and homes have so much space around them. The market has a parking lot twice the size it needs.

There are folks living around the town in seclusion, I guess, but those who live in the town itself, who *are* the town, probably number in the low hundreds. Other than that, it's just a waypoint. Folks heading up to the mountains stop through and keep all the businesses going, but they never stay long. They're always on their way to more romantic locations or heading back through on their way back to the coast. The town itself holds together through the need to provide for all those who would only pass through. All those people on any one day, and it's still a small town.

I've started painting again, too. Starry Night has a drop ceiling and each tile is painted a different color. After I mentioned having been a painter in my "past life," Stefan, the owner, perked up and sent me home with a blank tile, along with a few crusty tubes of acrylic and a brush that hadn't been used in a while.

"Go nuts," he said, and so I did. Background of green and a symmetrical tree in black, limbs splitting into branches that became whisker-thin toward the edges of the tile. The leaves were vague suggestions of white that broke the symmetry. An idea of a tree. Just the type of stuff I painted up until four months ago.

Stefan loved it, and here I am working on my second tile.

This—working jobs all but off the grid, body mods, looking like a hippie—isn't what I'd pictured when I unwound my previous life. Now, when I look back on it, on all my planning and scheming, I don't think I had pictured anything.

★

I've taken to working mornings at Starry Night and heading back to Adam's after lunch to run the desk there. If it's needed, I can even head back to Starry Night after to help out a bit more. We're well into the busy season, so both the long-stay and the cafe are happy for whatever help they can get. An accountant running the till is a weird fit, but at least I'm fast at it.

It's interesting to watch the ebb and flow of traffic through the town.

Starting about six in the morning, folks start trickling into town, but within an hour, it becomes busy, then frenetic. From there, it climbs steadily until about nine-thirty, dips for an hour, then picks up for lunch.

I head out by one-thirty or two to dash back to Adam's and start getting folks checked in and out while Adam does property stuff. Usually, he's out repairing the drive to the units (and the little one-room cabins in back, one of which I now inhabit). He's intensely focused on that drive; he's talked with me about the upkeep and maintenance of a dirt road for an hour or more on multiple occasions. I don't drive anymore, so I just have to trust him.

Things clear up by five, and sometimes I head back to Starry Night. At that point, it's mostly a social thing. If I'm not chilling out back of the office with Adam, I'm here at the cafe. If not either, I'm painting. I've gotten about a third of the ceiling tiles done.

The movement of people is fascinating up close, following the ways in which people move and change throughout the day. The before-coffees and the nine-AM-bounces and the post-lunch-siesta. The perking of ears and the bristling of whiskers. The droop of tails and stifled yawns.

When you zoom out, though, it's grains of sand just below high tide. The tide rolls in, and there's a chaotic dance of spiraling movement. Each wave brings cars cycling around parking lots, small collisions of bodies, crimped tails, tantrums weighing down parents.

And then tide rolls out, and the town settles back down into its ground state. Grains of sand compact nicely when left to dry, a comfortable stasis until the next high tide.

In the midst of it all, the regulars provide a sense of weight, anchoring high and low tide to provide a sense of continuity. There's Adam, of course, and Stefan. I suppose I'm slipping into that role too. We are the wave-polished stones.

And then there's Aurora.

We've only talked once or twice in earnest, her voice familiar and quiet, but I watch her every day. She has a table all but reserved in the corner of Starry Night, farthest from the door but right in the elbow of two of those ridiculous single-pane windows. To her left, one window looks out over the parking lot and, across the street, the parking lot of the market. In front of her, three trees that have been planted too close to each other, forming a tiny grove between Starry Night and the back fence.

She wafts in around six thirty and orders a latte, a soda water, and a pot of hot water for her and one of the teabags riding shotgun in her jacket pocket. If her table isn't free, she'll sip her latte at the bar until it is, and then set up camp.

She drinks the latte first, then the soda water, then the tea.

Once she's finished the soda water, she pulls out a pen and either a book or a stack of printouts and a clipboard. I've never figured out what she does for work, but she's always either taking notes or marking up printouts. A teacher, perhaps? An author? Editor?

At noon, she orders another soda water and another pot of hot water for the second teabag. Some days she'll pull out a sack lunch, some days she'll order something from me—we serve a few simple sandwiches—in her comfortable contralto.

She eats the lunch first, then drinks the soda water, then the tea.

Once she's finished the soda water, she settles back into the chair and stares out the windows. Mostly, she just looks at the trees, but sometimes she'll rest a cheek on her fist and look out toward the market, her long canine ears canted cozily back. Something about the sight always has me watching her in turn. Something familiar, comfortable.

Then the coyote gets back to work, and, before long, I duck out to help Adam. On the few occasions I've stayed, Aurora will close out the shop with us, saying little but saying it kindly. Her silences, I expect, are a matter of course. They are absolute, and absolutely part of her. A stillness I can only dream of.

I've never seen her out of the shop, but I think about her every time I walk or bus back home. I'll have inevitably forgotten by the time I get inside, though, as she's context-shifted around a corner of my mind.

*

I'd imagined I'd done such a good job of cleansing my life of who I used to be when I left, that each time I'm confronted by something I'd accidentally brought along, it's jarring, or even frightening.

Undergarments had been the first such instance. I hadn't thought to grab any new panties before leaving town. This was probably fine, I reasoned, because anything missing would have been noticed. Unfortunately, this left me with only one pair—the ones I left in—and I'd had to visit the "essentials" aisle of the supermarket early on to grab a pack of bland panties. They fit so poorly, I'd largely stopped wearing any.

What had me jittery, though, was seeing that old pair every time I did laundry. One last reminder that I'm no longer who I was.

I threw them out soon after.

Each time I come across some remnant, it reminds me of what I've done, in a very tangible way, even if not necessarily why. The "why" had already begun to blur on the bus ride, and I've never been able to make it gel again.

It's not always negative, this process, but it's never positive. Other than a few useful items—the jewelry, for instance, kept for something pawnable in an emergency—I throw everything I find away almost as soon as I find it, stopping only to destroy it for the catharsis. It's all too much risk to keep around.

Thus me, crouched on my haunches behind Starry Night, hyperventilating as I try to destroy my old driver's license.

How this had escaped me before was something of a mystery. An actual legal document bearing my actual legal name, tucked within my old wallet in the back of my suitcase, was not something I should have missed.

This caromed straight into fear. Into terror. Into that agonizing sickness that settles into one's gut and closes off one's throat. I'd stopped crying as much, recently, and started smiling more, but I'm on the verge of panicked tears now.

I can't say what made me tuck the wallet into a pocket at the start of the day. It was an interesting artifact, perhaps, nothing big or important, that I decided to keep on some whim. The credit cards that had once filled it lay scattered by my abandoned car back home, after all, so I figured it must be safe.

The license won't tear. That was my first instinct, but my pads had slip off the slick plastic too easily, and my claw tips only scrabble ineffectually at its surface.

I can bend it, at least, and I crease it this way and that in an attempt to fatigue the plastic enough that maybe I can snap it. ID cards are, apparently, designed to last, and despite repeated folds, I can't get enough of a grip to tear the card, much less snap it, though the ink along the crease fades and warps into whiteness. I don't have the leverage necessary to crease along my name, however.

This isn't working.

I stuff my wallet back into my pocket and dash over to the dumpster, flipping up the lid. I had intended to tear up the license and toss it in with the coffee grounds and banana peels, but the thought of it slipping out of the dumpster or falling out of the trash truck feels inescapable. With all the people going through the cafe during the day, though, there has to be...

I tear through two of the shop's thin garbage bags before I find what I'm looking for: a cheap plastic lighter, yellow and scuffed.

The rasp of the wheel against the flint sends my whole paw to buzzing, the snap of the spark too loud for my frazzled nerves.

I flick at the lighter a few more times. It's almost certainly dead, thrown away for a reason, so I just have to hope there's enough fluid in there.

The flame finally catches, only barely peeking above the rim of the lighter.

It'll have to do.

Holding my breath and struggling to still my shaking paws, I carefully bring my driver's license above the tiny flame, letting the diffuse glow settle beneath the photo of my face, the weasel there looking startled, back-lit by flame. The plastic browns, sags, then starts to char and bubble. By the time the smoke, reeking of burning plastic, starts to make me cough, the image of my face and much the identifying details have melted away, the ink burnt off by the low flame of the lighter.

Motion in the shadows cast against the dumpster catches my eye and I whirl around, Aurora startling back a half-step at my sudden movement. We stare, uncomprehending, at each other for a moment.

"I—" I croak. "Hey."

"Hey, uh...you okay back here?"

I look around, down to my mangled license and the shitty yellow lighter in my paw, back to the coyote, struggling to come up with an explanation. A half-truth is the best I can manage. "Needed to, uh...expired credit card and all. Melting it, I mean."

The quotidian mundanity of such an activity seems to click things into place for the coyote. She perks up and smiles, "I'd never thought of melting them before, I always just cut them into little pieces."

The lighter is finally starting to cool down in my paw after it's extended use, which is good, given how much I keep fiddling with it. "Couldn't find my scissors once I got out here, figured this would work."

She nods, squints toward my paws, then back up to me. "You from Idaho?"

I gape, crumpling the license as best I can within my hand.

"Just looked like my old card, I mean."

I do my best to keep my ears from flattening and tail bristling, only to catch myself panting. So much for acting cool. "I...yeah," I gasp. "Moved a while back."

"Hey, no stress. I won't pry," Aurora laughs, holding up her paws disarmingly.

I manage a smile, hoping it's convincingly embarrassed. "Sorry," I say, stuffing the lighter and warped card back into the garbage bag, before hauling the whole thing back into the dumpster. "I guess it's just a weird thing to get caught doing."

Head tilted, Aurora grins at me a moment longer, then shrugs. "I guess, yeah. See you inside?"

I nod, struggling to calm my breathing as I watch her round the corner to the front of the shop with a flick of her tail.

When I make it back inside to prep her usual latte, Aurora smiles at me. I beam back to her.

Something about the encounter by the dumpster has left me feeling giddy. Perhaps it was the thrill of nearly being caught, or maybe the relief of being rid of the thing. It's one fewer identifying thing about me that I need to worry about, after all; and beyond that, it got Aurora laughing.

Why that makes me so happy in turn is beyond me.

⋆

My brush-strokes are confident, each one is a smooth arc describing edges and boundaries, or perhaps reinforcing color.

The tile had been given to me burgundy, and I'd chosen to leave it that way, painting within that dark red surface rather than covering it up. I painted in black, and I painted only shadows, not details, as though the scene were blown out towards white and the contrast turned to a hundred percent.

It had started as an abstract gesture of a face, angular and canine, but had slowly headed toward something more concrete. Not realistic, but perhaps something from a comic. Hard-edged lines, but true to form with no liberties taken.

Aurora at her table as seen from the espresso machine, cheek on fist, staring out of frame. The shape of her muzzle, the tilt of her ears, both familiar and new.

My brush-strokes are confident. Black and red, no need for another color.

"Season's winding down."

"Mm."

Adam laughs and shakes his head, plopping down, then melting further into the deck chair.

"S'good to see you painting, you know."

"Mm." I perk up as my mind parses meaning out of those sounds, and then flatten my ears. "Sorry. I got kinda into it. What'd you say before?"

"Said season's winding down."

"Yeah, seems like," I say as I carefully shift the painting off the table to lay it flat on the ground next to me, replacing the bucket of ice in its spot. My poor-weasel's easel of the table between us returns to its former state as drinking space. I pour us both a drink.

The otter has moved on from rum and is now trying his paw at whiskey. We've been cycling through batches over the last few weeks. The taste is far sweeter than I would've expected, but Adam says he doesn't have the cuts quite right yet.

In my mouth, ice machine ice and homemade whiskey jockey for space with words. "Wha's li' in off 'easong?"

"Eh?"

I crunch down on the ice and brave the brain freeze to say more clearly, "What's it like in the off season?"

"Same but slower," Adam says, chuckling down to his glass. "Way slower, some days. You got here before season started, but weren't really here in the middle of off-season. I'll probably beg your help deep-cleaning some of the units."

"Sure thing, boss." I laugh as that gets me an ice-cube to the face. "Fine. Sure thing, master."

Adam makes as though he'll throw the whole bucket of ice at me, before we both settle back into our chairs with jars of whiskey and ice, grinning. In the silence, I paint my claws idly with the black acrylic left on the brush from my work on the ceiling tile. The condensation off the glass thins the paint and it starts to seep into my fur. My paws are covered with the stuff anyway.

The silence goes from comfortable to expectant, and when I look up, Adam's adopted a vaguely confused look with whiskers smoothed back, which he's directed toward his all-important drive. Just as I'm about to brush it off, he asks, "How'd you leave?"

Anxiety brushes up against me, breaking through the veneer of calmness. It takes me a bit to respond, and I try to fill that space by nervously stirring the ice into my white whiskey. "If I just say 'very carefully', will that be enough?"

The otter's expression softens and he shrugs against the back of his chair. "I s'pose. Doesn't mean I don't still want to know."

"I just...I don't know. I spent a lot of time thinking about all the different parts there were of my life and thinking about what I'd be without them." I brush my paws over my cheeks, heedless of the paint. My fur has almost grown back completely, and the freeze-brand has indeed come in white. Still, it's become a habit. "And then I just set a date and went around to all those parts one by one, turning them off or throwing them away."

"No going back, then?"

"Not if I want to stay out of jail." I don't think this is true, but it sounds good.

"So you turned off or trashed all these parts of who you were," Adam mumbles, pouring himself another inch of whiskey. "What's left?"

I don't answer.

I don't *have* an answer.

When I think about it, there's just nothing there. It's like trying to see the inside of my eyelids. Just nothing there. I tore down what I was without any thought of what would be left. Even my license, that last proof of me-that-was, had long since burned. There was nothing after that. It was more a form of suicide than I'd wanted to admit.

Finally, I shrug. "Just me, I guess."

Adam laughs at this and stretches his legs out, splaying webbed toes. "Fair enough. You do a good job around here, though. It feels like you belong now. I don't know what you were like before, but you were scared out of your whiskers when you got here. Now you're just you."

"A punky weasel living off the grid in a hippie town?"

"That too, yeah. Took you a while to grow into the punky bit, but you're getting there."

My turn to laugh. "Just missing the get-up, I guess. Second-hand shirts and jeans miss the mark a little."

"Mmhm. And you ought to get a piercing." Adam slides out of the chair and stands, using his thick tail to give the leg of the table a thwack. "And it's good to see you painting."

★

For the first few months I was here, I'd get a little twitch in my paw when someone mentioned something off the Internet. A twitch in my paw and a little shift inside me at a sudden-yet-averted context-shift. *I could look that up,* I'd think. *I could answer their question, or laugh at their picture.*

For a while, I'd countered it with lies. An "Oh yeah, ha ha" here and a "Yeah, I saw that" there. The anxiety that I'd mess up and be called out got to be too much for me, though, and I switched from that to nervous silence.

I replaced that twitch early on with the gesture of brushing back over my cheeks. At first, it was obvious why: when I got to town, my face was still freshly shaved, and for the first few weeks, the freezer-burnt marks of the brand were plain. Soon, though, it became more of a habit than a coping mechanism. I'd brush my pads over the fur and feel the edges of the shaving, and once they became imperceptible, I'd trace my claws through fur, trying to sense where the brown fur ended and the white, branded fur started.

Anything—*anything*—to keep from touching the Internet. It would be too easy for me to just log back on. The temptation to peer into a life that no longer existed was too great. My very existence here in this town depends on that life no longer existing. I'd destroyed it, and destroyed all that tied me to its remains.

And yet here I am, panicking in the bathroom at Starry Night.

There's a soft tap at the door, and I rush to straighten my skirt and apron, peeking in the mirror to make sure I haven't visibly cried.

Aurora's there when I open the door, standing a scant few inches taller than I.

"Sorry, I'm..." I shake my head. "I'm all done."

The coyote tilts her head quizzically, a movement that brushes against old memories. "You okay?"

"Yeah, I am." I stand up straighter and smile apologetically to her. "I will be."

We slide past each other and I make my way behind the bar again, busying myself with wiping down the already-clean espresso machine, just to give my paws something to do. Not many people ordering coffee at six at night. This late in the season, the sun sets early too.

Stefan hikes himself up onto the bar, the wolf's tail flagging off to the side. "You alright there, kiddo?"

"Yeah." I nod eagerly, then decide eagerness isn't what I should be going for, and turn it into a shrug. "Just stomach stuff. Nerves, maybe." I laugh, and it sounds too loud.

"You bolted right off, yep. Anything bring it on?"

I look around, checking on the occupants. We're down to me and Stefan, a young fox couple, and Aurora of course. "Just...just something a customer...something that bear said. Or saw. I don't know."

Stefan's brow furrows, and I watch his tail-tip tap arrhythmical against the wall where it joins the bar. "Saw? How do you mean?"

"He had a tablet, and I guess I caught a glimpse. He was talking about it to someone. Someone on the phone."

"Mm, yeah, I remember. What'd you see?"

"I saw my—" My words catch in my throat. *I saw my husband. I saw my name. I saw the picture from my ID.* "I saw my hometown."

The wolf grins and leans back on his paws. "Home, eh? You don't seem like the girl who's eager to go back."

At this, I laugh in earnest. "No. Not at all."

"What about it piqued your interest, then?"

I hide my racing thoughts with a shrug, and come up with a half-truth: "The headline had the word 'police' in it."

Nodding, Stefan slips down from his perch on the bar. "Fair enough. Weird day in here, anyway. I'mma close down after this—" he gestures vaguely toward the customers, "So feel free to head out whenever you want."

I think of the bus back to Adam's and being alone with my thoughts. I could walk, but that'd just mean more time turning that glimpse of an article—something about "police" and my old name, something about how long it had been—over and over in my head. "I'll stick around, help clean up and stuff."

Stefan shrugs, "Sure thing. Maybe I'll take off early, then. You okay closing up?"

"Mmhm," I nod, tamping down anxiety with a jokey grin. "Wipe everything down, put all the food away, put the chairs up, steal all the money from the drawer..."

The wolf laughs. "No more than ten percent, please. And girlie," he reaches out and pinches my ear between his claws. "Get your ears pierced with all sorts of crap or something so you can turn into a real punk. You're too wholesome-looking to be thieving."

"Adam suggested the same thing. This town must be in sore need of a punk."

"Yeah, all we've got is Aurora."

The coyote flips him off without even looking away from her book. He laughs.

⋆

Stefan's really good at disappearing when he's not needed at work anymore. If he doesn't have to be there for closing, he'll be nowhere to be found.

Oh well, that's fine. I don't imagine I'll be here much longer anyhow.

I start by cleaning down the bar and arranging all those bottles of flavored syrup for the drinks. Next comes flipping over the "open" sign and wiping down the empty tables, stacking chairs upside-down atop them.

The fox couple picks up on the hint quickly and we settle their tab.

I make a quick pass of the bathroom, but it's clean enough as is, so I mostly just wipe down the sink.

Back out in the cafe, I turn off the soft indie pop on the house speakers, and then something clicks within me.

I clutch at the edge of the bar as all of those emotions, eight or nine months of them, crash into me. All those months of living in at least some state of fear, all those days of holding back on feeling anything else, they all add up to time past-me only borrowed. All those past-due feelings make themselves felt *now*.

My grip on the bar tightens as I gasp out a stifled cry, and then I'm crumpling to the floor, wedged between the milk fridge and the end of the bar where Stefan had been sitting only a half hour ago. Anxiety crescendos into panic, and then far, far beyond that.

My muscles are tensing, and my perception of the world, my entire awareness, is shrinking to something the size of a coin, chalk-white pain smelling of snow.

I come to on my side, gasping for air and choking on sobs. I'd been sobbing the whole time, apparently, as my cheeks and the sleeve of my shirt are soaked. Drooling too, from the looks of it.

My body hasn't figured out how to move, yet, but I can see a dark, angular shape above me. I try to push away, but all I can manage is to tense up further.

"Hey, hey, chill. It's okay." Aurora. It has to be.

"Mmnglh."

"Let's get you upright, at least a little. See if you can stand." She helps lever me up until I'm leaning back against the bar. "Come on, legs out. You uh...you fell over. Let's at least get your legs in front of you."

I can't figure out how to work my voice, so I just continue to moan and sob as the coyote helps get my skirt untangled and my limbs out from under me. She slips her paws up under my arms and starts to lift.

"*N-nnn,*" I manage and clutch at her arms—far too tightly, if her wince is anything to go by. Too filled with terror, too struck by a sense of impending death to control myself.

She relents and settles back down, then gives into my tugging and slips her arms around my shoulders instead. There's a little uneven rocking motion as she slides her legs out from under her, and then she's drawing me in against her.

I don't really know how long I stay like that. The only thing describing the passage of time is my sobbing. Aurora is a warm bulk against me, something to wrap my arms around, some bit of stability. She doesn't coo or shush, just rests her head against mine in silence. A kind, patient silence. A silence with no expectations.

Eventually, I run out of sobs, and settle into a gentle, almost calm sort of crying. Aurora gives me a bit more time before carefully leaning back. Letting our arms slip from the embrace at least enough so that she can look at me. Her smile's kind, rather than pitying. "Come on, let's get you up, okay?"

My joints are loose hinges, too well oiled. Finding a way to be upright without wobbling onto the floor again proves difficult. It takes a few tries, but I wind up with my butt parked against the edge of the bar, tail crimped behind me. I leave my shoulders leaning forward to maintain my grip on Aurora. I'm loath to let go of her, so it takes another fumbling second for me to find a way to do so.

"Sorry," I croak.

She shakes her head and rests her paws on my shoulders. Once she's sure I'm steady, she steps away and grabs a plastic to-go cup from beneath the bar and fills it at the sink. She takes one of my paws in hers and guides my fingers around the cup, making sure I'm holding on before she lets go. "Drink. You cried yourself empty."

I nod and sip at the water. It feels too full in my mouth. Too thick. It slides around like oil. When I swallow, I realize how thirsty I truly am, and finish the rest of the cup in one go.

Aurora, meanwhile, finishes closing up; all that was left was her table, so there's just two chairs to put up.

I refill my cup from the tap and straighten up, trying to dispel the wobbliness in my hips and knees, to shake off the dark sense of panic. "Thanks Aurora, you didn't have to—"

"But you're in no shape to," the coyote cuts me off, laughing. She tucks her book and papers back in her bag and slips back behind the bar again. Shrugging her bag's strap up further, she snakes an arm around my back. "Let's get you home, though, okay? You good to walk?"

"Mmhm. I can take the bus, though. Don't need to walk."

"I meant to my car. I'll get you home."

If I open my mouth, I'll start crying, so I just nod.

★

Aurora's car is very...*her.*

I don't really know how to put it otherwise. It's sensible, as she is; it's filled with books and stacks of paper, as her bag is; it's not messy, but it's got a lot going on beneath its simple exterior, like her.

Still sniffling, I wait as she moves a sheaf of papers held together with a binder clip from the passenger seat to the back. Then I swipe my tail and skirt out of the way and slouch into the seat, clumsily clicking the seat belt in place with one paw, the other still holding the half-full cup of water.

The car smells of her too. My nose is doing about as well as anyone's would after so much crying, but I can tell that much. It smells like when she held me. It smells familiar, like something from years ago. Years and years. I have to swallow down a rising wave of guilt and terror.

The coyote settles into the driver's seat and gets all buckled in before giving my thigh a squeeze in her paw. "Adam's, right?" she asks, smiling. "One of the cabins?"

I nod. "Thanks again for driving me."

Aurora waits until she's reversed out of her spot and turned onto the road before answering. "No way I'm letting you walk, and goodness knows I know how awful crying alone on a bus is."

"Yeah, probably not a good look," I say. I can't quite laugh yet, but I do manage a rough sort of "heh."

"You are a bit of a mess."

I look down over my shirt and skirt. They're both rumpled. My shirt's still damp from my tears, and my skirt has picked up a stain from the floor behind the bar—probably old coffee. I can only imagine how my face looks. I grin. "Fair."

I let Aurora drive as I focus on re-hydrating. I want to just gulp down the water, but I've made enough of a mess of myself tonight. No sense risking a spill. Probably better for me that way, anyway.

It's about a forty-five minute walk from Adam's to Starry Night, and about twenty-five on the bus. I never realized how long the bus took, though, as it takes us less than ten minutes to get back to the long-stay. I laugh at the thought.

"What's up?" Aurora says, pulling into the dirt-road drive, heading around the back of the suites toward the cabins.

"Just thinking. First time I've been in a car here. Only ever ridden the bus or walked."

Aurora grins and pulls into a space in front of the cabin I point out. "Bit faster, yeah. Still, it's a pretty enough walk."

The car turning off leaves us in relative silence, my ears buzzing in my stuffed-up head from the lack of noise. My thoughts seem to be surrounding a blank space. Circling and swirling around it, around nothing. A black pit containing all the things I could think about my old life, of being discovered, of having to go back.

"Hey." Aurora. She's smiling. That's a good thing to think about instead, that smile. "Let's get you inside."

I fumble for my buckle and start to protest, but stop before I say anything. The coyote, the scent of her, it's all so comforting; might as well let her help. A few more moments together, at least.

Aurora levers herself out of her seat and strides quickly around the front of the car. I've got the door open by then, but there she is, ready to help me out of the bucket seat. I grin, feeling bashful, and take her offered paw.

She's got a bit of a wag going on, too, but I try not to read too much into that.

I lean on her as we walk the handful of steps to the door of the cabin. Once there, I fish in my apron pocket for my keys—I'd taken to wearing my work apron with the skirt for the utility of pockets—and let myself in.

Let *us* in. No discussion about whether she's coming in, too. She just is.

I flip on the lights and cringe, both at the sudden brightness against the dusk outside and the mess. I've been using my suitcase as my clean clothes drawer since I moved in. It's just got a day's worth of clothes in it, though. Next to it on one side is a pile of dirty clothes, and on the other, a folding drying rack holding a pair of jeans, a shirt, and two pairs of panties hanging off the corners.

Fuck.

I turn to apologize to the coyote, but she hasn't noticed the laundry at all. Doesn't even seem to notice me.

I follow her gaze, then cringe in earnest.

Fuck.

"Holy shit. Those paintings are yours?"

"Yes," I say, trying not to sound *too* humiliated.

"The coyote?"

I can't come up with a reply. We stand in expectant silence: Aurora's eyes locked on the paints and ceiling tile, burgundy, with her silhouette in black; and me, with my eyes locked on the floor and my tail tucked in against my leg.

She turns, mouth open to ask again, and I grab at her paw and rush to cut her off.

"Yes, I mean. Yes. You're just...you're just always there." My eyes well up with tears—I'm surprised I have any left—as words keep coming, and I keep holding onto her paw. "You're just always there and so familiar and I don't know— They let me paint the ceiling, and I don't know— I should've asked, I'm sorry— I don't know, you're just one of the only constants in my stupid fucking life and I didn't even talk to you until I—"

"Whoa, hey!" she says, raising her voice to cut off my stream of babbling. She looks startled, but not angry. "It's totally okay, but—hey..."

I've started crying in earnest again. *Looking a fool, standing there holding a girl's paw, tears pouring down your cheeks.* I manage a strangled laugh, though it's caught up in a sob. *Looking fucking crazy.*

Perhaps as an echo from the cafe, Aurora takes charge. She guides me over to my bed and sits me down on it before settling in next to me and just holding me, arms around my shoulders.

It doesn't last long, and doesn't get a tenth as bad as the crush of panic at Starry Night, but it still takes me a few minutes to get to the point where I can speak again. "Sorry, Aurora." I pace myself, so I don't just start babbling again. "Didn't mean to do that. Just such a mess today. My life's a mess, and it all hit at once."

"Tell me a bit about your life, then," she asks, low voice kind. "I want to hear."

I feel my face tighten in an ugly rictus, teeth bared and whiskers bristled. It's been months, but the freeze-brand scars over my cheeks give a twinge of protest. "There's nothing." As the sobs pick up again, dry now, I have to eke out words between. "There's nothing there. I'm just...paper. Paper thin with no substance. No substance at all." I trail off and take a few gulping breaths to calm myself, forcing my expression into mere hopelessness, rather than that grimace of self-loathing.

Aurora watches me, and, after I've gotten my crying under control, opens her mouth as though to say something, then seems to think better of it and leans in to kiss me instead.

I jolt and tense up. I hold my breath. My mind goes blank. That sensation of being about to cry fills my chest, never mind the fact that I'd already crying.

Then I just lean into the kiss. Return it. No discussion about it; it feels familiar, fulfilling. I'm calm. Still at last.

Aurora seems comfortable taking the lead, using her paws and subtle shifts of her weight to guide me to lay back on the bed. Once I'm there, she leans up from the kiss and grins down to me with just a hint of silliness. "You feel substantive to me."

I'm wrong-footed by this and it takes a moment to parse. Once it clicks, though, I giggle. "Thanks." I feel stupid just leaving it at that, though, and add, "That was nice."

"Mmhm." Still grinning, she leans into give me another quick kiss, then moves to kneel on the edge of the bed, tugging me by the paw. "Come on. Scoot."

I laugh and swipe at my face with the sleeve of my shirt—I must look a mess after all of this. Still, I scoot further up onto the bed at the coyote's bidding. "Alright, alright. How come?"

Aurora shrugs, her grin softening into a kind smile. "I got you thinking less about whatever's up with your life, right? I hope so, at least." I nod, and she continues, "The least I could do is also let you be comfortable on your bed instead of half hanging off of it."

"Good point." I grin and haul myself up onto the bed, flopping back against the pile of pillows. I'd bought more once it was clear I was staying here a while, and I'm thankful for it now.

Aurora moves too; as I make room, she moves up onto the bed to kneel next to me. "Doing better?"

"Yeah, thank you." After a moment's thought, I ask, "Why'd you do that?"

The coyote frowns down to me, ears splayed in embarrassment. "I wanted to. It felt like it would work, and like it would be okay after seeing the painting. I should have asked, though. I'm sorry."

"No!" I realize how loud that was and smile sheepishly up to her. "No, it was nice. Real nice."

That slightly silly grin comes back, tugging on buried memories. Memories of a latrans smile. "Good," she says, leaning in to press another kiss to my muzzle. I return this one more readily than the last, sliding my arms up around her shoulders.

This goes over quite well. Aurora seems to have taken it as a sign, and leans down over me more assertively, paws planted to either side of my shoulders. After a moment's hesitation, she leans up a little further onto her knees and shifts one up over me until she's straddling my waist. She's bigger than me, weighs more than I do. Maybe it's the way she carries herself, but her weight is more comforting than heavy.

"Wait," I murmur, twisting my head slightly to pull away from the kiss.

Aurora immediately tenses up, ears laying flat. "Uh, sorry, I don't—"

"No, no. You're fine," I mumble, searching for words. "Don't know why...why this is...doing what it is. Working. Stopping me from crying and all. Taking my mind off stuff."

She stays silent above me. An expectant silence she waits for me to fill.

I hunt for words as best I can. "Maybe I just...I don't know. I haven't touched—or been touched by—anyone since I made it out here. Before that, even. It feels dumb to say, I guess."

Aurora gives a short bark of a laugh at that, then lays her ears back again apologetically. "Sorry. You mean not at all?"

"Well, sure, I mean. I shook paws with Adam and Stefan, whatever. I've *touched*, yeah, but just nothing like this."

At that her expression softens and she nods. "Been a while, huh?"

I nod.

"And this is okay?"

I nod again and lean up to give her a quick kiss. "Yeah, very."

She nods, muzzle dipping to turn that motion into something of a nuzzle, and I can feel her nose tracing along one of those white bands of fur on my cheek, then under my chin, dipping down to tease at the coil of blue fur—faded now to a pale aqua—peeking up above the scoop-neck of my shirt. Her soft, low voice is muffled by my fur. "This is okay, too?"

Without tucking my muzzle uncomfortably low, all I can really see are her ears, so I lean forward to place a kiss between them, fur and familiar scent tickling at my nose. "Mmhm." I've given up saying more.

Aurora responds with a kiss of her own against my sternum. It's a ticklish sort of feeling, and my squirming gets a giggle, muffled as before against my chest. She settles down from her crouch above me, bringing her paws from by my shoulders to brush along my sides as she rests more fully against my front. I slip my own arms from around her until it's just my paws on her shoulders.

The sheer exhilaration of physical contact seems to be filling my mind—or at least that empty void within that I've only been able to tiptoe around—with something new. Something else. Something other than low-level anxiety. I can close my eyes and not wind up in some horrible hopelessness. I don't have to think, I can just be here. Goodness knows why, but I can just be here.

I jolt to awareness from my wandering thoughts and tense up, and Aurora's paws pause halfway up my sides. Her fingers and claws are buried in my fur with t-shirt cloth bunched around her wrists. We both hold still in that silence, a few long seconds of just our breaths. For once I don't rush to fill it with words, and simply settle back down, relaxing into her grasp.

The coyote hesitates a moment longer before edging her paws upward further, inching shirt up over fur. Keeping my paws on her shoulders as best as possible, I arch my back enough to let her slide my shirt up.

The exploration continues in fits and starts from there. Kisses along the blue diamond and down over my chest. Aurora shifting her weight. Me tugging my shirt off to keep it out of the way. Soft coyote nose tracing spirals in my fur. One lasting sensation, a singular point of focus.

The skirt, though, requires coordination. Aurora and I have to exchange a few glances, one or two half-words, and some soft giggles before the garment winds up bunched around my waist, spilling in pools of cotton to either side of me. And then there we are: me, with shirt off but for one arm still stuck through a sleeve, skirt bunched around my waist; and Aurora, looking nervous but excited, wagging as she looks up at me along my front over a pile of rumpled skirt.

"So uh..." I begin.

"Mm?"

"Mm."

Soft noises. Gestures of paws. The warmth of a tongue, slender and attentive. Finely-tapered coyote muzzle. Lithe, arched weasel back. Quiet moans and subtle shifts to express what works and what doesn't. Paws finding places to rest, to touch, to brush and stroke.

And then something new, something different clicks within me. A rising swell of pleasure, and a sudden, uneven tumble of memories. A shuddering gasp and an attachment of name to place to time. A contraction, then relaxation of muscles and a line drawn between two points. A connection.

Panting to catch my breath, and glimpses of high school, of nervous first times. Memories of a muzzle and an attentive tongue. That same muzzle, that same tongue.

A warm glow, and a name surfacing to memory.

I collapse back onto the bed, slack, and stare down over my front. Aurora stares back just as intently shifting her weight forward once more, retracing her route of kisses in double time.

"Wait, you're–"

"Aurora. I'm Aurora."

I start to speak, but she cuts me off.

"I'm Aurora. You're you."

I swallow convulsively, feel fear caving in my insides, terror at having been recognized, caught. "But you were...we–"

"I know who you *were*, and you know who I *was*, but I'm Aurora. You're you."

I fall silent, paws clutching at the duvet in search of something solid. Aurora leans up for the final kiss, more tender than heated, more earnest than fumbling. I smell her, and taste myself.

⋆

"We all have reasons to disappear," Aurora murmurs.

We've settled back onto that stack of pillows I've collected. My skirt's still bunched up between us, but I've managed to toss my shirt to the side. She's gotten her arms around me once more and her cool nose-tip is teasing along those brands again from where she lays beside me.

"I suppose," I begin, then shake my head as if to throw away a bit of the non-speech. "So you came out west and transitioned out here."

A faint nod, nose exploring a line perpendicular to the stripes of my brands. "I tried back home, a bit after high school and, uh...us. My heart was half out here by then anyway, though, and no one wants a mopey, trans coyote, least of all my parents."

I nod. There's still that hint of a name—I can think it, but would have a hard time saying it—and that memory of a tapered muzzle between my thighs.

Memories from nigh on twenty years ago.

A high school fling. Two dates, a night together, and drifting apart. She had seemed so uncomfortable with herself. We'd... Well, tonight had more than made up for that.

"And you?"

"Mm?"

"Why'd you disappear?"

"I don't know."

Aurora lifts her head a little, a hint of a grin turning the corner of her mouth. "You don't know?"

"I don't." I tilt my head to press my nose to hers. "I think that's what got me today. I saw that thing on the news. About Jarred, about myself. About home."

She nods, nose against nose and stifling a yawn.

"And I just don't know why," I murmur. "I unwound all of that life and came here, and I think, when I saw it, I realized I don't know why I did it."

"Were you happy, back home?"

"No."

Aurora tucks her muzzle up under my jaw and hugs her arm around me a little tighter. "Neither was I."

I brush my fingers across her arm, plowing a furrow in gray-tan fur, then smoothing it back down. I push down memories of that gawky and shy coyote, and revel instead in the comfort of Aurora.

So many months of panic following so many years of discontent. So much time alone. And now, comfort and peace.

Muzzle tucked over hers, I ask, "What about me did you remember?"

"Your paintings."

"Have I changed that much?"

"I mean, you looked like someone who could've been, uh, who you were. But it was your paintings." She yawns in earnest. "The lines. The shapes."

The burgundy-and-black ceiling tile is behind me. I think of looking, of disentangling myself from the coyote's arms, but there's something much better here in front of me.

"And you?" Aurora sounds sleepy. "What tipped you off about me?"

I think of all the things I could say—the warmth of her breath, the trail of kisses, the way her nose drew lines through my fur. The way she rested her cheek on her paw, staring out the window. The softness of her form. Her very scent.

We lay together in silence. A comfortable silence. The first in a long time.

Fisher

Alv pinned his ears back against his head as he stomped down the length of the block. His boots were too much for the drizzle that the weather offered, but it was that or his threadbare sneakers, and some tiny part of his mind had done the calculation without the rest of him knowing, and he'd tugged the heavy things on for the walk.

The air inside had grown too stuffy for the old fisher, or perhaps his eyes had grown too tired of reading, or maybe it was something in his joints, a feeling of too much space that needed to be compressed down. The solution, no matter the problem, was to move.

His third time around the block, knees and hips aching from walking in work boots that were never meant for the task, and Alv still hadn't figured out what it was that kept driving him out of the house. He'd walk, day after day, until his tail drooped and his feet started dragging. Sometimes, like today, he'd circle the block. Some days he'd drive the mile to the supermarket and walk aimlessly up and down each aisle, eventually picking up a drink or a snack, just to make the trip worth it. Other days, he'd just pace in his building's parking lot.

He didn't think.

Or maybe he thought too much. Maybe that was it. Maybe the fisher's every step was taken to crush too many thoughts beneath the soles of his boots, pressing the life out of them through the sheer weight of his restlessness.

He didn't know what it was that, day by day, drove him to his feet, drove him to walk until he couldn't walk anymore. He just knew that if he didn't, that ache within him, that burning, that itch would continue to grow, and he'd start to feel like his heart was being extruded through his rib cage, like his fur was coming out in clumps, like he couldn't possibly breathe deep enough.

His wife, gone now these five years, had been fond of calling him a restless soul. He wasn't sure that he was capable of believing in a soul, nor that this increasingly restless state of being was confined to something so intangible. He was just restless.

Just. Only.

That's all he was. There was nothing to him except restlessness. After Naomi's death, he'd slowly become less and less of a person, until all that was left was the urge to move, the terror over being confined to one place for any length of time.

His tail starting to sag, the fisher could feel all the calm he'd accumulated through the walk start to ebb, the tide of anxiety creeping in from the edges, from his fur inwards. One last trip around the block, he figured, was all he could manage before resting again.

By the time he made it around to his building again, Alv was well and truly sore, knees and hips aching from the repetitive motion of stomping around the block. Still, he couldn't bring himself to head up to his apartment quite yet. The idea of being closed in such a space held negative appeal. Something about the thought of four walls was actively repulsive.

So he sat on the damp stoop and watched the trees across the street.

The drizzle had dried up—though he hadn't noticed when—and all that was left was the occasional *pat* of drop on leaf as some bit of water got too heavy and sought a new home closer to the ground. There was just that gentle sound. Despite the hour, the street was empty of traffic, as though the shoddy weather had chased everyone inside.

"Would that my soul were that calm," he mumbled to the bare street at last and levered himself up creakily, climbing the rest of the stairs to head inside.

Centerpiece

"Hey E," Aaron mumbled, the cat nudging the turn signal lever up to make his way toward the right lane.

"Mm?" Erin peeked up from her book to see how far they'd made it into their journey. Still about twenty minutes. She lowered her gaze once again.

"Put any more thought into the idea of a donor?"

Slinking lower into the passenger seat, Erin gave a half-hearted shrug. "Not really any more than before. Just want someone we know already and who we trust. Don't want to go to a bank."

Aaron nodded and settled back into his seat as they made their way onto the highway. "Anyone you can think of, minkypie?"

Erin caught herself about to shrug again and shook her head instead, "Only really know a few other minks out there—the Redstones from work, and there's that Matthew guy from your office...Matthew Lederer, was it?—and I don't know if they swing or not. Come on, though," she laughed. "Figure out something sexier to talk about. We're supposed to be getting psyched for a night of debauchery, not figuring out sperm donor paperwork."

Erin and Aaron had been one of those couples that had been insufferably cute when dating. When they'd been friends, they'd been teased about it enough, but when it turned to romance, it all seemed a bit much.

It was the names that got most people, of course. They'd react in a few very predictable ways when they found out that the couple had homophonic names. Most folks would gush over how adorable it was, asking how they referred to each other when alone, what they'd name their children if they could have any, and so on, The rest seemed to fall into two camps: those that would ask, "doesn't that get confusing or weird in conversations?" and those that would make some lewd comment about sex, whether referring to threesomes or whether they'd ever played with another Aaron or Erin or something like that

The answers were all fairly straightforward, too, especially after several years of being asked the same questions. They would say that they called each other by their names like regular folks; they'd joke that if they had kids, they'd name them Erin and Aaron; they'd say that conversations were made easier when eye contact signaled which individual was being talked to; they'd say their sex life was private but give a wink.

Below the surface, though, were the more intimate truths. In private, they really only used each other's first initials, going by E and A respectively. They'd done the threesome thing quite a bit, actually, and even once with another Erin; it had been really rather nice, and they were looking forward to seeing her again tonight. And perhaps the most intimate truth was just how sore a subject parenthood was for the two of them, how much being an interspecies couple got in the way.

Aaron laughed and nodded. "Alright, alright," he said. "You looking forward to being a useful mink tonight, then?"

Despite all the planning and negotiation that had gone into tonight, despite all the times she'd heard it before, being called a 'useful mink' right before the first night in far too long where she really would be useful had Erin squirming in her seat, ears pinned back against her head.

The cat in the the driver's seat laughed, "I'll take that as a yes, then. Tell me what you're looking forward to most, then."

"Being...being useful."

"Mm, so it's more the serving others than the bondage?"

Erin felt her tail start to frizz out, something she could never seem to help when agitated. A fact that Aaron was always keen to exploit. "Mmhm...mink wants to be useful more than anything."

"More than anything?" Aaron asked, risking a glance away from the road to grin at his wife. "More than the pleasure of the act, you just want others to use you to feel good?"

If his goal had been to make her flustered, Aaron was succeeding. If it had been to get her more worked up, it was also very, very much succeeding. "Yeah," she began, voice thick with embarrassment. "Yeah, mink wants...wants people to come away feeling fulfilled, mink wants to be a tool to help them feel that way." The mink thought for a moment longer before slipping out of character, as it were, and adding, "The sex is good too, you know I'll enjoy that, but being useful is what I want."

Aaron nodded. "Not to drag us back to where we were, but is that part of why you want to be a mother so badly?"

"Mmhm, at least a little part of it. It feels like the strongest, highest, and, well, purest form of being useful."

"Well, that makes sense," Aaron said with a chuckle. "So..."

" 'So...' what?" Erin sat up within her seat. "What are you planning?"

"Nothing, nothing!" Unable to lift his paws from the steering wheel, the cat did his best to imply a disarming gesture with his shoulders. "Only, I was wondering, what if you got to be useful at a party like this one, and that led to a child?"

The mink in the passenger seat sat, mouth open, for a moment before finding the words to respond, "You...you're sure you're not planning anything?"

"Promise. No plans, or we'd be negotiating a hell of a lot harder."

"Well, I...I don't know." Erin realized that she was fiddling too much with her book, bending the pages, so she set her bookmark in place and slipped the paperback into her bag. "It would be a lot to process. But I'm pretty sure all of it would be good."

Aaron grinned toward the road, making his way over to the rightmost lane once more—they were just about to the end of the freeway stint of the trip, Erin guessed, so probably just a few minutes left. "Well, alright then. So if we wind up at a party like this and there just happens to be another mink there-"

Erin cut him off with a quiet whine, her tail bristled from base to tip and swishing against the back of the seat. "A! Come on!"

The cat's grin turned to a laugh. "What do you mean, 'come on'? You'd love it, you said so. You'd love to be a Centerpiece and come away with motherhood, I know you would! And you know I'm game, too."

Brushing furiously at her tail in an attempt to soothe her nerves, Erin let a stony silence fall, fighting to sort out a turbulent mixture of embarrassment, arousal, and that longing she'd always associated with her drive towards motherhood, biological imperative and otherwise.

Erin's silence and Aaron's grin lasted the next few minutes until they parked at the curb before a squat, suburban ranch house.

Aaron turned off the car and tugged up the parking break, leaning over to kiss his wife on the cheek, "Sorry if that was too far, E."

When she didn't respond, the cat reached for Erin's paw, twining fingers with her. She smiled bashfully to him.

"No, was just thinking," she murmured. "I *would* love that."

The cat's grin snapped back into place almost immediately, along with the start of a quiet purr. He leaned over to give another quick kiss before slipping his paw away and swinging wide the driver's side door. "Come on, then, grab the bin and let's get inside, catch up with folks."

★

Those who travel among the play parties, orgies, and swing groups often think of themselves as being sexually liberated.

However, they'll all be the first to admit that the time before the play party begins can be the most awkward part. Milling around with a plastic cup of too-sweet spiked punch in one paw and a little plate of store-bought cookies in the other sometimes made it feel a little too much like a social function put on by a group of employees.

The hosts of this party, another couple that Erin and Aaron had known for a few years now, two ferrets named Elise and Joan, had set up a few things to help alleviate that feeling, though there's not much that could make it go away entirely. For every bowl of chips or plate of cookies, there was a bowl of condoms (with several different sizes present) or lube packets (silicone or water based). The cooler of drinks, normally holding just beers and sodas, also contained a few drinks made from stronger things. Small, printed signs listed the rules (play safe, wear clothes outside, and so on) near every doorway. The plans for segueing from "party" to "play" involved strip poker.

Despite all of the effort, there was still some difficulty in loosening up. This was due in no small part, Erin suspected, to anticipation for later. Even the most sexually liberated could be awkwardly shy in the time leading up to sex.

Thankfully, as Centerpiece, she had little to worry about, in that sense. For her, the start and end to the night were clearly delineated. No strip poker for her. It would start when she was bound, gagged, and blindfolded, and it would end when she tapped out or was set loose, whichever came first. That would come soon, and the gear was all in the bin that Aaron had dragged in and set in the living room next to the neatly decked mattress that would be her spot for the night.

"First things first," Aaron said, once Erin had gotten a drink. "Lift your chin."

Erin did as she was told, letting her husband deftly swing a collar up around her neck and fasten it in front. Although she couldn't see the collar, she knew what it looked like—black nylon webbing with some yellow nylon woven into it to spell 'TOY' along the back and a tag saying the same in front. Feeling the weight of it around her neck, the slight constriction of her fur beneath it, Erin tensed up and swished about, her short, rounded ears splayed.

"Finish your drink, minkytoy," Aaron continued, waiting for the mink to down the rest of her soda before clipping a leash to the D-ring at her throat.

When the cat gave an experimental tug, Erin felt herself jerked forward an inch or two by the collar at back of her neck. Beyond that, though, she felt that latent arousal that had been dwelling within her the last few days finally begin to assert its presence, felt sub-space start to surround her like a warm blanket.

Her husband grinned at the obvious change and leaned in close enough to whisper to her, "Mm, cozy there, pet?"

Ears pinned back, Erin gave a bashful nod.

"Going to be a good pet tonight?"

Nod.

"Still comfortable with this?"

Another nod, more vigorous this time.

"Going to be useful for everyone tonight, no matter what?"

Erin mewled quietly, tucking her muzzle down toward her chest and hunching her shoulders as though she could hide her embarrassment that way. "Yes owner," she murmured, tail lashing this way and that. "Will be useful."

Aaron grinned haughtily and wound the leash around one of his paws a few times, giving another little tug to help reinforce his position over her. "Good mink. Let's go see who you're going to be useful for, then."

Erin felt them quickly slip into a feedback loop of power dynamics. The more dominant that Aaron got in showing her off to the party's other attendees, the more submissive she felt. The more submissive she acted, the more that seemed to egg Aaron on. Before long, he was encouraging her to spin and show off, to curtsy, to make small confessions to the other attendees.

This was one of the other things that Elise and Joan did to loosen up their guests. Each party—and there were several a year—

included one guest who would be the Centerpiece. The Centerpiece had become a coveted role in the circles that attended this party, one that had to be applied for ahead of time.

And it was indeed a role to play. The Centerpiece was the one who had to start moving the atmosphere from party to play while the two ferrets tended to more mundane things such as maintaining snack levels and ensuring that the rules were followed. Once the atmosphere had shifted, the Centerpiece (almost always a known sub, but once or twice, a more dominant figure had surprised the group by serving) was to become literally that: a fixture at the center of the party, immobile. A figure to be discussed or a toy to be used in a public fashion.

Although this was Erin's first time being the Centerpiece, the role fit her naturally. Elise had leaped at the chance to feature the mink for the party. To have a willing critter who was already a well-known sub (and already quite knowledgeable in bondage) made the hostesses' jobs easier and the party more fun.

By the time they had made the rounds of the patio, Erin knew that she had done well. The timbre of the party had shifted according to plan, the curtains had been drawn, and the game of strip poker had already begun in the den. The mink was buzzing with a mixture of arousal and pleasurable embarrassment, along with a base note of that nearly primal need to please.

Which is precisely when her smirking owner and husband tugged on her leash to get her to look up, saying, "And this is Matthew. Matthew Lederer. I believe you've met."

Erin found her gaze sliding up along the slinky form before her, hidden by a half-unbuttoned dress shirt, to the soft features of the other mink. He was sleek and well groomed, whiskers bristled as if caught in the middle of searching for an intriguing scent. As everything from the earlier conversations clicked into place, she found herself tense at the end of the leash.

Another mink.

And here she was, smelling of arousal and desire: the Centerpiece, the offering to the party.

Matthew's mind seemed to be going through some similar calculation, as his gaze shifted from shock through bemusement to hunger, grinning at the slender mink-toy being presented to him by the cat, giving an appraising glance over the rims of his glasses.

Erin watched him turn to face her husband, "Good to see you here, buddy! And yeah, I believe we have." That grin widened, showing the mink's pointed teeth. "Wasn't expecting to be so lucky in my choice of toys for tonight."

Looking positively smug, Aaron tapped the tip of his wife's nose with the end of the leash, nodding. "Mmhm. Was my turn to bring the Centerpiece. Just about to go get her all trussed up. But here, stand up straighter, minkytoy."

Able only to muster a soft mewl, Erin nodded and stood up straighter, her tail flitting about erratically.

"The Centerpiece should greet all her guests while she still can. Go on."

Erin nodded and leaned in to give the other mink an embrace and a whiskery, bashful kiss to the side of his muzzle. "W-welcome..."

Matthew returned the kiss with a grin, seeming to pick up on some of Aaron's bravado. "Thank you, ah..." he reached a paw up to lift the tag on the smaller mink's collar to read it. "Thank you, toy. I'm sure I'll be most welcome indeed."

⋆

"I thought you said you didn't have anything planned," Erin said, still shivering from the mix of humiliation and arousal as she tugged her shirt off.

Aaron, already nude, looked up from where he had been rooting in the bin of bondage gear, "I didn't, E, I promise. I didn't know he was coming until he showed up just then. Didn't even know this was his scene."

Erin nodded, anxious. She slipped shyly out of the last of her clothes and knelt, nude, on the mattress.

"Do you want me to call in Elise? We can tap out, if it's uncomfortable, or Elise can ask him to not interact with you as the Centerpiece."

The mink felt herself flush beneath her fur, whiskers bristling. "Mmnf..." she managed, then, "N-no. I mean, now I'm all curious. I've...never been with another mink before, after all."

Aaron grinned and sat down on the edge of the mattress, holding a pair of soft, locking bondage cuffs and a snap hook connector—two lobster clasps joined by a strip of nylon with a D-ring situated in the middle—for binding them together. "Oh, so you're eager, then, toy?"

Erin squirmed at the pet name. She hadn't quite left subspace, hadn't wanted to, and so the words played readily into that. "I...maybe," she admitted, squirming tensely.

The cat's grin widened as he turned and crawled over the mattress to her, muzzle tucking in against her cheek, his paws working to fasten one of the locking cuffs around her wrist. "Toy sure *smells* eager," he breathed.

Tilting her cheek to her owner's muzzle and lifting both of her paws to offer her wrists to him, Erin whined quietly in return. "Can't help it," she mumbled, her breathing picking up.

"I imagine not." Aaron continued slipping the other cuff onto the mink's other wrist, making a show of checking the locked status of each before attaching the connector to the exposed D-rings of the cuffs, effectively locking Erin's paws together. Although cuffs were a common accessory for her, she always got a thrill out of having them put on by someone else.

"Hopefully not too obvious?" she asked.

"This is a play party, E, it's kind of expected," Aaron said. The cat's laugh made Erin lay her ears all the way back. He tugged on the strap connecting her cuffs together pulling her up onto her knees and then onto all fours, his paw pinning the snap connector to the mattress. The laugh turned into a low growl as Aaron murmured, "And besides, toy, everyone noticed." With a soft nip to her ear, he lowered his voice further to a soft purr, adding, "Everyone."

Any distance Erin had managed to gain from the sexual dynamic to ask about plans was quickly obliterated with the firm treatment and teasing words. She quickly found herself back in that cozy submissive mindset, her paws clutching at the sheets of the mattress, held only as far apart as the cuffs would let them. "Was toy useful?"

Dragging the tote of gear closer, Aaron nodded, his voice muffled slightly by the fact that he couldn't hold back a purr. "Very useful. You got everyone up and moving. Lots of needy looks when we left to get ready." The cat brought up another snap connector and with an insistent paw, pushed Erin's shoulders down until her chin nearly touched her paws, clipping this connector between the D-ring on her collar and the one on the first snap connector, leaving the mink with her backside hiked up and exposed. "But you're only just getting started, minkytoy. You're going to be very, very useful by night's end, aren't you?"

Erin nodded, her breathing quick and shallow in anticipation. She could smell her own arousal quite strongly, now, as well as that of Aaron, a scent she was well accustomed to. "Yes, owner," she panted, breath tinged with a whine.

There was a bit more fumbling in the bin before Aaron lay a few more items out in front of her, close enough to see but not touch. A ring-gag. A blindfold. A small remote control type device. A bowl of condoms. Two laminated signs—one with rules, the other with a space for tallying just how the mink had been useful. A marker to go with the signs.

Kneeling before her, Aaron took the blindfold in one paw and the gag in the other and leaned in closer. The familiar scent of the cat's arousal was filling Erin's nostrils, his stiff shaft dead center in her gaze, but, again, just out of reach. The scent of him was overpowering the scent of herself, but she could feel that burning arousal in her belly, feel the cool air against her groin, caressing warm and slick flesh.

"Even that mink? Matthew?" the cat asked. It was hard for Erin to pick apart whether her owner was purring or growling, or perhaps a little bit of both. "Are you going to be a useful toy for him, too?"

Erin felt her fur bristle, that perennial reaction to humiliation no longer restricted to just her tail, but creeping up her spine to her neck and ears, heckles raising. "Toy will," she whimpered. "Mink'll be usef-*nngh!*"

She was cut off quickly. She'd been so focused on Aaron's words and the sight of his arousal in the center of her tunnel-vision that she hadn't noticed the paw with the ring gag.

With one deft movement, the cat had taken advantage of her open muzzle to slip the gag in place, wedging her muzzle open with the ring of stiff rubber. His fingers quickly traced the straps of the gag to their ends, Velcro straps that looped around her collar to hold the gag in place.

"I know you will, toy," the cat growled—and it definitely was a growl this time. A commanding, possessive, domineering growl that ensured she knew her place.

Erin could only whine and pant, huff and whimper. She nodded shakily, as much as the straps restraining her neck to her wrists would allow.

Those teasing growls continued as Aaron set up, clearly leaving the blindfold in his paw until last so that she would be forced to watch. "I wonder if toy will be able to tell it's him," he said. "By shape or by noise. Or maybe he'll lean forward and whisper to you how he's taking you. Maybe he'll just scruff the toy. I bet his teeth are sharp."

Whimper, pant, squirm. Erin couldn't manage a whole lot more, as she watched her owner set up the signs. "Please use condoms; no damage; Centerpiece will use buzzer to tap out" read one. "Cum count: In sex—In muzzle—In fur" read the other, the pen laid neatly at its base.

"Maybe it'll trigger something in you," Aaron said. He picked up the remote control and gave its single button a quick press, the small box emitting a surprisingly loud buzzing noise, annoying by design. Slipping the buzzer into Erin's paw, he leaned in closer to continue, "Maybe your body will know him by his species. Maybe you'll know what it is that you're missing out by him using a condom with you, by being that close to having his kits."

A more drawn-out whine this time, low and needy, as her owner sought out and tickled each and every one of her kinks in turn.

She was gone. Totally lost in sub-space. And he was driving her deeper and deeper.

"Press the button, toy."

Shaking, Erin fumbled with the remote, getting the button aligned under her thumb before pressing it. She got a loud buzz in response.

"Good. Don't forget that, toy." Aaron grinned and reached once more into the tote of gear. "I'll watch when I can, but I have my own fun planned tonight."

With that, Erin watched as the cat stood, making as if to open the door for everyone, letting the play of the Centerpiece begin, still murmuring, "Maybe toy will find herself needing him, hmm? Craving that mink within her, fitting so nicely like only another mink can. Maybe some day you *will* wind up with his kits."

The cat paused and turned back, looking as if he'd just remembered something. Erin noticed the blindfold left in his paw and squirmed against the bed, knowing that the sensory deprivation would only serve to drive her deeper into Useful Mink territory.

Aaron knelt before her once more and lifted the blindfold, then set it to the side and instead lifted his other paw. In it was a safety pin, something from the emergency sewing kit in the gear tote. Holding his paws deliberately within her gaze, Aaron opened the safety pin, exposing the sharp point. With his free paw, he reached down to grab one of the wrapped condoms from the bowl.

"And who knows," he said, grinning widely as he drove the

point of the pin through the package, the condom inside, and clear through out the other side of the package. "Maybe he'll get this one."

The condom dangled briefly from the safety pin directly before Erin's eyes. She watched, unable to speak even if she hadn't been gagged, as the cat slid the needle-thin pin from the condom and massaged it with his finger-pads, leaving it looking intact and unmolested. He then tossed it almost casually into the bowl of condoms, mixing them up lazily with his paw. Aaron closed the safety pin and dropped it back into the tote with a small rattle.

Realizing that she had been holding her breath, Erin let it out in a gasp and a shaky moan before swallowing dryly, making a soft *gllk* noise with the gag in the way. She could feel Aaron hesitating, watching her for any sign that she would need to back out.

Her mind was reeling, her breath coming in ragged pants, her arousal out of control, her body coursing with what felt like electricity. But she gave a slight nod of consent.

Her last sight was of Aaron grinning as he reached down to fasten the blindfold over her eyes, clipping that, too, to the collar so that it couldn't easily be removed. Sight gone, she could only rely on touch, scent, taste, sound.

The rustle of Aaron standing, the feel of the mattress shifting beneath her.

"Remember your buzzer, toy."

Footsteps.

The scent of her owner's arousal fading, the scent of her own taking over.

The sound of the door.

Traces of other scents, other people, other species, other arousals.

Voices, soft applause.

And Aaron's voice, "The Centerpiece is ready."

You're Gone

— Sunday, March 30 —

1:39 PM Markus
Doctor Maura told me I should start journaling when this whole crazy process started. She said it would keep me grounded, let me set milestones of memory, some BS like that.

1:40 PM Markus
I told her I'd give it a think and then promised myself I'd forget about it.

1:40 PM Markus
But now, you're gone.

1:40 PM Markus
You're gone.

1:40 PM Markus
Oh god.

1:40 PM Markus
You're gone.

— Monday, March 31 —

12:10 AM Markus

I made it home from the hospital a few hours ago. My hand hurts. My heart hurts. So much paperwork to let someone go.

12:11 AM Markus

They say I'll have to sign more tomorrow, and that I should get a lawyer.

— Tuesday, April 1 —

7:12 AM Markus

I keep expecting you to still be here.

7:12 AM Markus

It's not trite, like it sounds like when others say it.

7:13 AM Markus

Not like I'm expecting you to come around the corner or come through the door.

7:13 AM Markus

More like

7:13 AM Markus

You're still at the hospital.

7:13 AM Markus

You're still just at chemo.

7:13 AM Markus

You're out of the house.

7:14 AM Markus

You lost your phone.

7:14 AM Markus

I guess that's trite.

7:18 AM Markus

Though I turned off your phone.

7:18 AM Markus

I could hear it vibrating every time I messaged.

7:28 AM Markus

Couldn't tell if that made me feel sad or stupid, or both.

7:32 AM Markus

Both, I think.

— **Wednesday, April 2** —

2:30 PM Markus

You made it to the funeral home.

2:30 PM Markus

In one piece.

2:30 PM Markus

Hah hah.

2:48 PM Markus

Nice skunk working with me there is irked that I keep texting.

2:49 PM Markus

Just showed him this.

2:50 PM Markus

He got quiet and smiled and said, "You can keep texting."

2:50 PM Markus

Feeling slightly less stupid, but no less sad.

3:08 PM Markus

Cremation and all that goes with it is expensive.

3:08 PM Markus

I mean, not super expensive. Cheaper than the other stuff.

3:08 PM Markus

But we didn't really plan this well.

3:09 PM Markus

Oh god.

3:09 PM Markus

I almost made a suggestion.

3:09 PM Markus

Oh god.

3:28 PM Markus

You're gone.

— **Thursday, April 3** —

10:02 AM Markus

You came home in a plastic bag in a box.

10:02 AM Markus

Lol

10:08 AM Markus

this is dumb

10:08 AM Markus

cryinf ovef a bvox

3:43 PM Markus

Service Friday 4pm call Maru dad mom mil Jenna Jeff Selene flowers
664-1140

3:43 PM Markus

...

3:44 PM Markus

Thought you should know, I guess.

3:44 PM Markus

Kick me from beyond the grave if I start using this as a notepad.

3:44 PM Markus

I know you would, too.

— **Friday, April 4** —

9:51 PM Markus

Okay.

9:51 PM Markus

So.

9:51 PM Markus

You know I hate your mom.

9:52 PM Markus

I think that's supposed to be some Thing, that a husband must hate his wife's mom.

9:52 PM Markus

But you know that, because I'm pretty sure you hated her too.

9:53 PM Markus

I mean, you never said so to my face or anything, but you did all you could not to be in the same room as her.

9:53 PM Markus

(I know you hate your dad)

9:53 PM Markus

*hated

9:53 PM Markus

fuck

9:54 PM Markus

sorry

9:54 PM Markus

...

9:56 PM Markus

sorry

— **Saturday, April 5** —

12:21 AM Markus

Anyway, that bitch was there at your service.

12:21 AM Markus

Of course she was, I mean.

12:21 AM Markus

But I call her a bitch because she was.

12:22 AM Markus
She made it sound like I killed you.

12:22 AM Markus
She said if her daughter had married another cat, it would've been fine.

12:23 AM Markus
But no.

12:23 AM Markus
You married me.

12:23 AM Markus
And I don't know how, but somehow it became my fault that you died.

12:24 AM Markus
We went from crying together over supermarket snack trays to terse arguments in surprisingly little time.

12:24 AM Markus
She thought that if she'd married a cat, she would've had kits and a happier life.

12:25 AM Markus
I don't know where the cancer came in, but she was convinced that this was somehow the cause of it.

12:26 AM Markus
Marry a coyote? Get cancer.

12:26 AM Markus
I mean, duh.

12:26 AM Markus

She really wanted grandkits.

12:26 AM Markus

(didn't tell her about the ligation. You never did, so I promised I wouldn't)

12:26 AM Markus

Anyway.

12:27 AM Markus

I'm really upset.

12:27 AM Markus

The service wasn't meaningful. It was boring.

12:27 AM Markus

Your mother aside, I think that's the most upsetting thing.

12:27 AM Markus

Your service was boring.

12:27 AM Markus

I got home at nine or whatever, and I just sat on the bed.

12:28 AM Markus

I fell asleep in my nice clothes.

12:28 AM Markus

Now I'm sitting on the bathroom floor waiting for the water to heat up, and it's already hot, but I'm still on my phone, just like you hate.

12:28 AM Markus

*hated

— **Sunday, April 6** —

10:10 AM Markus
Thank you for leaving a will.

11:12 AM Markus
Met with MiL again, this time with lawyers.

11:12 AM Markus
Thank you for leaving me everything.

11:12 AM Markus
Even your ashes. Your mom hated that most, I think.

11:13 AM Markus
You left me with all of our debts, but you left her with nothing.

11:13 AM Markus
Surprised I don't feel self-righteous or whatever. Just resolute. I didn't "win". If anyone won, it was you.

11:14 AM Markus
But if I'd had to cede to your mom and stepdad that would have hurt.

11:16 AM Markus
Thank you.

— **Monday, April 7** —

2:18 PM Markus
I formed your ashes into a rock by mixing them with water and baking until they got hard, and then I skipped it across the university pond.

2:19 PM Markus

Kidding.

2:19 PM Markus

I know you asked for that.

2:19 PM Markus

I also didn't dump your ashes out in the parking lot of your office.

2:20 PM Markus

I didn't dump them in the plaza fountain or flush them down a toilet at your office, either.

2:21 PM Markus

Sorry. All your last wishes gone to waste.

2:24 PM Markus

I took your ashes and drove up into the hills, because I decided this wasn't for you, it was for me.

2:25 PM Markus

I'm sorry.

2:27 PM Markus

I drove up into the hills until I got to one of those pull-aside rest stops, and I walked down to the river there, and I just sat for a bit and cried.

2:27 PM Markus

And I wasn't thinking.

2:28 PM Markus

And I cut open the bag of ashes and scooped a few pawfuls of water in there and mixed it up to a sort of smoothie consistency.

2:29 PM Markus

And I poured it out on the river bank.

2:29 PM Markus

And I kinda mixed and kneaded and massaged it into the river mud.

2:29 PM Markus

And I just kinda cried and gave you up bit by bit.

2:30 PM Markus

The water would splash up on the banks and I just let you be carried away bit by bit.

2:30 PM Markus

Until there was nothing left but a messy spot on the shore.

2:30 PM Markus

And I washed my paws.

2:30 PM Markus

And it was super cold.

2:30 PM Markus

And I only had my jeans to dry my paws on, so I just sat there like an idiot.

2:30 PM Markus

Crying and puffing into my paws to try and warm them up.

2:31 PM Markus

You'll be proud to know that it was disgusting.

2:31 PM Markus

there's you all over that river bank

2:31 PM Markus

and all over my paws

2:31 PM Markus
and stuck in my fur

2:31 PM Markus
and probably on my muzzle

2:31 PM Markus
and the steering wheel of the car

2:31 PM Markus
and the doorknib

2:31 PM Markus
asnd your all over now

2:32 PM Markus
and i thought I was saying goodbye

2:32 PM Markus
and your still here

2:32 PM Markus
i miss you

2:32 PM Markus
i love you

— **Tuesday, April 8** —

12:01 PM Markus
Okay.

12:01 PM Markus
So.

12:01 PM Markus

Not only was that a mess, but it was apparently illegal.

12:03 PM Markus

I slept and feel better, and now I'm giggling like an idiot over the fact that I did something meaningful to me, and it turned out I was breaking the law the whole time. You're not supposed to scatter ashes in water.

12:03 PM Markus

(And even if it were legal, there's probably a better way to do it than what I did.)

12:04 PM Markus

So there you have it. I thought I was going to snub your goofy wishes but your idiot husband wound up going along with them all the same.

— Wednesday, April 9 —

9:41 AM Markus

Back at work today.

9:41 AM Markus

Everyone was nice.

9:41 AM Markus

Calm.

10:21 AM Markus

And I do feel better, PS. I think I got more out of that than I can put into words.

— Thursday, April 10 —

4:54 PM Markus

I miss you, sweetheart.

4:54 PM Markus

I remember when you got diagnosed and we both had a good cry over it, but then it all turned out to be so boring after that.

4:55 PM Markus

It was hard having that hang over us both, I know, but it all got routine

4:56 PM Markus

Awful, but routine

4:56 PM Markus

And then things got better.

4:56 PM Markus

Until they didn't.

4:56 PM Markus

Everything got so bad so quickly.

4:56 PM Markus

Your mom didn't even come and see you.

4:56 PM Markus

Oh well.

4:58 PM Markus

Starting on the rest of your will and such tonight.

5:20 PM Markus

Looks like you just left me everything.

5:20 PM Markus

Which is good.

5:22 PM Markus

When my sister died, everything was a mess, because she had two wills.

5:23 PM Markus

Neither had been updated.

5:24 PM Markus

Oh god, and her husband and my parents were a mess trying to figure things out with the house and title and stuff.

5:24 PM Markus

Renting is making things easier.

5:24 PM Markus

And your "everything to Markus" will.

5:24 PM Markus

Your mom's pissed.

— **Friday, April 11** —

6:43 PM Markus

Okay, your mom's -really- pissed.

6:43 PM Markus

She says that a lot of your stuff is rightfully hers.

6:44 PM Markus

I've yet to find anything that could rightfully be called hers.

6:46 PM Markus

She wants to go through your desk with me, and I don't know what to say to her. She says she's got books and papers that are hers in there, and I don't know what to do about that.

6:46 PM Markus

I wish you were here to tell her off.

6:48 PM Markus

She keeps sending me messages in all caps that are half about your stuff and half about how I'm the wrong species, and that you deserved a cat who would take care of her and give her grandkits. She says I'm garbage and disreputable and that I tarnished the reputation of your family.

6:48 PM Markus

Which I don't get.

6:48 PM Markus

You guys aren't famous

6:48 PM Markus

Forwarded message from Xiuying (Lee Mom)
GARBAGE YOUR GARBAGE I CANT BELIEVE YOUD KEEP ME FROM MY DAUGHTER

6:48 PM Markus

Forwarded message from Xiuying (Lee Mom)
You took our name and DRAGGED IT THROUGH MUD YOU TOOK LI AND DRAGGED HER THROUGH MUD GIVE ME WHATS MINE

6:49 PM Markus

Though I guess I did drag you throuugh the mud.

6:49 PM Markus

Har Har

6:50 PM Markus

I don't know what she means about keeping you from her.

6:50 PM Markus

I thought I knew what hatred felt like, but damn, Lee.

6:50 PM Markus

How did so sane a cat come from so crazy a family?

6:52 PM Markus

I was going to go through your clothes first, because those felt like they'd be easy, but I'm going to go through your desk instead.

— Sunday, April 13 —

9:03 AM Markus

There is literally nothing in your desk of interest.

9:04 AM Markus

I took all our bills and boxed up everything and gave it to your mom.

9:05 AM Markus

Seriously. You had some notes printed out about research, two planners, and 12 blank books.

9:05 AM Markus

I counted.

9:05 AM Markus

I swear to god, Lee. I miss the hell out of you, but 12 blank books?

9:06 AM Markus

I just kept your laptop.

— Monday, April 14 —

4:21 PM Markus

Your mom's yelling at me again.

4:21 PM Markus

She wants to go through my papers now, too. And my books?

4:22 PM Markus

I love you and miss you so much. You were always so good at telling her to go away. She won't listen to me at all.

4:42 PM Markus

Called a probate lawyer.

4:44 PM Markus

She said it should be straightforward if the will is in order.

4:44 PM Markus

Didn't tell her about your mom though.

— Tuesday, April 15 —

3:53 PM Markus

Your stepdad is meeting with me after work.

3:53 PM Markus

We're meeting at a coffee shop, don't worry.

5:23 PM Markus

WHAT THE FUCK WHAT THE FUCK

5:24 PM Markus

Your stepdad was nice enough, we talked about memories of you. He said he knew about your feelings toward him, and that he wished he'd done better by you.

5:24 PM Markus

But then I got home and YOUR MOM HAS BEEN IN OUR APARTMENT

5:25 PM Markus

I guess I got home faster than they thought, but I think your stepdad was keeping me occupied while your mom BROKE INTO OUR PLACE

5:26 PM Markus

I ran into her in front of the building and she started yelling and hollering at me, and I was so confused.

5:26 PM Markus

She said I was hiding your stuff from her and that she would be calling her lawyer.

5:28 PM Markus

AND THEN SHE HIT ME

5:28 PM Markus

SHE SLAPPED ME

5:29 PM Markus

I yelled that I was going to call the police when Jun screeched up in a car and she jumped in and drove off

5:29 PM Markus

What the FUCK

5:30 PM Markus

I'm calling the cops to get her away from here

5:58 PM Markus

They took a report and said to call again if she shows up, that way they can talk with her, and worst case, then I can get a restraining order.

5:59 PM Markus

She trashed our bookshelf and dug through our closets.

6:00 PM Markus

I don't think anything's missing. It's just a mess.

6:00 PM Markus

The cop took a report, though.

6:00 PM Markus

Don't know how she got a key.

— **Wednesday, April 16** —

11:03 AM Markus

Now she wants your laptop.

11:03 AM Markus

I had it with me at coffee even.

11:04 AM Markus

I don't have the password, though, no idea what she'd do with it.

11:32 AM Markus

I think I may destroy it.

— **Friday, April 18** —

11:03 PM Markus

I miss you so much, Lee.

11:04 PM Markus
I think it's really starting to hit me.

11:04 PM Markus
You're gone.

11:04 PM Markus
You're dead.

11:04 PM Markus
You're never coming back.

11:05 PM Markus
Your mom went quiet, and now I'm finally starting to digest this.

11:08 PM Markus
I wish I could take your place.

11:08 PM Markus
I wish I were dead.

11:08 PM Markus
I wish I was gone.

11:11 PM Markus
Oh god.

11:11 PM Markus
I keep getting stcuk crying and

11:11 PM Markus
its so hrad to keep going sometimes

11:11 PM Markus
i want to die without yowue

11:12 PM Markus
oh god

11:12 PM Markus
lee

11:12 PM Markus
oh god

— **Saturday, April 19** —

12:44 AM Markus
I miss you

— **Sunday, April 20** —

2:21 PM Markus
I can't believe you set your password to that!

2:21 PM Markus
I could spank you for that, miss prissy whiskers.

2:21 PM Markus
You're such a dork <3

— **Monday, April 21** —

1:02 AM Markus
Lee

1:02 AM Markus
Lee I'm so sorry

1:02 AM Markus
  I'm so sorry

1:02 AM Markus
  I'm reading it now

9:20 AM Markus
  stayed home

9:21 AM Markus
  cant stop crying

9:21 AM Markus
  sorry

9:21 AM Markus
  im so sorry lee

4:11 PM Markus
  I could kill him

4:11 PM Markus
  Kill your fucking dad

4:11 PM Markus
  I WOULD fucking kill him right now

4:28 PM Markus
  I would destroy him and your mom for all they've done if I could

— **Tuesday, April 22** —

12:31 AM Markus
  I won't

12:31 AM Markus
  But I could.

12:31 AM Markus

I'm sorry Lee

12:41 AM Markus

I wish I could go back in time and help you.

— **Wednesday, April 23** —

6:43 PM

Lee sent you a file "should-I-pass.txt"

6:43 PM Markus

Sorry, wanted that on my end, so I sent it from your account.

6:48 PM Markus

Apparently your account expires after six months inactivity.

6:48 PM Markus

I wonder if I should keep logging on once a month to keep it active?

6:49 PM Markus

Or

6:49 PM Markus

Maybe I should let it expire

6:49 PM Markus

And set that as a date to let you go

6:49 PM Markus

Oh god Lee

6:52 PM Markus

oh god

6:52 PM Markus

i miss you

6:52 PM Markus

you made me whole

6:57 PM Markus

don't want to tgo on weifthout oyu

6:57 PM Markus

sdf

7:20 PM Markus

sorry

— **Friday, April 25** —

5:10 PM Markus

I'm calling your mom and Jun today.

5:11 PM Markus

I'm going to invite them over this weekend and confront them.

5:12 PM Markus

You're right in that it's just a document. No signature, no verification.

5:12 PM Markus

Biot I need to do right by yuo/ i miss yuo, and i want to do right by you

5:12 PM Markus

you tolfd me not to fight

5:12 PM Markus

and i wont

5:12 PM Markus

im just goin to tell thm i know

5:12 PM Markus

tey need to know that someone else knowds

— **Saturday, April 26** —

11:01 AM Markus

Your mom and Jun are coming over tomorrow.

11:01 AM Markus

I think I'm going to just tell them plain and simple, what I found.

11:02 AM Markus

I hate them. I loathe them.

11:03 AM Markus

But I owe it to you to not make it a big fight.

11:03 AM Markus

Not on my part, at least.

11:03 AM Markus

If they get angry, whatever. I'm just going to read it.

11:03 AM Markus

Most of it.

11:03 AM Markus

Read it and watch and make sure they understand that I know.

11:08 AM Markus

I'm starting to second guess this.

11:18 AM Markus

Like, obviously I'm upset, and obviously you wanted me to know that your parents are awful.

11:18 AM Markus

But I'm starting to second guess what I'll get out of this.

11:19 AM Markus

Even when I said I wouldn't make it a big fight, I was still coming at it from a vengeance standpoint.

11:19 AM Markus

I wanted to hurt them.

11:20 AM Markus

Still do.

11:20 AM Markus

I just don't think that's totally right.

2:18 PM Markus

I thought about it more, and I think I still need to share what you wrote.

2:19 PM Markus

It'll hurt them, and it'll probably hurt me more than it already has.

2:19 PM Markus

But I don't think any of us will be able to start grieving with the current state.

2:19 PM Markus

...I'm going to call Dr Maura.

2:48 PM Markus

I wasn't expecting her to get back to me, but she actually picked up her phone on the first ring.

2:48 PM Markus

I don't know why that strikes me as weird.

2:49 PM Markus

We talked for a bit about what I should do.

2:40 PM Markus

I told her about the letter you left. She agrees I should share with your parents, if only to give closure, like I said before.

2:50 PM Markus

She says she's worried about me and wants to talk more soon.

2:58 PM Markus

I told her about this, too.

2:58 PM Markus

About sending you messages, even though you'll never respond. Just talking to you.

3:00 PM Markus

She says it can be a healthy coping mechanism, but only to a point, and that I shouldn't lean on it too much, or I won't stop grieving.

3:00 PM Markus

Makes sense.

3:01 PM Markus

I promised I'd let your account expire, and would do my best to start moving on sooner than that.

3:02 PM Markus

We also talked about getting through grief in stages. She says there are a few different lists of 'stages of grief', but that they're all just loose guidelines.

3:03 PM Markus

She says it sounds like I'm going through some healthy stuff, but that she wants to meet again to make sure I keep going.

3:05 PM Markus

She says that things could wear me out and make me depressed, or that things could be super easy and I could finish all the work I need to do, and realize you're truly gone and get depressed.

3:05 PM Markus

I countered that I was depressed now, but I'm not sure about that anymore. I think I'm sad, and that depression will come soon.

3:06 PM Markus

I'm sad, Lee.

3:06 PM Markus

I'm sad and I'm tired and I want you back.

3:06 PM Markus

I'm sitting on the floor waiting for the shower again. My tail's fallen asleep. I'm gonna go before you get mad, even if that isn't possible.

3:07 PM Markus

I don't care if that's me grieving in an unhealthy manner or anything, I'm going to go before you get mad.

3:07 PM Markus

I'll try to only write again after things with your parents.

— Sunday, April 27 —

4:05 PM Markus

This is weird

4:21 PM Markus

Taking a break, this is still weird.

5:33 PM Markus

WHAT THE FUCK, LEE

5:33 PM Markus

THE POLICE JUST ARRESTED YOUR MOM

5:33 PM Markus

What the FUCK

5:43 PM Markus

Gave the police my report.

5:43 PM Markus

What the fuck.

5:46 PM Markus

Okay, writing this all down before I forget.

5:47 PM Markus

We met at that same coffee shop I met Jun at before. The Book and the Bean. It's got a bookstore in the back, I think we've been there before.

5:47 PM Markus

Only this time, Jun looked sincerely upset and sorry.

5:47 PM Markus

Like

5:48 PM Markus

I don't know how to put it. He looked upset for me, not at me?

5:48 PM Markus

And your mom looked extra pissed.

5:48 PM Markus

And I don't know what happened, like maybe they got into a fight before getting here?

5:49 PM Markus

So we were really quiet and Jun was looking down at his paws a lot and your mom was glaring at me a lot and I was tired.

5:49 PM Markus

I hate coffee, but I got a mocha or whatever, because Lee, I've just been so tired.

5:50 PM Markus

this isn't helping, i'm sorry.

5:50 PM Markus

i miss yuo

7:32 PM Markus

Sorry, I'll try again and get more to the point.

7:33 PM Markus

So the more I thought about what I had planned, the less I really wanted to go through with it. So I tried to just sit there and talk with your parents about you and all the good time and stuff.

7:33 PM Markus

I tried earnestly to patch things up, but your mom just told me she remembered things differently.

7:34 PM Markus

And it was stupid, because I could tell Jun was sad.

7:34 PM Markus

After everything.

7:34 PM Markus

After everything in your letter and after the dumbass break-in attempt and everything.

7:34 PM Markus

He was sad.

7:35 PM Markus

He would smile a little at a memory I brought up, then look off away from your mom like he wasn't going to cry.

7:35 PM Markus

And then your mom would get huffy, and he'd nod at her, and go back to looking at his paws.

7:35 PM Markus

I don't know.

7:36 PM Markus

I feel like he's as exhausted as I am, but for different reasons.

7:36 PM Markus

So we took a little break because I felt like he and I were headed for a different conversation than your mom.

7:36 PM Markus

So we got some more coffees and such.

7:36 PM Markus

And I just kinda buckled down and did it.

7:36 PM Markus

Before, when I was feeling more vengeful, I thought maybe I'd print off some copies and hand it to them all formally and wither them under my glare or whatever.

7:37 PM Markus

But I just sat down and told them about the file and how I found it.

7:37 PM Markus

How you'd written it to me, and locked your computer with a password for me.

7:37 PM Markus

oh god haha

7:37 PM Markus

fuck

8:01 PM Markus

I'm supposed to keep it together to finish this.

8:02 PM Markus

How you always called me 'crazy face' but only over text because it sounded silly to say.

8:02 PM Markus

And how you set that as your password, and addressed the letter to me.

8:03 PM Markus

(I didn't tell them I called you 'prissy whiskers' in return.)

8:03 PM Markus

And I told them what the letter was about.

8:04 PM Markus

And as I started to talk about all that your dad had done and all that your mom and Jun did to cover it up I started to loosen things up

8:04 PM Markus

And I started to feel lighter.

8:04 PM Markus

And I started to wake up.

8:04 PM Markus

And your mom started looking strange and scared.

8:04 PM Markus

And Jun was actively crying now

8:05 PM Markus

and don't know

— **Monday, April 28** —

12:03 AM Markus

Sorry

12:03 AM Markus

And then I started talking about your mom and her attempts to cope and how she blamed you, and she lost her mind.

12:04 AM Markus

It was like something snapped.

12:04 AM Markus

That sounds cliche, but it's true. Like, she was gripping the table tight and all set to pounce, and whatever tension was in her muscles snapped violently and she threw the table.

12:05 AM Markus

It sounds so fucking ridiculous to say it now, hah

12:05 AM Markus

It was scary as hell then, though. She threw the whole table to the side and then threw her coffee cup (empty) at my face and then hit Jun with her purse.

12:06 AM Markus

And I thought she was done because everyone was shocked and staring at us.

12:06 AM Markus

But then she started shrieking and ran to the book shelf we were sitting by and started throwing books at us.

12:06 AM Markus

(paperbacks don't hurt that much, but hardcovers do)

12:06 AM Markus

And Jun seemed to snap out of it too and jumped up to grab her.

12:07 AM Markus

He grabbed her around the middle and sort of lifted her up and turned around so that he was between us.

12:07 AM Markus

This is dumb, but it was sorta like when I'd pick you up when you were being a fuss and carry you off to bed, laughing.

12:07 AM Markus

So I guess that runs in the family in a creepy sort of way.

12:07 AM Markus

Anyway.

12:07 AM Markus

Jun got her turned around and hauled her outside, hollering at us to call the ambulance on the way out.

12:08 AM Markus

And the badger at the bar already had the police on the phone, so she added something about an ambulance.

12:08 AM Markus

And then the police were there and the fire truck because they're the first responders.

12:08 AM Markus

And they fucking handcuffed your mom and put her in the back of the cruiser.

12:08 AM Markus

And no one was hurt, so the fire truck left

12:08 AM Markus

And the police came in and started taking reports as Jun and I and the badger started picking up the books and putting them back.

12:09 AM Markus

And all the while your mom was alternating between sobbing and throwing a hissing fit in the back of the cop car.

12:09 AM Markus

And then I gave my report, and then Jun did

12:10 AM Markus

And I just kinda waved at him and left while he was giving his report.

12:10 AM Markus

Because how awkward of a goodbye would that have been?

1:21 PM Markus
I met with Dr. Maura today, and we talked about the weekend a lot.

1:21 PM Markus
She says that she thinks I did the right thing, and that this is a turning point in our relationship

1:22 PM Markus
our=me and your parents

1:22 PM Markus
And she said that it's time to work on letting you go.

1:23 PM Markus
She said that it's not because my relationship with you has changed, or if it has, it's gotten stronger. She says that it's important that I use the energy I've had when it came to your parents and your estate and put it to work on myself.

1:23 PM Markus
And I told her how tired I was and she smiled and said that I felt better after giving the letter to your parents because that was the first bit of letting you go.

1:24 PM Markus
And I think she's right.

1:24 PM Markus
I think I'd been holding you close to keep you safe from what I perceived as danger.

1:24 PM Markus
Rightfully so!

1:24 PM Markus

But your mom was right in that I was keeping you from her, to some extent, and largely at your request.

1:24 PM Markus

So I think I need to start working on that.

1:24 PM Markus

I'll never forget you

1:25 PM Markus

And I'll never stop loving you

1:25 PM Markus

and i'll never stop missing you

1:25 PM Markus

but she's right

1:35 PM Markus

I need to start working on myself, too.

— **Wednesday, May 1** —

9:38 PM Markus

I gave it a break for a day and spent yesterday cleaning the apartment.

9:40 PM Markus

Well, after work. I'm back there full time, and that's starting to feel normal again.

9:40 PM Markus

But after, I tore down your desk and turned it into a bookshelf, best I could.

9:40 PM Markus

Not sure how long that will last. I want to set up my gaming rig there, just to piss you off <3

9:44 PM Markus

Anyway, I'm going to keep doing this less and less.

9:44 PM Markus

This texting you.

9:44 PM Markus

I already threw away your phone and stored your laptop.

9:45 PM Markus

So I don't have access to your account anymore, and it'll expire.

9:45 PM Markus

(and yes, I did try 'crazy face', but you hadn't changed it, which is good, miss prissy whiskers.)

9:45 PM Markus

So...

9:45 PM Markus

I'll contact you in a week after the probate thing and see where things go from there.

— **Tuesday, May 7** —

6:11 PM Markus

I

6:11 PM Markus

shit, tomorrow

— Wednesday, May 8 —

7:58 PM Markus

I was going to text you yesterday because I got a call from Jun.

7:59 PM Markus

Your mom was released that same weekend, of course, but she got charged and had to go do a trial or something and has community service and therapy.

7:59 PM Markus

And Jun sounded like he'd perked up some, too.

8:00 PM Markus

So we talked about you and sort of had the conversation that we were going to have without your mom.

8:00 PM Markus

You know, memories and good stuff and rebuilding bridges.

8:01 PM Markus

And he said that he'll probably be getting a divorce from your mom after the letter (I emailed it) and coming to realize just how much your mom was after him as well as you, keeping him in her service and using anxiety as a tool.

8:01 PM Markus

So that was good.

8:02 PM Markus

Or maybe not good, I imagine divorces suck.

8:18 PM Markus

Anyway, it's been a week of caring for myself.

8:18 PM Markus

I did move the gaming rig.

8:18 PM Markus

Sorry not sorry.

8:19 PM Markus

And I started putting the stuff that was yours but worth keeping into a few boxes, which are now in my closet, and the rest of your stuff is gone.

8:20 PM Markus

Well, there's probably more, but it's gone.

8:20 PM Markus

And hell, I miss you, Lee.

8:22 PM Markus

Until next week <3

— **Wednesday, May 15** —

5:07 PM Markus

I met with Dr Maura again today.

5:07 PM Markus

It was REALLY good.

5:07 PM Markus

We were talking a lot about the stages of crisis and such.

5:07 PM Markus

Which we've done before, of course.

5:08 PM Markus

And my role in it all.

5:08 PM Markus

How it's sometimes my choice to move between stages.

5:08 PM Markus

Like, I can park myself in depression for a while.

5:09 PM Markus

Or anger, or bargaining, or whatever.

5:09 PM Markus

I could just stay there because it's easier to stay than moving on.

5:09 PM Markus

Not that those stages aren't necessary!

5:10 PM Markus

Just that it takes effort to leave them when you're ready.

5:10 PM Markus

And I'm trying.

8:22 PM Markus

We were pretty spot on in terms of music tastes, you know that?

8:22 PM Markus

Going through your library.

8:22 PM Markus

Sorry not sorry <3

8:28 PM Markus

We could've made a rockin' band, you know?

8:28 PM Markus

Miss Prissy Whiskers and the Crazy Faces.

8:28 PM Markus

Though that sounds like an old punk band.

8:28 PM Markus

And we seem to have done mostly prog.

8:28 PM Markus

...

8:29 PM Markus

And neither of us played any instruments

8:29 PM Markus

So maybe not a good band.

— Thursday, May 16 —

12:38 AM Markus

i miss you

12:38 AM Markus

i love you

8:22 AM Markus

Sad night last night.

8:23 AM Markus

Taking Maura's words to heart.

8:23 AM Markus

Going to choose to go to work.

8:23 AM Markus

Choose to get better.

8:23 AM Markus

Holding off until tomorrow, if I can.

11:01 PM Markus

This needs to stop.

11:12 AM Markus

I think it's time.

— **Friday, May 24** —

6:58 PM Markus

I miss you, Lee.

6:58 PM Markus

I always will, and I'll always love you.

6:58 PM Markus

But you're gone.

6:59 PM Markus

You're gone now, and I'm working to find a way to live with that.

6:59 PM Markus

I've been slowly washing the apartment of your presence.

7:03 Markus

Not that you'll be gone entirely, of course. I have your picture in a few places.

7:03 Markus

But I got rid of all the stuff that was -yours-.

7:03 Markus

and washed the bedding several times.

7:04 PM Markus

To get rid of the smell of you.

7:06 PM Markus

Christ, this is hard.

7:07 PM Markus

Good, in the long run, I hope, but hard.

7:18 PM Markus

I'm not done grieving or mourning.

7:18 PM Markus

Not by a long shot.

7:18 PM Markus

But I'm working on it. I'm working on finding a way to accept that you're gone.

7:21 PM Markus

Not to forget you, but, tacky as it sounds, honor you.

7:21 PM Markus

I'm working on getting to that stage.

7:21 PM Markus

So.

7:21 PM Markus

I'm going to start journaling.

7:21 PM Markus

And delete your contact.

7:21 PM Markus

Though I saved our messages.

7:21 PM Markus

And write for myself, and not for you.

7:21 PM Markus

With Dr. Maura's blessing.

7:22 PM Markus

And, hopefully, yours.

7:22 PM Markus

I love you.

7:22 PM Markus

I miss you.

7:22 PM Markus

I always will.

7:22 PM Markus

But you're gone.

7:22 PM Markus

And you're not at the store.

7:23 PM Markus

Or at chemo, or still sick at the hospital.

7:23 PM Markus

You're gone.

7:23 PM Markus

And it's time for me to work on that.

7:24 PM Markus

So goodbye, Lee.

7:24 PM Markus
Sleep well, miss prissy whiskers.

7:24 PM Markus
Crazy face, out.

You're Gone was originally released as a work of interactive fiction, which is available at `http://makyo.io/youre-gone`

Overclassification

"Some would say that the primary goal of folkloristics is one of anthropology, of understanding a culture's view of itself. I, naturally, disagree." Professor Haswell's voice droned on even in sleep, even these many years later. Dani hated it, hated these dreams. "Folkloristics works from the other direction. It constructs a semiotic niche out of so many *umwelten...*"

How damning was it to have such boring dreams?

Dani would write this one down on a fresh page in the morning, as she always did. The entry would be noted in the book's index. It would be given a series of tags. "School", "Haswell", "NGNB"—that boring category of "neither good nor bad"—and probably "work". Should she put "work"? Was the dream even worth it?

Perhaps, one of these days, she would build her own folkloristic taxonomy of dreams. Tonight, she would think, *I'll dream 002.010.001 (work, current job, nonspecific), 004.011.001 (school, past, nonspecific), and 035.103.002 (person, school professor (own), important but no overt pressure),* and that would be it.

Maybe if she reduced her dreams to a simple list, she could skip the actual process of dreaming them and wake up well-rested. An otter, sleek by design, efficient in all possible ways.

By the time she had actually woken up, written her dream journal entry, and stretched her way out of bed, she was left with only the grumpiness. Coffee was the first order of business, and then grooming. Neither of those were dreams, both could be easily taken care of without over-thinking.

The otter's apartment was small and, surprising no one, quite orderly. It wasn't neat, per se. It wasn't pretty or aesthetically pleasing, but there was some unnatural level of order to it that was immediately noticeable. Where many homes would slowly settle into a comfortable sort of messiness, into that "I know it's messy, but I know where everything is"-ness, Dani's seemed resistant to that particular form of entropy, in some intangible way. It was occupied, but, as a space, gave no sense of being lived in.

The kitchen was tight, and the plates stacked as anyone might stack plates, but in such a way as to not permit bowls in their proximity. The DVDs stacked on the shelf were of all sorts of genres, but one would be hard pressed to return one out of alphabetical order. Something about the vanity in the bathroom disinvited one from placing anything on its surface.

It wasn't the apartment, of course, it was Dani. Even that was obvious: one could no more place that blame on the apartment than one could place a dirty dish on the counter rather than in the sink.

It wasn't OCD, her therapist had explained—and she had explained in turn to an ex-girlfriend—so much as an aspect of personality.

This was back in her undergrad, and she'd initially been hesitant to accept that. Surely an ICD10 code would help. A bold *F42— Obsessive-Compulsive Disorder.* If only she could stack all her problems up into a banker's box and scrawl *F42* across the top in permanent marker. That she couldn't felt like an indictment that she wasn't fixable, just weird.

In grad school, she had met a vixen with OCD in one of the classes she TA'd, and she'd immediately dropped any pretenses of *F42*-dom for herself. She lacked the raw, primal anxiety that went along with such a thing.

She *was* just weird.

"Maybe it's not OCD," her ex had said, at her explanation. "But that doesn't make you any less crazy."

Ah well, 'ex' was just another shelf onto which one could put a relationship.

By the time she was coffeed and groomed, all dressed in the usual natty slacks-and-shirt-and-bow-tie-and-pea-coat, the otter was quite thoroughly sick of this glum mood. There was no reason to expect that work would change that, nor that Friday would bring any relief.

None of the countless others had.

*

When Dani was younger, she got caught stealing a pack of blank cards that were used for the card catalog at the Sawtooth Library. That was the only time anyone had ever pulled her tail, too, before it'd gotten too unwieldy to pull. The librarian had caught her under the catalog desk with a pencil in hand and a fresh pack of cards half-opened, and had yanked her out.

When her mom had hauled her out to the car, tail still aching, she had argued that the library *didn't even use the card catalog any-*

more and *the books weren't even in order anyway* and *why did Miss Weaver have to pull so hard?*

"It's still stealing, Danielle," her mother had sighed. "And I'll have a talk with Miss Weaver. Why were you even stealing cards? We've got lots of paper at home."

Dani had sulked and grumbled something about wanting to organize things.

The incident had been forgotten for years until a nineteen year old Dani announced that she would be adding a library sciences minor to her anthropology degree. Her mother had laughed so hard she'd had to hang up and call back only when she could talk once more. She still had the pack of catalog cards (which Miss Weaver had grudgingly let young Dani keep) and would mail them soon.

The discovery of the utility of categorizing, sorting, and cataloging things—an act which previously had felt so pointless—had been validating in a way she could never explain to her mother. There were boxes. Things were put into them. Sometimes you had to work out which box to use, or if there were actually *two* boxes the thing went into.

Her degree had turned into one focused on folkloristics, a field she desperately loved, but, unless she went hunting out of state, one dominated by the tireless Doctor Haswell. She'd declared a master's degree to be quite enough and moved, full circle, to working in the campus library's archive department.

It was fulfilling work, but, as predicted, did little to lift her mood. It was fulfilling without being good. Comfortable without being pleasant.

She made it through the day, categorizing high-resolution scans of glass-plate negatives, and drove home to another night of plain dinner and a movie she'd seen dozens of times already.

Her movie habit had started out of necessity for her degree, classifying the stories that she saw and how they were presented. Many of the movies that had wound up on her shelf had done so not out of enjoyment, so much as for part of one assignment or another.

She would be hard pressed to tell why she kept watching them, though. She'd park herself on her beanbag, rudder canted off to one side while she poked her way through a plate of pasta. The DVD would be set to play and she would...well, she didn't really watch the movies.

She didn't watch the movies, she didn't taste the food, she didn't think about whether or not she was comfortable. It was something more than a habit, but less than participation.

Meditation, perhaps? The voices that she heard offered no companionship, but did so companionably. She could hear voices on the TV and know that other people existed in the world. Rather than making her feel lonely, perhaps the movies made her feel alright to be alone. One didn't talk during a movie, so if she didn't have anyone to talk to, that was okay.

As she cleaned up her plate and put the rest of the pasta away for tomorrow, she found herself in a cloud of glass-plate negatives, of catalogs and movie dialog. The static of her day was louder than the closing credits of the DVD.

No amount of sound could drown out that sheer lack of feeling. No voices could add to Dani's life. The drunken slur of a fox in film, the sharp retort of his wife, none of those were more than unimportant variations in that thick static.

The otter washed her paws, and stood at the sink a while longer, toying with the stream of cold water, brushing it up along her forearms, and watching the way it beaded atop her fur.

She thought of how her mother used to get her soap in the shape of crayons when she was only a kit. It gave her a bright-red way to scrawl across the bathroom that was easy to wash off, and which—theoretically—got her clean in the process.

Her mother had been exasperated when all Dani had done was draw that point of soap crayon along the lines of grout between the tiles in the bathroom. It had turned the walls (and part of the floor) into a pleasing red grid. When pressed, her mom had grumbled about the grout being more difficult to clean than the tile itself.

Dani had always wondered at that. Sometimes, she would stand in the shower, water beading along far more of her than just her forearms, and draw along the grout with a bar of soap she bought for such purposes. She never used the stuff, hated the very texture of it in her paws, but she did spend shower after shower seeing how well it rinsed out of the grout.

The dishes were finished, her paws were plenty clean, and still she stood, trying to figure out if she could draw lines in the sink.

> Life within a comfortable grid.
> Parallel lines
> > Interrupting narrowing circles
> > Of birds in flight.

A snippet of poetry tugged at memory, some bit of drivel she'd written in her undergrad. Something to try and put into words just how her life was organized, how she made sense out of chaos.

> Travel in straight lines.
> Turn at right angles.

Trace the roof of your mouth
With wet tongue.

She did that now, finding comfort in the ridges of her palate, each describing a successive concentric arc radiating from her throat.

She turned the TV off and wafted into her bedroom, driven by some part of her she couldn't quite access for all that static. *002.010.001* she thought. *I'll dream of (work, current job, nonspecific)*. A small mantra, or maybe a supplication to the Oneiroi: *may I dream less and rest more.*

★

There's something tinny about the smell of oncoming snow. Something metallic.

Some days, it would stick around for a day or so, maybe a day and a night, right before a snow storm. It would be the herald of six or eight soft inches of perfectly dry, unpackable snow. The weather would be too cold to admit any of the moisture that was required in building a snowball.

Some days, it would give one a scant hour to prepare for the oncoming weather. A cold front would move across the land in a swift gallop to the Rockies. Two quick inches of drive-by snow.

Dani had read that the scent of snow was actually the lack of scent, of an air too cold and dry for the nose to pick out anything in particular. The opposite of petrichor. She wasn't sure that she'd believed it. That study had all been canines, and had focused specifically on temperature.

Today, there was none of the expectancy that came with the scent. It was just a lingering miasma around town, that non-scent that spread on the breeze. There would be no snow, at least not yet. There would just be cold.

Dani bundled up to take her usual walk. As otters went, she was bog standard. Lithe enough, a bit soft without being fat, with short, oily fur. None of which did anything to protect against the cold.

A walk was a walk, though.

She lived two blocks or so from the 13th street plaza, and every weekend, at least twice, she'd take a walk down to the plaza and, at the very least, walk it's length. Some days, she'd grab a coffee from the bookstore-*cum*-coffeehouse that anchored the far end of it.

It was only three blocks long, with a fountain set in the middle of the middle block, just outside the courthouse. Not really an arduous hike, but it was enough to get out of the apartment for a bit and stretch her legs, disengage from the monotony of a screen held at a fixed distance in front of her. In summer, she'd dangle her bare paws in the fountain, watching the streamers of water as she sat facing it.

The fountain was off now, of course. Nigh on February, and it was too cold to be running water through pipes outside.

The plaza was empty, silent.

Sawtooth liked to talk about its homelessness statistics. It was a strange thing to be proud of, these folks living without a place to call their own, but here the council was saying that only about a hundred and fifty were homeless out of fifty thousand.

In the winter, this maxed out the homeless shelters in town and taxed the soup kitchens. Those who made it in were provided the barest of necessities, doubled up in the Open Door Mission, and offered approximately fifteen hundred calories per day from Mercy Kitchens.

In the summer, it seemed as though all hundred and fifty were out in front of the courthouse, making the benches their own, using the fountain for covert sponge baths.

Dani talked with them. She readily admitted that she worked at a campus library and made less than she probably needed herself, so she had little to give, but she would talk.

It was strange, when she thought about it, how few of them she wound up knowing. She'd talk, sometimes spending an hour or so talking with one person, and then never meet them again.

"You folks always go away," one had said, when she brought it up. "Talk's all well and good, but we can't ever expect to see you again. Y'all are, pardon, full of shit."

Still, she kept at it. Or, perhaps, that was the wrong way to word it. She kept coming back. There was no conversion to be made, no minds to change, just a tacit agreement that it was best for both parties to talk to someone. No strings attached, just engagement.

The scent of the oncoming snow had chased everyone indoors. Dani clutched at a too-hot coffee from The Book and the Bean and wandered back to the beginning of the plaza, thinking of non-scents. Her eyes tracing the herringbone pattern of the walkway, she marveled at the dryness of it all. Maybe that's what the scientists had thought. The scent was the recognition of just how cold and dry the world was, not of anything so concrete as snow.

She made her way through a few cluttered shops, browsing the windows of the mod parlor and thinking of a movie she might pick up at the Discount Video at the corner near her apartment building.

She was sick of documentaries. She needed something false.

⋆

Sunday was cold. Way cold.

The weather had turned into a full-on cold snap. It was too dry for frost to form, but one didn't need to see that fine latticework on the windows to know that it was nearly twenty below outside. It was cold enough that one could walk past a window and pass into a brightly-lit cold-shadow in the warmth of a room.

Dani spent the day holed up within her apartment, curled on the couch with a movie playing. To keep herself from getting too bored, she set one running in a language other than her own, meaning her eyes had to track the subtitles. It kept her from wallowing into nothingness with the voices registering on some subconscious level.

The glum adherence to ridged lines had lessened, at least. She found herself wishing she had done more with herself, instead of wishing she could chart life on a sheet of graph paper.

All the same, a movie alone wasn't enough to keep her satisfied. There was no way that she knew to achieve such a feat.

Once the movie started to bore her, the otter stood up in a huff, donning her jacket and gloves—gotta keep the webs warm, they vent so much heat—so that she could head out on a walk.

No sense languishing at home, she thought. *Well, no sense in anything, but at least I'll be moving.*

By the time she made it to the plaza, Dani was pretty sure the walk was a mistake. The dryness of the cold air burned at the inside of her nostrils until she was sniffly, and at her eyes, until she teared up. Her paws were warm enough, and her pea-coat helped her plenty, but her legs were more exposed, and the cold seemed intent on pulling warmth down through them. An eager cold. A hungry cold.

Just think of the coffeehouse at the end.

By the time she'd made it to the fountain, the otter wasn't sure she'd make it even that far. She promised herself she'd soldier on, but was caught up short by a bundle on the far side of the fountain.

At first, it looked like a backpack someone had left there. One of the camping types, with a frame. On top of the backpack, a puffy anorak had been cinched down.

Cold as it was, Dani detoured around the fountain a ways to at least get a better look.

"F-fuck you want?" the bundle growled.

Dani skipped back a pace at the sudden expletive.

The bundle un-bundled itself enough to become recognizable. There was a small...Dani guessed a young woman, by her voice, buried within the jacket. She'd tucked her knees up and pulled the jacket down over them. It looked like her tail had done similar, curled into her lap underneath the jacket.

"Holy shit, are you okay? It's cold as hell."

"Y-y-you're te-telling me." A snout poked out from beneath the hood of the coat, pointy and tan and masked. "Ch-change for c-coffee?"

Dani shook her head vigorously. "Screw change, come on. I'll buy you five coffees." She pinned her ears back and added, murmuring, "And another layer of clothes."

The laugh from within the coat was pained, desperate. "N-normally, I'd tell you to f-fuck off, but alright. I th-think I need it."

The stammering speech seemed to be getting worse, and the shape shook awkwardly as it stretched out. The frame of the 'pack' under the form's anorak was a bundled up sleeping pad atop a simple school backpack beneath that.

The young woman stood up, tottering and shaking. A banded tail bristled out from beneath the coat, curling as best as it could around tattered-jeans-covered legs.

Dani reached out to help, then rushed in at the sight of the shaking. She wrapped her arms around the ringtail, rubbing her gloved paws briskly over the form's sides, unsure if that was actually helping. "Come on," she tutted. "Coffee shop's only a block, then we can figure things out from there."

It was hard to tell with the shivering, but she was fairly sure bundled-up form nodded.

Still clutching the lumpy and shaking form close, Dani guided them both down the street to the cafe.

*

The baristas in The Book and the Bean were good folks.

There was a sort of unspoken rule that the homeless in Sawtooth were welcome in for about an hour at a time before they were expected to be on their way. Still, they offered what they could. They even had a community "coffee pool", where those with a bit of extra cash could pay into it a coffee at a time, and those without could 'withdraw' from it.

The frowzy badger behind the bar got one look at Dani and the still-indistinct form under the jacket, and leaped into action.

Dani and the ringtail were guided to a table and made to sit down. The barista disappeared for a few minutes and returned with a mug for the bundled-up bassarisk.

"Here you go, dear," she'd said, voice flush with concern. "Lemon and ginger and honey. Just tap warm for now. We'll get you a proper hot drink soon, don't want to shock the system." The jumbled speech trailed off as the badger padded back to the bar to start prepping the properly-hot drinks.

Dani tugged off her gloves and tucked them into the pockets of her coat, the better to help guide the ringtail's paws around the warm mug. It smelled spicy and citrusy, and Dani wanted to breathe that scent for hours to soothe her nose.

Those tan paws had a hard time holding the mug still, shaking as hard as they were. The otter kept her own paws nearby in case of spills as the young woman sipped at the drink.

"Fuck. C-cold."

The badger bustled back up with two steaming mugs. Both of them were stronger versions of that same lemon-ginger-honey tea. "Cold? Freezing. Nineteen below, out there. Surprised you're not frozen solid. Don't drink this yet."

Dani took a selfish moment to breathe in that steam, sating that craving and soothing her poor, dried out nose.

"Y-yeah, sorry." The shivering seemed to be picking up, and the ringtail was having a hard time saying more than a word at a time.

"Just hold onto your cup," the badger said, helping the ringtail out of her coat and pulling up a chair to sit with them at the table. "Gonna get worse before it gets better. Switch to the hot one once you can hold your hands still."

The three sat in unsteady silence. Both Dani and Malina, the badger, tucked themselves in against either side of the shaking form, adding to the warmth. As Malina said, the shuddering turned into a ragged jerking before settling back into what one might call a 'shiver'.

Dani made a mental note to look up stages of shivering when she got home.

"Thank you both for helping. I thought if I bundled up and stayed still, I'd be okay."

Malina shook her head, "You'd freeze no matter what, dear. What's your name?"

The preparation of a lie showed in the moment's hesitation before the ringtail mumbled, "Anne."

Dani nodded. "Do you have a place around here?"

Anne shook her head.

"What about the mission?" Malina asked.

"Full." The ringtail looked uncomfortable as she added, "Or at least it looked full."

Dani could sense Malina shutting down. She knew the badger was endlessly kind, but she also knew how fiercely protective she could be of the coffee shop.

The otter spoke up, "Well, either way, you're not fit to stay out there. Let's get you to my place and we can start calling around and see what's out there."

Neither Anne nor Malina seemed overly happy with this, but neither brought up any objections.

★

The walk—or perhaps stumble—back to Dani's apartment had been a rushed and urgent affair. After the coffeehouse and the spicy-sour-sweet tea, neither had wanted to go back out into the cold.

Still, they'd made it, and while both were shivering by the time the otter had latched the door behind her, neither were frozen.

Anne stood just inside the door, looking shy. Dani shrugged out of her pea-coat and helped the ringtail out of her own to hang them both together by the door.

After a moment's hesitation, Anne also shrugged her backpack off and propped it up against the wall right next to the door. Beneath her coat and pack, she was wearing a hoodie over a T-shirt that had obviously seen better days. The ringtail was smaller than Dani's initial estimate; a few inches shorter than herself and slight almost to the point of waifish.

"So..."

Dani laughed, "Sorry, didn't mean to space out like that. Pardon the mess."

Anne tilted her head to the side and grinned, "Your place is kind of the opposite of a mess."

"I sometimes get extra organized," the otter demurred. "Make yourself comfortable, though."

Anne nodded. They stood for another few moments.

The silence grew weird.

"I, uh," Dani straightened her shirt. "I don't have anyone over all that much. Can I get you anything?"

Anne moved cautiously to sit on the couch, perched at the edge of the seat. "If you have any...I mean, I don't want to trouble–" She shook her head and gave Dani a bashful smile. "Do you have anything to eat? I can work to pay you back."

The otter straightened up and grinned, "Oh! Yes, sorry, and don't worry about paying me back."

Dani cooked in silence. It was well past dinnertime by now, it needed to be done. She usually cooked three portions anyway, so she just wound up making one of her regular meals.

There was no getting around the strained tension in the apartment. Dani's place was small and neat, and obviously built for one and organized tightly to that one's specifications. She couldn't afford much, loans being what they were, and yet she felt obnoxiously wealthy, with a homeless girl sitting on her couch.

She also felt obnoxiously awkward. It had been easy enough for her to help Anne from the fountain to The Book and the Bean, and from there to her place, but now it was obvious that she really *didn't* have anyone over all that much. Or at all.

She suspected that neither she nor Anne were all that good at engaging with others, and each had led to its own outcome. Dani had buried herself in school and work as an attempt to cope with a disordered mind that wanted everything else to be in order, one that didn't really cope well with others around. She was pretty sure that Anne wasn't all that keen on being around folks either, though she couldn't guess why.

Dani brought two plates piled high with pasta over to the couch where Anne had parked herself. "It's not much, but it'll be filling. Let me know if you need more, too. There's a whole other serving still on the stove."

"Thank you," the ringtail said, whiskers and tail both bristled out at the opportunity for food. She seemed to be watching Dani for cues, but when the otter took a bite, she dug in. No prayers for either.

It was easy to tell that Anne was doing her best to keep from just wolfing the food down. She looked like she was focusing on forking up reasonable amounts of pasta and chewing thoroughly, but her hunger showed in her movements. And as predicted, she cleaned her plate.

"Thanks again," she said, paws clutching at plate and fork tightly. "For everything, I mean. I was colder than I thought out there. Fucking freezing."

Dani set her plate down on her lap and nodded, "I thought you were a backpack at first, all bundled up like that."

Anne laughed. "Kinda, yeah. Was hoping I could just conserve all my warmth under my jacket."

"I think you'd probably need more than a jacket out in that level of cold, and it wasn't even dark yet."

"Fuck. Yeah." The ringtail looked down at her plate for a moment, then shrugged. "Dunno what I would've done."

"And Open Door was full?"

"I guess. Kinda."

" 'Kinda'?"

Anne frowned at her plate.

"It was full, then," Dani said quietly, trying to settle the matter before any of the ringtail's obviously complicated emotions needed to be put in words. "Is there, er–another place with beds?"

"I dunno," Anne mumbled. "I only just got here last week. Had been staying at Open Door."

"Where'd you come from?"

"Out east a bit. Making my way out to Oregon, nice and slow. Was born here in Idaho, figured I'd get a good look at the state before fucking off."

Dani laughed. "Fair enough. Never been out of state myself."

Anne nodded, "I seen a few, but mostly saw a lot of brown grass and pine trees. I wanna go west, see all that green they have there."

"You, ah–" Dani hesitated, trying to think of the best way to ask. "Bussing? Hitching rides?"

"Mostly hitching. My...well, we came in with a guy who drives between towns once a week."

Anne was loosening up with the food and warmth. Her speech coming more fluidly, and language less stiff and formal. There were things still being held back, but the otter figured it wasn't really for her to know.

"So you landed here." Dani stood and took Anne's plate as the ringtail held it out to her. "Pretty cold time for hitching out west."

"Yeah, it's crazy out. Been through cold snaps before, but not stuck out in one like that."

Dani stacked the plates in the sink, right where they belonged, and thought of Anne. Here was this sudden ringtail-shaped kink in her life. She felt confused and anxious and tense. She'd have work tomorrow, and this wasn't how she'd pictured her Sunday would go.

"Listen, I–"

Anne jolted upright. "It's late, sorry. I can head out, I think there's another shelter in town."

Dani blinked away a moment of confusion and shook her head, whiskers bristling out in a grin. "I was going to suggest you stay here for the night." She gestured to the couch and beanbag. "Plenty of space, and I don't think either of us want to head out again."

"Thank you," Anne mumbled, ears pinned back. "That wasn't what I was expecting, but thanks."

The quiet that followed was broken by a giggle from Anne. "You know, you remind me of one of my mom's friends."

Wrong-footed, Dani tilted her head. "What?"

Anne stood from her spot on the couch and nodded. "She was a fox, not an otter, but she was kinda like you. Neat, you know?"

Dani laughed and nodded.

"Do you have any blankets for me? I'll tell you while you look."

Dani nodded and padded to the hallway by the bathroom, opening the cabinet there to hunt around. Sometimes, she'd fall asleep on the beanbag rather than her bed. She'd always wake up with a weird kink in her tail or with memories of strange dreams, so she'd been trying to avoid it, recently. Still, she had some blankets of various thickness that she cycled through.

Anne continued her story as she followed along, trying to help where she could. "She was neat, like I said. She and her husband. Her husband would make things a little messy, but she'd put them in order. It was weird. Their place wasn't super clean, they had a lot of stuff, it was just all organized."

Dani poked through the blankets, before giving up and just grabbing them all. It was cold, after all, might as well make sure her guest was comfortable. She stuffed the blankets into Anne's outstretched arms before reaching back for the pillows on the shelf below.

"Anyway, they were super nice. But the guy, her husband, he got sick. Cancer or something. He passed away. Killed us all, you know? We all loved the guy. Mostly, though, it killed us to watch her. Her tail got all droopy and her fur would get matted and dirty, like she couldn't be bothered to organize again."

Dani wasn't sure where the story was going. It didn't sound like a flattering comparison to herself. Still, the ringtail seemed to be having a good time telling it. She wasn't so bristled out anymore, and was loosening up. "Did she wind up getting organized again?" Dani asked.

"Oh, definitely! You know, you get sad and stuff, and then things slowly get...I dunno, not easier. They get more comfortable. You can live with them better, you know?"

"Yeah, I get that."

"Anyway, they were super close, this couple. Two foxes who just couldn't live without each other. We thought this gal was gonna kick it soon after her husband. You know how that goes?"

Dani nodded, setting the pillows down on the couch.

"Someone told me once that girls outlive their guys, though. If the guy dies, the girl will keep going, but if the girl dies, the guy's not long after. So maybe we shouldn't have been surprised she kept on going."

There was a bit of a pause as Anne decided on the beanbag over the couch. It looked soft, she said, so she started piling blankets up on it.

"Anyway, poor fox. She gets her life back on track, gets her place all neat again, and starts lookin' for another guy, you know? You can remember your loved ones, but you gotta have company, and all.

"Anyway, weirdest thing, though. There's lots of foxes in the area and such, so she's not hurtin' as to selection, but she keeps turnin' down loads of them. Says she'll reject any who don't look like her old husband. Isn't that weird?"

Dani laughed and nodded. "Uh huh. Sixty-five."

Anne stopped fussing with the blankets and stared at her. "What? Sixty five?"

Dani nodded again and, with the cabinet door shut, moved to help Anne set up her bed. "Yeah. Number sixty-five. The suitors: woman proves her loyalty by only dating those who look like her dead husband."

The ringtail plopped down on the edge of the beanbag. Dani sat on the other side. "What kinda craziness is that?"

"You can organize stories. Take folktales and boil them down to their essences. The core to *that* story is number sixty-five on the list of, er...folktale essences. A story which proves a wife's faithfulness by how she remembers her husband in every new guy she dates." Dani realized she'd been rambling and smiled apologetically. "Sorry, I studied this in school."

"Putting numbers to stories?" Anne laughed.

The otter grinned, "Kind of. We would look at a culture's stories and see how the culture treated them. It would help us trace things back through history. That scale, the numbers, isn't really used anymore, but we all learned it."

"You majored in story numberology?"

Dani laughed. "Well, folkloristics. Part of–"

"Story numberology." Anne gave a firm nod, then winked to Dani, and they both laughed.

"Do you tell lots of stories, Anne?"

The ringtail shook her head. "My name isn't Anne. It's...hmm." She made a show of thinking up another, then grinned, "Alex. You can call me Alex."

Dani tilted her head and frowned, "Well, okay. Going to take me a bit to unlearn 'Anne', then."

Alex grinned, "It'll do you good. And yeah, we tell stories a lot on the road. True ones. Made up ones. Ones that are a bit of both. It's good to tell stories to friends, and even better to tell them to strangers."

"How do you figure?"

"You didn't laugh or anything until I told that one, did you?"

Dani thought for a moment, then shrugged. "You got me there."

Anne– Alex grinned and nodded, "See? It works. Your turn, though."

"My turn?"

"Yeah, tell me a story."

Dani froze. She knew stories. She knew tons of them. Each was stacked on a shelf of its own category, each had strings running from it to a list of motifs, each thoroughly cataloged.

And all of them suddenly inaccessible.

"I, uh-"

Alex shook her head and laughed. "It's tough, don't worry. I'm good at this. Gotta get through the days somehow. It's only...what, eight? Just tell me something about you."

Dani uncrossed her legs to get comfortable on the beanbag, leaning back against the couch where it was nearest, hips canted over to keep from resting solely on her tail. "About me? Hmm."

Alex took her cue from the otter and stretched out on the beanbag. Dani felt strange emotions tugging at her. Here was someone she'd—literally—brought in from the cold, and now it felt like they were in the middle of a high school sleepover.

"Doesn't have to be you, I guess." Alex stretched out, then sat up and took her hoodie off, as though that were a serious barrier between her and comfort. Her shirt said 'Ladies is gender neutral'. "Mine wasn't about me. Just it's usually easier to talk about yourself."

Dani nodded and smoothed her whiskers back thoughtfully, then shrugged. "I got caught stealing, once," she began, and told the story of Miss Weaver and the card catalog.

Alex looked on thoughtfully, then nodded. "Clearly a three twenty-eight."

Dani snorted. "The treasures of a giant?"

"Well, okay, I made that up." Alex laughed. "It's not wrong, though, is it? You stole things from Miss Weaver."

"Usually it's something more important. Something you go out of your way to steal. Treasure and such."

They both grinned. Alex shrugged, and began a simple grooming of herself, brushing through tan and white fur. It was soft-looking, almost downy, but certainly no protection against the cold. Not that Dani's was any better. "There you were," she said. "Concocting your secret plan to steal organization itself from the very lair of the beast, a treasure to keep for yourself."

Dani laughed and urged Alex on with a gesture.

"You saw the giant before you, the symbol of the system, of all things more powerful than wee little Dani. You snuck...uh, not up the beanstalk. You snuck around the counter, and there you saw it. The golden pack of catalog cards. 'From these,' you thought. 'I can rule over all of my toys. Each will have a number.'"

"I did, too." Dani thumped her tail against the ground. "With an iron fist. I was a dictator."

It was Alex's turn to laugh. "Alright. And so then you did it. You reached for your goal, and you took it in your hand. You were caught! Poor Dani, at the whim of a giant! Little did the giant know, you'd learn to master all of her organizational powers and unseat her!"

Dani made as if to buff her claws, "And I did. Though Miss Weaver is still on the Sawtooth Library board here. I see her whenever we do archival work for them."

"You grew up here?"

"Yeah. Born here, did my undergrad here, and came back after grad school."

Alex looked around the apartment, "You went to grad school and you live like this?"

Dani rolled her eyes. "I probably owe more in student loans than this building is worth."

"Yeowch."

"Yeah. Yeowch."

The chatter continued between the two for another few hours. By the time Dani looked up, it was nearly ten.

This was a surprising feeling, this talking the hours away. She had gone into the weekend filled with gloom, her mind unable to provide her with anything but static. A noise of delineated things, a sound of overclassification.

And now here she was, chatting away like a kid again with, of all people, a homeless girl she'd rescued from the cold snap.

There were problems to be sorted, of course. Dani was pretty sure she trusted Anne/Alex. There was nothing for the ringtail to steal. She could take the TV, which would suck. She could take the DVDs and would probably be doing Dani a favor. This was no *Les Miserables*.

Or maybe it was to a fault. If Alex was going to steal anything, Dani would forgive her. What use had she for the things she kept? She would reorganize her life around the loss.

Either way, they ought to find Alex something a little more permanent. Dani could certainly help with warmer clothing, as she had offered, and she certainly had no qualms in hosting the poor girl longer, if it left her feeling this good by the end of the night. Would it even be okay to ask her to stay?

Maybe what they had to sort out was how much each of them would get from this.

They yawned themselves to sleep, that night, and once Alex had dozed off, Dani wafted back into her bedroom. *Tonight, I'll dream of 035.028.000 (person, stranger, important in a positive way).*

She didn't remember her dreams.

★

Dani's alarm went off too early on Monday. It was the same six AM as every other weekday, but getting up proved harder.

She silenced the alarm and sat up in bed, groggy. She had a kink in her tail. Not an auspicious start to the week. The cold, the soreness, the weekend.

It took a few minutes for her brain to unfog enough to remember that Alex—or was it Anne?—had claimed her beanbag the night before.

Well, okay. The cold, the soreness, the weekend, *and* the homeless girl camped out in her living room.

Dani groaned. She'd not thought this through well enough yesterday. She had work, she couldn't do that *and* help out a refugee from the cold. She'd either have to call out from work or find a place where Alex to stay. Maybe both.

The otter levered herself up out of bed, stretching longly and trying to work the kink out of her tail. Tweaked it over the weekend, perhaps, or just slept on it funny. Made it hard to walk without wobbling.

She tugged her phone from its charger on her desk and swiped a pad across it to unlock the screen.

Two new voice messages. One from late last night, one from an hour ago.

"Hi Dani, this is Erin. I got a call from facilities saying that they were having problems with the steam plant. You're usually first in, can you check on things first thing and call out to others if there are any problems in the building? Thanks a million."

Dani furrowed her brow and skipped to the second message.

"–all employees and students. There will be an inclement weather closure on Monday the 30th of January. This closure affects all employees and students. There will be an inclement weather closure on–"

Her furrowed brow turned into an outright frown. Still standing in the middle of her cold room, she pulled up the university website on her phone. Right at the top of the page in bold, red text, an announcement.

Inclement weather closure
Monday, January 30, 2017

On Sunday evening, a boiler in central heating ceased working. The back-up boiler was brought online, but cannot heat all campus buildings to a safe temperature. Crews are working to replace the boiler.
Temperatures have reached -30, stay inside and keep warm."

"I guess that solves that," Dani mumbled.

Remembering her guest, she slipped on a loose pair of pants before heading out to the kitchen and living room. Alex was a lump of clothes and blankets on the beanbag, the only visible part of her being the tip of her tail peeking out from beneath two layers of blankets.

It *was* cold, Dani thought, and checked on her thermostat. She bumped it up a few degrees, wary of the outcome if it got too low. Hot water baseboard heaters were nice and all, but the last thing she wanted was for one of them to freeze and for the pipe to burst. She set about making the quietest cup of tea she could manage, waddling around the kitchen as best she could with the ache in her tail. She was normally a coffee drinker, but that'd wake the ringtail in the living room. Tea would do fine, though, if she didn't have to race into work.

Alex grumbled from beneath the covers at the sound of the water boiling in the electric kettle, but, as far as Dani could tell, kept on sleeping.

The otter spent the next few hours holed up in her bedroom, sipping her way through a mug of tea. She poked through news and stories on her phone, before pulling down the book of folklore classifications.

Her life was in disarray, she knew. Alex had thrown a wrench into things, into her neat little life and her neat little apartment. It brushed up against all sorts of weird desires to keep both life and home organized.

Not that the bassarisk had been a problem. She'd set her backpack down where backpacks go, she'd given Dani her plate when she was done, had used the bathroom once or twice. She had, in fact, not budged from her spot on the beanbag otherwise.

And yet this all felt like some intrusion.

Perhaps it was the way in which Dani approached it. Perhaps it wasn't Alex at all, and it was all just on her. She was the one who had taken Alex in. She was the one who was stuck thinking about this. For Alex it was nothing, she could keep clean and to herself. It was Dani who was having a hard time classifying things.

She realized she was doing the same with her book as she did with her movies. Her eyes scanned over the words in the thin workbook, but none of the text made it further into her mind. She covered each line, recognizing letters, before turning the page.

I should just put it up, she thought, feeling grumpy. *I'm not getting anything out of it. I could take a nap.*

She shook her head to shake wandering thoughts into a sense of order, and turned back to the index of folklore motifs.

Maybe she could come up with a story to tell Alex.

*

The silence—or at least quiet snores—from the living room slowly morphed into soft rustlings, and then from there to audible yawns and the sound of padding feet heading to the bathroom.

Dani levered herself quietly out of bed and snuck into the kitchen before Alex could make it back out of the bathroom.

"Coffee?" Dani asked when Alex stumbled back to the beanbag. The ringtail sat down heavily on the cushion, looking mussed up from her night's sleep.

"Nngh. Mmhm."

The otter nodded and flicked a switch on the little counter top espresso machine, then set the grinder to run for two shots worth of grounds. The tea had helped, of course, but she suspected the coffee would help all the more.

"You're chipper," Alex grumbled.

Dani nodded. "Been up a few hours already. Dad always used to get us up early for the sunrise. He said it wouldn't rise without us kids. Someone had to be there to see it."

The otter finished pulling one shot of espresso, and walked it over to the ringtail on the couch. "Let me know if you need milk or anything."

Alex shook her head, sipped gratefully at the bitter coffee.

"Anyway, one day we all got sick. One of those bouts of the flu that catches the whole house at once." Dani tamped down the grounds in the portafilter, using the tamp to brush the grounds off the rim. She paused to lick a finger and sweep up a scattering of grounds that had missed the used-grounds container she built the shot over and wound up on the counter, flicking the gritty coffee back into the container.

"We all slept in to–" She leaned back to look at the clock on the microwave. "Until about ten thirty. We were all so surprised when we saw the sun had risen without us."

Alex laughed as Dani pulled her own shot. "Oh yeah? And which number is that?"

Dani leaned back against the counter and laughed, wincing at the strain in her tail and clutching her little demitasse in her paws. "You got me. One hundred fourteen."

The ringtail held onto her empty cup with one hand and leaned back onto the other, grinning up to the otter. "I'll give your delivery an eight out of ten, but the story needs work. Did you rehearse it?"

"A little," Dani admitted, ears and whiskers both canted back in embarrassment. "Was it that obvious?"

"To me, yeah. But I live off stories. You get a feel for truth, lies, and the right mix, you tell enough stories. You can hear when one's being told on the spot."

"What about mine didn't work?"

The ringtail shrugged and leaned forward to pass over her cup when the otter held out her paw. "Your truth-to-lie ratio was good. Lemme guess," she said, tilting her head. "You got up with your dad, but don't have any siblings."

Dani laughed. "Yeah, that's it. How'd you guess?"

"The way you talked about your mom last night, about stealing office supplies." Alex shook her head. "It wasn't that, though. Like I said, that was good. The, uh...what's it. How much the story means..."

"Consequence?"

"Yeah, it was inconsequential to a good level. You tell a story, and if you're trying to weave one, you don't make it too consequential. You told me a true story last night; those can be consequential. A tale should make you care enough to laugh or cry, but not much more."

Dani thought for a moment. "When we'd talk about folktales, we'd talk about what tied them to one culture versus another, even if they'd share a common core. That feels pretty consequential."

"I guess a little." The ringtail shrugged and stood up once more. "But you're not imparting deep wisdom. They're all just stories, still. They gotta be light, inconsequential—and yours was—but they also gotta be, um...spontaneous."

"Extemporaneous, maybe?"

"That's it. They gotta be on the spot. Yours was just too rehearsed."

Dani grinned and shrugged, "I'm not sure if I could do that."

"It's not for everyone. You–" She paused for a moment, thinking before continuing. "You're too organized. Too OCD to pull a story out of thin air like that. Hey, can I grab a shower? I know you're probably sick of me, but I really need one."

The OCD comment caught Dani off her guard. She had so many thoughts, countless words, about how she was or wasn't that. She didn't have the F42 required for F42-dom. All of those had disappeared, as they always did at time of need.

She just nodded and waved Alex into the bathroom.

★

"So, it's gotten down to negative thirty. I know I was going to offer to help you get more layers, but I think it's too cold for even that."

Alex nodded and kept quiet. She looked as though she were preparing to be kicked out.

Dani hastened to clarify, "I don't even want to go out to the car. Plus, my tail hurts too bad to do much more than sit around. You alright just staying in until things warm up this afternoon? I can get you to Open Door or another place if you don't want to."

The relief was writ plain on the ringtail's face. She nodded. "Yeah, that'd be good. I don't want to go out either. Really don't want to go back to Open Door. Can I, uh...can I help out any? I don't have much to pay with, but I can do work or whatever."

"There's not really much to be done, I don't think." Her expression softened. "You're just welcome to say until things warm up, Alex."

"Amy."

Dani blinked.

"You can call me Amy today." The ringtail grinned.

"First Anne, then Alex, now Amy?" Dani laughed.

"A real name holds power, right?"

The otter thought for a moment, then nodded. "Five hundred, yeah."

Alex–er, Amy rolled her eyes. "They really did include everything in that catalog, didn't they?"

Dani nodded as she waddled over to the couch. "Yep. Five hundred is a trickster who will be defeated by someone knowing his true name. Fuck," she interrupted herself. "How the hell did I fuck up my tail? I don't think I did anything to it yesterday."

"Well, it *is* big."

Dani laughed, changing trajectory to the beanbag and laying down on her front. "Yeah, it is. Still, I didn't think I could sprain a tail this bad."

"Well, doesn't that just make us a pair? I don't have the gear to go outside, and you can hardly walk."

"Guess it was good fortune, then."

"Does your catalog of tales have anything to say about this? Is three hundred and eighty a story about an injured person being stuck with someone who can't go out in the cold?"

The otter shrugged. "I don't think so, no. And there isn't a three eighty. They're all organized into a hierarchy, and they leave some numbers unassigned so that they can add to them later on."

Amy grinned. "How do you even know all this?"

"I went to school for it."

"And they made you memorize it or something?"

Dani rested her chin on her folded arms, a motion to conceal some embarrassment. "They didn't make me. I did because it was fun."

The ringtail stared in disbelief, then motioned for her to continue.

"I really like organizing things, and–"

"I could tell."

Dani smirked, then continued. "–and I like the way things can be categorized while still retaining everything that makes them unique. Like, the five hundred from earlier? That's a vague classification that can be applied to many stories, which are all different from each other."

"Sorta like putting things in a box, then?"

"I guess. Or writing them down on a sheet of paper with a specific heading, then putting that sheet in a folder, which is put in another folder. At the very top, you give rules for how to get to what you need."

Amy looked thoughtful for a moment, then nodded. "Makes sense, then."

"What does?"

"Your inability to be, uh...extemporaneous. You can't pull things out of thin air, 'cause you're rifling through a catalog."

Dani stayed silent.

"I mean that in the best of ways!"

Dani shifted over onto her side enough to look at Amy more directly, trying to look as kind as possible. She had no idea how to take this being told that she was uninventive.

"Well, listen," Amy continued. "You have OCD, right?"

"I don't know. I've been told I don't."

"But, like...look at you. Everything about you is based around order, around the need for things to be in their place, all classified."

"Well, sure," Dani demurred. "But OCD requires anxiety that I don't have. You have to feel anxiety about things that you obsess over, and you have to have the compulsion to fix them at all costs. I don't have those. I just classify things. That's just what I do."

Amy looked thoroughly sorry for having brought the topic up. All the same, she persevered. "Okay, well, maybe not OCD, but my ma, she told me that there's all these disorders around anxiety, and each has a personality disorder to go with it." Her voice was fast, as though she were rushing to fill a hole she was digging herself into. "Maybe you have that? Obsessive-Compulsive, uh...personality disorder?"

Dani reached out a paw to rest on Amy's. None of this was too terribly surprising, it was all stuff that made sense. Still, Amy had talked herself into a tizzy. The ringtail looked absolutely panicked. "Maybe," Dani allowed. "What does this version entail?"

Amy took the hint from Dani's paw on her own. She smiled bashfully and made a show of calming down. "They, well," she straightened up, organizing her thoughts. "They are like the regular dis-er, they're like the regular ones, but without the anxiety. The life is ordered, order is the obsession, but without, uh...without the pain. Like, it's...like the obsession is a good thing.'

The otter thought it over, spending a few seconds grooming her whiskers back. "I guess that makes sense. It's something that isn't eating me alive, but it's still a big part of me."

Amy nodded, turning her paw up to let Dani's paw slip into her own, resting the her free paw on top of it. "I really do mean that in the best way."

Dani laughed and rolled the rest of the way onto her side, letting her aching tail rest against the side of the beanbag, taking some of the weight off. "No, I get that. It really does make sense. I saw someone about it years ago, on an old girlfriend's suggestion."

Amy tilted her head, though whether at the 'girlfriend' part or the 'seeing someone about chronic neatness' part, she couldn't tell.

"My doctor said it wasn't OCD, just part of my personality. Not something I felt bad about, something I felt good about. My ex still thought I was crazy, though."

Amy patted at the otter's paw in her own, then gave it a little pet, brushing fur that was already straight all the straighter. "Can I confess?"

Dani laughed. "Of course. I'm no priest, though."

"I didn't think so" Amy laughed. "Anyway, I guess I saw how neat you were, and that's why I've told you so many names. Just add a little disorder to your life."

"None of them real?"

"Of course not." The ringtail grinned as mischievously as she could. "I can't tell you that, remember?"

Dani laughed. "Right. Five hundred."

"How many of those classifications are there, anyway?"

The otter started counting mentally, then perked up. "In the bedroom, there's a book on the bed. I was reading it after yesterday. That should have the catalog in it. Go grab that."

"Uh, me?"

"Yeah, you." Dani laughed, "My tail hurts too much. I'm laying down and you're sitting. I'm older than you, probably. Just because."

★

"Okay. Fourteen seventy five."

Dani had found a few comfortable spots on the beanbag, alternating between stretching out on her front and laying out on her back with her tail resting between the folds of the cushion. "Right, hmm. Back when I was a kid, my dad used to take all of us to church.

The preacher was a kind old guy, but one day, he got it into his head that it was best to keep it in the town.

"He saw us girls sitting in the front row and asked us all to come up on the stage. It was so embarrassing. He made us promise to God and the congregation that we weren't to be married to girls in other parishes.

"Everyone laughed and laughed. *Girls marrying,* they'd say. *Good joke, preacher.* But there I was, standing up there with my sisters, saying I'd never marry a girl from another town. All my hopes and– I'm no good at this, am I?"

Amy laughed and slapped her paws down on the page. "No, you're good! You came up with that better than I thought you would'a. You just got all stiff at the end, is all."

Dani grinned. "Makes sense, I guess. I kind of get the rhythm, but it's hard for me to just pull it out of nothing. I get part way through and start thinking about my story too much, about what other categories it fills. I start thinking, *oh, that's four eighty, the kind and unkind girls* and then I'm totally lost."

"Yeah. I can tell. You get this look on your face when you get to let go. You get all confident lookin' and then you fall apart, and I can almost see the filing cabinets in your eyes."

They laughed together.

Contrary to expectations, the outside thermometer had pegged itself at thirty below for a few hours and then, around noon, started to drop even lower. They had eaten a late lunch. Amy asked if she could wash her clothes while she was here, and Dani had found her a shirt and pair of pants that would fit meanwhile. The temperature stayed cold through the afternoon.

Neither were keen to go outside and see just how cold, so they'd parked themselves on the beanbag with the catalog of folktale types.

Amy had said that she was going to teach Dani how to tell a story, but that was a thin excuse for a continuation of the sleepover atmosphere. What would be more 'sleepover' than telling stories and a friendly competition?

Dani was losing, that much was obvious.

"Alright, ninety one," she said. "When someone is caught for their heart (or paw, or eyes) as a remedy—like one's heart or fingers being the only cure to an illness—but convinces the antagonist that they left it at home."

Amy grinned and launched right into the story. She would always win, so long as she could jump right in like that. "Oh yeah, that reminds me of one of my daddy's stories. He laughed about this all the time, said one day, this cat came to him. One of those all black ones, the uh..."

"A panther?"

"Yeah, that's the one! Daddy would always say hi to this guy as he walked his property. He used to walk the perimeter of his property and make sure all was okay, but it got him to talking with all his neighbors.

"Anyway, one day, one of his neighbors takes a shine to his tail, says, *Dang, you know, I wish I had that tail. My wife left me some years ago, you see, and I bet the gals would be all over me, I had a tail like that.* Dad would laugh, we'd all laugh at that. Poor old Mister Lincoln, he looked like a shadow in every picture, like someone had cut out someone, wherever he went.

"Now dad, he can sense Mister Lincoln starting to get more insistent about things, and one day, on a hunch, he grabs a handful of soot from the fireplace—we hardly ran the thing those days, but the soot was still there—and rubbed it into his tail."

Dani laughed, picturing Amy rubbing soot into her tail, turning the stripes all black.

Amy grinned. "So dad, he's got this all-black tail. It was nearing night, so it wasn't too out of place, but sure enough, once he runs into Mister Lincoln, out walking his property, the big old guy grabs dad by his collar, starts shaking him, asking for his stripes!

"Dad doesn't know what to do, starts squealing, just as sure as I would.

"Well, didn't take a genius to know Mister Lincoln was as drunk as he was plain. He thought he could grab the stripes off daddy's tail and take them for his own. Maybe he'd put them on his face and gain some features. Maybe he'd put them on his paws, so he could always see where his hands were. Maybe he just plain wanted dad's tail."

"And he left it at home?" Dani asked, giggling.

"Of course he did! Dad, he told Mister Lincoln he left it in the trunk by his bed. *No stripes today, sir,* he said, kind as could be. *Talk to me tomorrow, though, and I'll hook you up!*

"Well, Mister Lincoln, he looked pleased as peach, said that'd be real nice. Dad, he had something like ten stripes. Golly, Mister Lincoln would'a been able to do plenty with that!"

Dani clapped her paws gleefully at the story. "Wonderful! You've got the entire thing set up, right there. I feel like I get close so often, but I just don't quite get it to stick the whole way through."

They were as two girls at a sleepover, stretched out on their fronts on a beanbag, a book propped up before them both.

It was Amy's turn to laugh. "You do get close, yeah. You're just missing mechanics. Like, y'gotta start telling little side stories, no more than a sentence long, to buy yourself some time. We don't care what Mister Lincoln does with the stripes, but we make something up to give us time to, uh...stick our landing, I guess."

"Yeah, I can't even begin to think of how to do that." Dani shrugged, stretching her tail out carefully and wincing. "If I don't go into the story with the whole thing already written, I'm more than likely just going to run myself in circles trying to think of all of the archetypes."

Amy looked as though she was cuing up a response to that, perhaps some list of improvements for Dani to follow. The otter interrupted, both of her paws clutching at Amy's. She almost had the ringtail clocked. Shelved, cataloged, organized.

"You, see, you're eighty one. Here you are, plowing through the world, and you're doing really good. You find yourself on the road, and you got yourself some friends, or maybe just one. Just someone you're traveling with."

Amy shut down at this outburst, her expression going blank and her paws going slack in Dani's.

The otter persisted. "You said, *It's so wonderful out now, I must be all set for the next year.*

"But you were with someone, weren't you? Someone at Open Door? He had a home, or money, something he could offer, he could..." Dani trailed off. "Shit, I'm sorry. I went way too far, there."

The otter tried to tug her paws back to herself, to withdraw. Drunk on storytelling was a new sensation for her. She hadn't expected it would lead to such an overreach. She hadn't expected it to drop her barriers around classification.

Amy clutched at Dani's paws, shaking her head. It was a confused gesture, a sad gesture. "No, you're right. He's down at Open Door."

Ears pinned back and whiskers sleeked in against her cheeks, Dani continued haltingly. "You didn't...you didn't prep for the winter because summer was easy. He had, so he kept you in his debt."

The ringtail's grip tightened around Dani's paws.

There was nothing the otter could say to continue.

"So he pulls me aside, he says *we just need to keep ourselves warm.*" Amy's voice was quiet, hoarse. "And that sounds good to me. But I have to do something in return. Something for him. So I think to myself, *Aha, I've got a plan.*"

Dani returned the squeeze of paws. Amy wasn't looking at her any longer, staring toward the blank wall with a smile that's more grimace than the jolly grin her story would imply.

"*Don't worry. I'll hold up the roof,* I tell him. So I hide myself away up in the attic, tell him I'm doing something useful, when all the while, I'm making sure I can get away without giving him everything he asks."

There was a silence between them, then. True silence. Neither had anything to say, and neither could offer any path forward.

It took a good five minutes for the moment to pass. Amy's expression cycled through vacant amusement, thinly veiled anger, and despair. Dani, frozen where she was with the strained tail, could only hold on to the ringtail's paws and hope that she hadn't fucked up too badly.

"That-" Amy coughed, clearing her throat and sitting up. "That got a little too real. Alright if we switch to a movie or something?"

Dani nodded and bowed her head, gesturing in the direction of the shelves of DVDs. "Take your pick."

★

Dani stayed silent through the movie. Amy had chosen a thriller, something with enough action to hold their interest without demanding it. Not *too* actiony, not too cerebral.

The ringtail had shrunk in size, Dani noticed, all her confidence drained away. The jokey story-telling exercise really had gone too far, and although she stood by her assessment, she realized she probably should have been a bit more careful of providing it.

All of that openness that had grown over the past few hours, all of that was slowly unwound. She had built up this stanchion of confidence, only to find she'd planned the bridge in the wrong spot. She'd hoped to understand Amy.

She hadn't had a goal in this companionable storytime, but even so, she'd fucked it up.

She spent her time pretending to leaf through the book of motifs and tropes. Amy sat where she had been, watching the TV over Dani as the otter poked through her book. She didn't have quite what it took to look Amy in the eyes.

Perhaps I should find her a place to go, she thought. *Perhaps this whole thing was a mistake. We don't know each other, neither of us know how to share.*

And yet they stayed there. Amy watched her movie, and Dani's eyes traced lines of text without reading them.

Dani perked up enough to watch the climax of the movie, angling her ears back enough so that the movie isn't all she heard. She'd seen it dozens of times already. She was more interested in Amy's thoughts than in the movie itself.

The denouement of the film was swift. A proper thriller, she decided long ago, should leave several threads hanging. Explain too much, and you get a detective story. Explain too little and you get...well, a mess. You get her life. Too many things independently explained which do nothing to provide a sense of the whole, nothing that adds up to a plot.

Amy seemed to melt beside her, slouching first toward one side, then stretching her legs out, and finally slipping down onto the beanbag. It was more of a collapse than a deliberate movement, but at least it was something.

"You okay?" Dani asked, setting her book down off to the side.

Nothing but the sounds of the ringtail settling into the beanbag bed. It was her bed, even. Dani's was around the corner in the bedroom.

The otter carefully squirmed onto her side, doing all she could not to tweak her tail more than she already had. She would need to get up to use the bathroom a some point, but for now, she considered herself stuck.

Might as well fix this, while we're here.

"You okay, Amy?"

"Amber."

Dani hesitated for a moment before murmuring, "Is that your name now?"

"No, that's my name. Just Amber."

The ringtail's voice was flat, her eyes downcast, and even then focusing on nothing. It hurt to listen to.

"Did I go too far?"

"No, you're fine."

Dani watched the way Amber's eyes went in and out of focus.

They never shifted the direction in which they were looking, but it was still plain enough to see her thoughts shifting instead.

"You want to know something?" Dani asked.

The ringtail lifted her gaze enough to look at Dani properly. "Mm."

"I don't think your story is eighty one, like I said. It's fifty eight."

Amy–Amber's ears tilted back. Short, sharp condemnations.

Dani pressed on all the same. She tried to pick up on the smooth confidence of Amber when she had told stories, tried to slip into the same casual language. "You're the one who sees something on the far bank that she wants. You have a goal, something you could really desire. Not just a passing fancy."

Amber's expression softened.

"So you think, *Ah, there we go! Just what I was after.* But it's on the far bank, right? So you look around and you see the crocodile. He's a good kid, you know. The type of person who would try to do right by you, even if he doesn't get the whole story.

"Well now, you've got a means, and you've got a goal, but you don't have the influence to make it happen. So you sit down by the crocodile and you say, *Great day out here, really nice.* And he says, *Yup.* And it's not a great start and all, but you know it's gonna take a while to sway the crocodile's interests to align with yours.

"*I always find myself thinking of the far bank, of what that would bring me, what I could gain by being there.* The croc frowns. Each bank is the same to him. The river is as valid as land, when it comes to crossing.

"*All I think about,* the croc says. *Is how I'm going to meet someone. Come to a river, and you've got a one dimensional dating pool. I can't meet anyone across the river I can't meet on this side. The river's not that wide.*"

Amber was grinning outright, though she stayed quiet to let Dani finish her telling.

"And that crocodile, well, you know he was kind of an asshole. All he was thinking about was what he'd get out of the deal. Sometimes that's good and all, like you want to get to the other side too, right?

"Still, you've got goals other than just *Hey, just looking for a lay.*" Amber's grin gets tight; a bit mean, but no less earnest.

"So you give it a bit of thought, and you duck off down the bank, and you put your hard-earned basket-weaving skills to use, and you come up with a present for the crocodile.

"*Tell you what, buddy,* you say. *I know a bunch of folks on both sides of the river. I've got a guy on the other side, he says he knows someone. I think she's even on this side of the river.*

"The croc laughs, and comes back at you with. *Why don't you just send her my way, then?*

"*Well, it's not that easy, duh, or I would'a. I don't know the girl, I just know my guy, he says he knows all sorts of these girls.* You give this big, exasperated sigh. *Look, just get me over there, and I'll get this all sorted out with my buddy. We both want that, right?*"

The ringtail was fully engaged now, laughing and rolling her eyes and nodding along with Dani.

"You can always tell when a guy's just after one thing, so you just need to point it out to him. Anyway, that's what you've done, and your friendly croc bud helps you across the river. That shit's deep, and you could swim, but that'd suck.

"Crocodile dude drops you off at the far shore, and sure as shit, you're closer to where you want to be. *Sweet, thanks,* you say. *My buddy here, he says that you've got someone already waiting for you on the other side. She's heard all about you, if you know what I mean. See? there she is now!*

"And you point across the river. There, just across on the other side, poking just out over the water, is the snout of another crocodile! Well, your dude, he gives you the biggest thumbs up and tackiest wink one could manage, and starts back across the river with your blessing.

"That's your crocodile on the other side, after all. You made her out of reeds, built up from whole cloth, and now here you are, where you need to be. What your dude does with his very flammable wife is up to him. You've done your part."

Amber laughed outright at that last bit, and Dani grinned happily in response.

"I'll give you a nine out of ten on delivery on that one," the ringtail said. "You sold me at the end there, but at the beginning, it sounded like an apology."

"Yeah." Dani grinned sheepishly. "I'm sorry, Amber."

"It's cool, I swear."

"So what about the story?"

"Oh, that gets a ten out of ten."

Dani laughed. "Oh yeah?"

"Of course! I think your earlier story was true, too, but this one's better. I got here, didn't I? I got what I wanted."

The otter went quiet at that, tilting her head. "How do you mean?"

Amber shrugged. "I got here. I made it across the plains, and I have a few more, uh...rivers to cross, but I got here with a bunch of help, like that dick back at the shelter."

Dani nodded, waited.

"It cost a lot. More than I want to say. But I can move on from that."

The otter gathered up the ringtail's paws in her own and gave them a squeeze. "You sure you're okay? You safe from that guy?"

"I think so, yeah." Amber nodded. "He's too 'interested in experiences, rather than people.' He can go off and get more of those, while I get what I want."

Dani nodded, and let the silence linger on. Finally, she screwed up the courage to add, "You can stay here, too, you know. Long as you need."

Amber laughed easily. "Thank you. You've done so much for me."

"Does that make me your crocodile?" Dani shot back, grinning.

The ringtail didn't respond verbally, but rather leaned in and give Dani a kiss.

Dani froze.

It was completely out of the blue, though perhaps some part of her suspected it was coming. The tension had been a thing, of course, but had always been on her end. She hadn't expected a homeless girl to be giving her a kiss, no matter the stories that surrounded it.

All the same, the otter relented, shifting more onto her side and ignoring the twinge in her tail. When presented with a kiss, there was no further categorization to be done. They were kissing, and that was that.

The moment shifted, and Amber leaning back away from Dani. The otter plastered her whiskers back against her muzzle with a little 'huff'. She couldn't hide just how much the kiss had affected her, but she could at least distract from the fact.

"Tell me your name."

Amber smiled. It was a soft and kind smile, open and honest. "Amber."

"I'm not going to wake up to a different name, am I?"

"Would you like to?"

Dani laughed. "Probably not. If your goal was to subvert me organizing everything too much, you did it. This, though–" and she leaned forward to give Amber another quick kiss. "I'd like to hold onto this."

The ringtail smiled, looking happier than before, with nose nearly pressed in against Dani's. "'Amber's real, don't worry. That's my true name."

Her whiskers bristling from the close contact, Dani smiled. "What power does that grant me, knowing that?"

"What power would you like?"

"Flight?"

Amber laughed.

"Seeing through walls, maybe?" Dani continued. "Precognition? Pyrokinesis? That might be nice with it being this cold."

"And dangerous, probably."

It was Dani's turn to laugh. "Okay, yeah, probably."

The ringtail propped herself up on an elbow, resting her cheek in her paw. "Okay, how about company, then? I can give you the power to not be alone, at least for a bit."

"I don't know if that's a power, really, but I'm more than happy for it."

Amber shrugged and grinned down to the otter, "Good. I don't feel very powerful. I don't grant wishes or anything, but it's good to be here."

"Mm," Dani agreed.

Amber paused, then laughed. "And this is the point when you kiss me again."

And so Dani did.

The otter would ever be herself, and she owned that. It was her place in life to classify the things around her, and so she took up the reins and did as she was built to do.

Amber, her fur was soft under Dani's paws. It wasn't pillowy or silky, but it fell into the category of dry-soft, similar to the way silt was soft.

F:S.03—fur, soft, dry and smooth.

Dani began her categorization with touch, as the two leaned in closer to each other. There had been the softness of Amber's paws in her own when they'd touched earlier, but now that they were leaning into more of an embrace, Dani's paws slipped up along the ringtail's arms, ruffling through clean fur, and then from arms to sides.

The ringtail was small—she barely fit in Dani's clothes, and the otter wasn't large by any stretch of the imagination. But one can wear oversized clothing in a number of ways. Amber didn't seem like a young girl wearing her father's clothes. She didn't seem like someone trying ill-fitted clothing. She was just comfortably two sizes smaller than Dani, and was wearing that clothing while her clothing was being dried off. That had to be a trope of its own.

S:Sm.03—size: small, by necessity (cute).

Neither otters nor ringtails were burdened by long snouts like some of Dani's friends. All the same, when the kiss broke—as kisses do—Dani tucked her muzzle alongside Amber's, nosing her way through fur from cheek to neck. The scent of the ringtail's fur filled her nostrils.

Sometimes, one comes out of the shower smelling not just clean, but bearing the Scent of Clean, patented and trademarked. Amber had just come out of the shower earlier in the day, but she smelled...not clean, but of herself, with nothing standing in the way of that.

O:C.10—odor: clean, pleasant (not perfumed).

Amber shifted up enough to let Dani settle onto her back. The otter slipped her arms around the ringtail's compact form. With clothing bunching up, her webbed fingers explored through soft fur, exploring the contours of Amber's back, lithe and strong.

She was responsive to Dani's touches. She didn't arch or wiggle or do anything so silly, but neither was she totally passive. Dani felt that she could drag her paws down along the ringtail's sides and front, and trust that she would continue to feel that confidence. Not eager, but willing. Not slack, but still. Not passive, but soft. Available and open to Dani as the otter moved against her.

R:5.05—responsiveness: consensual, familiar.

Nose twitched, ears perked, paws touched. Dani explored and investigated, gleefully categorizing as she went. Amber was middling ticklish, more quiet than not, and prone to stretching when touched. When they interacted, they were neither verbose nor silent, neither shy nor bold; just a comfortable commingling that was sensual enough to be labeled as such without being lewd.

Dani ignored the twinges of pain in her tail as she moved. It was more important that she find the ways in which they fit together than to hold her tail still. There are things, she knew, that she would regret the next day: stretches, actions, words. Each of those was duly labeled and set aside.

The otter focused instead on the things that made them both feel fulfilled. They were both all-in on this, they were both intent on one another, and that left her mind clear. There were a limited set of choices she could make—to touch here and kiss there, to taste, to stroke, to clutch—and she made them.

By the time the two of them settled down together once more, panting and laughing, Dani knew that her classification of Amber had been wrong from start to finish. The act, the moment, the motions—those had all been tagged and labeled, described and delineated.

The ringtail: not at all.

Amber had come into her life through both of their actions, as well as circumstances outside their control. Along each step of their journey, each had made choices and taken actions that wound up here, with each tangled in their own clothes and both tangled with one another, sharing pleasure and breath.

Every step of the way had been noted and slotted into its own comfortable box.

Dani, as a person, was easily classified, but Amber...she was wholly uncategorizable.

⋆

When Dani awoke early the next morning—very early, far before even her alarms—she was alone. Amber was gone.

When she thought of the last few days, she wasn't totally surprised. The parable from the night before had been accurate enough: Amber had gotten to the other side of the cold snap. Dani would be left grappling with the Amber-that-was, the Amy and the Alex and the Anne, for a while yet, but Amber was on her way.

Not surprised, but not happy. She had set aside that overarching need to categorize and order her life for someone, and now they were gone. It hadn't been a one-night stand, hadn't been a fling. It wasn't a relationship, though Dani would have perhaps welcomed that. It had been a closeness borne of cold and necessity.

She clumsily paced her apartment for a few hours, that Tuesday. The university was still closed for the remainder of the cold snap, though the temperature was now well above zero. She suspected it was more of an issue about the boiler than the temperature. Either way, she was still all wobbly from the strain in her tail.

She made coffee.

She took a nap.

There was nothing she could do to follow Amber. There was nothing she *would* do to follow her. Amber had moved on, and Dani was left to deal with what remained. Dani could no more follow her than the crocodile could. She was bound for the other shore, for more loneliness and more dreams.

She put a movie to playing.

She cleaned the kitchen and picked up all the blankets on the beanbag.

She checked the clothes dryer, but it was empty, with the clothes she'd lent Amber piled beneath, so she did a load of laundry

She slowly reorganized her life around this Amber-shaped hole, patching together feelings into a new whole.

And the only thing missing was her catalog of folktales.

Acts of Intent

Lines and curves, lines and curves. Beginning now.

Seven o'clock, and the 13th Street crowd was headed to dinner, or focusing on a postprandial stroll.

Jacob was focused on lines. On arcs and straight edges. On corners and angles.

The cans of spray-lubricant had clanked onto the counter, earlier that afternoon. Three of them, some of the cheap kind. The poor stoat behind the till scanned them numbly, seemingly on autopilot.

To see someone with such dead eyes had led down some strange alley and into what felt like second-hand embarrassment for Jacob. Second-hand to what, he couldn't tell. Either way, the transaction had itched, and he had shifted his weight from paw to paw until it was done.

Finally able to tap in the pin for his card, that itch had been scratched. The digits of the number across the pad always traced a pleasant, angular rune, and then the coyote was done, hurrying out of the store. The bag of cans had been

dumped unceremoniously into one of the panniers of his bike,
his tail clipped quickly to his thigh, and he had been off.

His breathing slowed and the jittery, speedy vibrations in his
mind smoothed out.

The heat along those lines grew, dull black iron turning first into
a burgundy red, then glowing, picking up more towards cherry.

Spring turning to summer had the days warm, but not un-
comfortably so. The air still held enough spring in it that the
light long-sleeved shirt Jacob wore never got too warm, even
with the exertion of the brisk ride home.

Eyes focused on surroundings briefly, hunting for a patch he
knew had to be somewhere here. Wander north, magnetic attrac-
tion.

Ducking into the apartment had taken only seconds, enough
for him to toss two of the purchased cans on a counter and
another into a backpack, then back out into the evening air.
Back onto his bike. Back on the road.

Cherry red and up to yellow, starting to put off enough glow that
it crept into his vision, a light-leak in the camera of his eyes.

Making it to the 13th Street Plaza had taken longer than ex-
pected, but perhaps that was for the best. The flames would
shine brighter in twilight.

North, north along Linden. North to cross the plaza. North to
pass the fountain.

Jacob had parked his bike at a rack in front of one of the 12th street shops, locking it with care. Of his two prized posses-sions, the bike was the most practical, and the thought of los-ing it was something he would barely allow to register. He would be more than just upset, he'd be fucked. The commute to work would go from twenty minutes to more than an hour on the bus system, a fact he knew well from when it was too cold to ride. He'd saved up for three months to get this bike, a fantastic upgrade from what he'd had in college.

He could barely see now. Yellow brightened, headed more to-wards white. A sun made of lines, graceful arcs and definitive straightedges.

The other prized possession was less immediately practical, yet even more dear than the bike. The small sketchbook, barely more than a few inches on each side, was truly irre-placeable. That sat snugly in his pocket; the backpack was too risky, even his apartment wasn't safe enough.

Toward the courthouse.

Jacob was panting now. Cool as the evening was getting, it was no match for the searing symbol locked in his thoughts. Burning, some part of him reddening, blistering, flaking and charring.

His Sigillarium sat distinct from his notes. Those were ash now, long gone. Their pages had held letters, all unique, warped and twisted through repeated passes of his pen, slip-ping and sliding together into some place between joy and fear, a place of too much meaning.

Past the courthouse now. And there, along the brick wall that surrounded the guarded parking lot. A place for moving the guilty to prison, maybe? There was the icy patch, freezing in the still-warm evening.

Once the meaning grew overwhelming—he'd know the moment when it came—the Sigillarium was brought out, opened reverently to the next blank page, and impressed with the new sigil. He used a dip pen with India ink into which he'd stirred several drops of blood. As the ink dried, Jacob did his best to start the process of forgetting.

Strange place, strange place. Empty, yet meaningful. Locked up. Guilty and innocent. Shackled, manacled, clanking and clinking in chains. The patch on the wall likely wasn't actually cold to the touch, yet he knew if he touched it, frostbite would follow.

Forgetting took days, weeks, months. It began with closing the Sigillarium, locking away intent and meaning while Jacob forgot the words themselves. He wouldn't look at the sigil again until the night before.

Obscured though his vision was, Jacob turned around, using his peripheral vision as best he could to check for others around. Empty street.

Doubtless there were cameras who had seen him, but intent never left a visible mark, so no one had ever come after him. Intent was psychological. Magical graffiti for no one to see and everyone to feel. He would begin internalizing the symbol the

night before, and hold it in his mind until the moment of, when
it once more became unbearable.

Smooth movements. Smooth and sure. He took the can, focused on the frigid patch, and began spraying. He couldn't do it too quickly, even if he did need to hurry. There needed to be enough penetrating oil left to burn.

Then he would bike and hunt for the cold he knew peppered
the town.

The sigil was one unbroken line. One line that contained all those arcs and curves and straightaways and angles and corners. All sprayed dead center in the midst of that patch layering intent over what meaning was already there.

Quickly, before he even capped the can, he fished his lighter out of his pocket and gave the wheel a rasp just at the final endpoint of the line.

Blue flames, tinged yellow at the tips, spread fast, curling along the sigil, branching and curving whenever it came across a point where lines crossed.

All that fire in his mind wound up on stone.

All that patch of ice began to thaw.

The coyote was already on his way back to the plaza, can of lubricant back in his bag and all that unbearable meaning seeping from him as he slipped into the evening crowd.

Every Angel is Terrifying

I take the bus to the edge of Sawtooth, basically as close as I can get to the highway on local transit. Beyond here it's all industrial. All warehouses and junkyards and hulking, silent buildings painted gray or beige, or not painted at all. Machine shops, garages, or simply anonymous buildings with rows of doors and loading docks. Beyond here, there is no living. It is a liminal space.

That's okay. I just need out of this town. This stupid fucking town. This brown and flat and sad town. This restless town. This home to ennui and melancholy. This scrub of buildings and people and emotions spilled in the middle of an apathetic landscape like hay from an overturned truck.

I walk from there.

I walk past the buildings until the parking lots are replaced with fields and, eventually, the buildings are too.

I walk until the sound of the interstate grows from the sound of wind to the sound of a waterfall, and from there to the sound of wheels on pavement.

I walk along the county road, across the bridge over the freeway. Halfway across, I fumble my phone from my pocket and let it tumble over the railing to the concrete below.

I keep walking.

*

At fifteen, I had been an anxious and gawky dog. Too anxious. Too gawky. I took to slinking around school from class to class in silence, letting my overful backpack propel me down the halls, walking close to the walls. Any time not spent in the desk furthest from the door daydreaming was spent in front of one of the computers in the lab.

Sawtooth High had a few computer classes, but none of them warranted the lab that the school had. Twenty relatively high-end machines—at least, higher end than would ever be needed for the two typing classes, the Pascal class, or the HTML class offered by the school—and my favorite, two Linux machines tucked away in a corner. Babylon and Enterprise.

I spent hours on those damn machines. Sometimes, it would be me, holed up in the lab itself, sitting in front of an aged CRT monitor, claws clacking on the keys as I taught myself one programming language or another, worked on homework, or just plain goofed off online. Sometimes, it was me me surreptitiously tabbing back and forth between what I was supposed to be working on in Pascal class and a terminal window opened to Babylon (Enterprise being the machine that ran the school's website, we were discouraged from actually using). Sometimes it was me sneaking out of bed once I was sure my mom had gone to sleep and, muffling the modem with my pillow, logging on remotely.

Most often, at those times, it was me logging into some text adventure or another. Where flashy video games had never caught my attention, I'd gotten hopelessly addicted to dungeon crawling with a small party over a MUD. Where instant messengers had failed to grab me, I would spend hours chatting on MUCKs.

The limitations of text only fascinated me, and though I never wrote with any seriousness other than a well-worn blog, more journal than literature, I learned to weave my tales and use my words in front of a crowd.

And it was there where I found love. There where I found love and lust and romance and flings. I dated. I TSed (we were, of course, too cool to use so vulgar a word as 'cyber'). I set up relationships for characters in our games, and I set up relationships that transcended that, two hearts touching through only those white words on a black screen.

Merlin and Marusin, The_Prof and rranger386, people I would dream about and likely never meet. We were all young. We were in love with each other in our own little worlds, serially and in parallel.

And while sometimes I would think about who they were beyond the screen, it was rarely for long. I was in love with Merlin the fighter who hated magic. I was in love with The_Prof the student who desperately wanted to be a professor when he grew up, and didn't care which subject.

Sometimes I would think about who they were when we TSed, would wonder what it would be like to have their paw instead of my own around my erection, but never for long. It was easier. It was safer to not bother with it.

But our relationships were as real as any collocated flings. More so, we told ourselves, for the purity of essence that came with no flesh to get in the way.

I'm sure we all hungered for touch.

★

I'm regaining my *I*. My *me*. My *self*.

I'm no longer just Derek, that monster, that hollow shell, that desolate vacuum. No longer watching him from the outside, watching him move with mindless purpose.

I'm regaining my I, and I don't like what I see.

I keep walking.

★

It was toward the tail end of high school that I began to get plagued with depression and mood swings.

I was a healthy collie. All the romance of a noble lineage had gone to my parents' heads, and there was simply no reason one of my standing should ever feel bad. Sure, the family had come on hard times financially, and Idaho had been an inexpensive refuge for us. Flyover state or no, we could keep our large house and happy lives. How could any dog be sad?

And yet I was. I was in spades. I would swing down for a few months, life slowly losing its color, until I'd feel nothing except an ache behind my sternum, eating only mechanically, and only when reminded.

Then it would pass. It would be dinner and I'd realize that I was actually *really* enjoying the curried chicken. I'd realize that it had been days since I'd thought about falling asleep and not waking up. I'd have energy.

I'd have a bit too much energy.

Mom would shrug and mumble something about boys. "Men in this family, always so moody. You'll grow out of it."

I mostly kept it to myself. When I did share it with friends online, it was to commiserate in the "Parents, eh? What do they know?" style that never goes out of fashion among teenagers.

Still, as awful as it was, I learned the rhythm of it. I'd spend a month or so feeling terrible, three months feeling pretty good, and then a month feeling great.

Not just great, *better* than great.

I'd spend all of my allowance in a week. I'd sleep three, four hours a night. I'd write page after page of backstory for my role-playing characters. I'd scribble ideas as fast as they came to me and still not be fast enough.

I still have a folder of those ideas. They're illegible, unnerving.

And then, over the course of a week at most, I'd be back underwater once more.

Depression is a strange thing.

I tried at several points to capture some sense of it in words, but nothing ever quite fit. Whenever I did, I found myself using a lot of ellipses just to fill in, textually, my fumbling for words with enough meaning. I came up with stuff like, "I dunno. My brain just isn't all me. Like... It's something else. It's there and exerts influence on me life, but it spends an inordinate about of time trying to destroy me."

Or poetry. I tried to throw that at depression, too, but it just came out sounding stilted and weird. I'd wind up talking about fire a lot. Fire and birds, for some reason.

Which was nonsense, really, but each in such a way that seemed to cover at least one small corner of depression.

Depression is big. It's vast and terrible and empty. Completely empty, and there you are, in the middle of it, feeling bad about nothing.

There's just no sense to it. No sense in trying to describe nothing. A 'nothing' which is also nonsensical.

And yet I keep trying.

All these words...

*

Every angel is terrifying.

The words start a whisper, a half-heard echo. They are a niggling thought, a loose tooth, a thread to be worried loose from a hem.

And before long, they're resounding within my head. They pound and boom in time with my steps, and I start murmuring them under my breath. "Every angel is terrifying. Every angel is terrifying."

As with all linguistic satiation, I can't tell when it is that they stop holding any meaning. It's as though I let my attention slip, and the next time the phrase rolls through my mouth, they're awkward shapes tumbling from my tongue, buzzing in my nose, brushing past my whiskers. Poetry reduced to its bare building blocks becomes as clumsy as any other guttural utterance, though they may stack better than most.

"Ein jeder Engel ist schrecklich," I try, hoping the original German might somehow waken something other than dread within me—it doesn't—and then I bark out a laugh, realizing maybe it's doing exactly what it was meant to.

The single laugh does not echo. It dies among the weeds and crumbly blacktop of the county road.

I keep walking. I keep murmuring my mantra. Keep muttering long after the words have lost meaning. Long after all that's left is a bottomless, emotionless nothing. Long after all thoughts have left my head, except for the realization that I desperately, desperately want to die. Realize it for the million, billion, trillionth time.

I keep walking.

*

"LTS, this is Derek, how can I help you?"

It was one of those staid lines, the standard greeting that everyone gets when they called our department, Library Technical Services. One of those lines that was so rote, such a patterned behavior, that I'd answered my own cellphone with it once or twice.

I'd worked at the campus library for a year and a half at that point, and eighty percent of the problems we take care of were reported through a form on the library's intranet. Even so, I'd gotten that line down pat. The line and the tone. I lowered my voice a few steps, spoke quietly and soothingly, sounding attentive. The people who called rather than using the request form were usually doing so for a reason: they wanted service right then, their problem was urgent, and usually affected more than just themselves. Most issues with customer-facing stuff—the public computers, desktops or laptops—were reported through a phone call.

"I...I can't find the photo editing program, and I can't find the page layout program, and I can't find email, and...and gosh darn it, you guys promised all of this would be on my new computer!" the frustrated voice whined from the receiver. I felt my ears cringe back and the fur at the back of my neck rise.

"Alright, ma'am, slow up a sec, everything's going to be alright, now–"

"No, everything is not going to be alright! I was told I'd have all the software that was on my old machine back again, and it's not, otherwise why would you guys ask for it?"

"Ma'am, please slow down, I think there's been a misunderstanding," I said. "When we upgraded your computer, you were upgraded to the new email suite, so your desktop shortcut is probably broken. I can fix that and install the other software items you need here in just a sec. Can you compile a list of all the old software you had on your computer?"

She was near tears by then. "I don't understand why you guys even asked me what software I wanted on the new computer if you're not going to install any of it!"

"That's where the misunderstanding was," I replied hastily, tail tucking out of instinct. "We were asking for a list of software to be installed on *everyone's* computer in Liaisons, not just your station. We install the same operating system image on everyone's computer in that area."

"Well, this is absurd. I need email back, and I need photo editing and page layout...ing!" She sounded so much like a petulant child, I dropped the phone.

No, tell a lie. I threw the phone. The portable handset skittered across the carpet and knocked against the far wall, battery cover snapping open and the battery pack tumbling free, smoking.

Bad sign.

I rushed to pick up the battery pack and hold the shorting wires apart so that I could tape them separately.

I shouldn't have thrown the phone, to be honest. It was just as childish and petulant as the employee I was talking to. No denying it felt good, though, that catharsis.

But that day hadn't been a good one. It felt like school and work were conspiring against me to make my life as hard as possible. Majoring in computer science had sounded so fun when I'd picked it, but the more I learned about computers, the more I learned to loathe them. The more I loathed computers, the more I loathed a key part of my identity, loathed myself as a whole. The more I loathed computers, the more I loathed school, the worse my grades, the angrier the calls home, the less I spoke, the more I hid.

The last thing I needed was an employee throwing a temper tantrum and blaming me for her non-issues blown way out of proportion.

We knew it was a non-issue, too. Her software had indeed been included on the list we were given with her name beside it, so we had checked her drive over the network and found that the last access times for the editing software had been only a few hours after their creation dates, more than a year ago. Always on a quest to trim down the size of the disk images, boss had gone on a bit of a spree—or the opposite of a spree, rather—pointedly not including software that people didn't use on the Liaisons image.

A minute and a half later found me sitting in my chair trying to fix the portable handset I'd just thrown across the lab with little success. The employee, a fisher, came peeking in through the door to LTS. I held up the phone toward her and mumbled something about having a little bit of trouble with the handset, simple mechanical repair, sorry for the dropped call. My boss peeked out of his office, glancing between us to see what the noise was.

"Matt," she whined to him. "When you gave me the new computer, I was told that I would have all of my old programs on it and they're not there!" She sounded a hairsbreadth away from tears, and my boss's eyes went wide at the tinge of hysteria, his muscles tensing as he backed away from this new threat. I noted with a small amount of satisfaction that the coyote's own tail tucks as reflexively as mine.

"I think there was a misunderstanding," he said carefully. "Everything will be alright, if you just give us a second, we'll–"

I was already wincing away from the conversation at his very familiar words by the time she stamped her foot. Her tail was already bottle-brushed out, and I could tell she was only a moment away from hissing. I took that as my cue and quietly ducked out around her to slip out of the library.

I walked around the building. I took the counter-clockwise route, knowing I risked being seen from LTS' view of the parking lot, but trusting my boss to have things in hand.

An unseasonably warm winter was heading toward a cold snap. I could smell it in the air, as though all of the moisture had been packed away for the weekend. Shortcutting through a grassy alley between the library and the psychology building, I crunched through dead leaves with paws buried deep in pockets.

I wasn't relaxed enough by the time I reach the front doors again and so I walked around the building a second time, thinking.

Most of the employees in the library were meek, older, librarian types. I didn't mind that. It made my job a whole lot easier. I told them to do this, not to do that, and they obeyed with a look of fear or reverential awe in their eyes. We had a few that were bad for thinking they knew rather more about computers than they really did; bad, because we got called in to clean up particularly broken messes.

Still feeling surly, I decided this particular librarian was the last type: the customer. The customer is always right, even when they're wrong, even when it's to the detriment of the those around them.

I really shouldn't have thrown the phone.

When I got back into the lab, my boss handed me a small stack of install disks and a list of downloadable software with an apologetic look. "She was awful...I think I'm scarred for life," he mumbled. "I'm gonna need you to install those for her. She went home for the day, though, so feel free to do it remotely."

"What's her computer again?" I asked resignedly. Fair's fair.

"N-W-A-I-T-E"

"Nora? Nancy? I forget her name. Guess I blocked it from my mind. Should probably email her an apology."

He gave an abbreviated wag, always a sign of trouble. " 'I moan' backwards."

I groaned, rolled my eyes at the strained humor, and set to work installing Mrs. Waite's software.

That night, I dully made myself a grilled cheese sandwich, poured a finger of precious, ill-gotten gin over stale ice, and holed up in front of my computer, wrapped in a blanket with tail draped limply from the back of my chair.

For an hour, perhaps, I scrolled through blogs and forums. I read up on my friends' brighter lives. I read threads I didn't care about. After a certain point, I didn't even read. I scrolled mechanically, and when I hit the bottom, I'd click the 'next page' button.

Or perhaps I read, I don't know. Perhaps the pattern-matching part of my brain that recognized letters and words and sentences kept on doing its job. Perhaps words and meaning did flow through my mind, but none of it found any foothold. None of it stuck.

It was a flashing icon in system tray that caught my attention, and I sheepishly clicked over to chat, wondering just how long it had been blinking at me.

There, tinted cyan amid the general stream of chatter in the room, was a private message. With a force of will, I crunched my mind back into gear, and read to understand.

```
Peter_P pages, "Hey, you okay?" to you.
```

Before I knew what I was doing, I was already well into my reply third reply, and by then, I had too much momentum to stop.

```
You page, "Yeah. I mean, I guess I'm depressed.
     Work is probably the highlight of my day
     if only because I have to be there and do-
     ing my job. Even with classes, I can just
     zone out in the back and feel bad al-
     most in private. I come home and avoid my
     roommates and idle on here." to Peter_P.
You  page-pose,  "Piree   sighs,   "I'm   okay,
     though."" to Peter_P.
You page, "Or my life is okay, I dunno." to
     Peter_P.
You page, "Shouldn't complain, I'm in a good
     spot. It's just hard when it all feels
     so pointless and empty. Sometimes I get
```

```
so desperately sad and everything hurts
or whatever, but this is just like having
my heart and brain replaced with cotton
balls. It's like thinking through gauze."
to Peter_P.
```

I realized, by the time I manage to lift my paws from the keys and cup them around my blunt muzzle, that I've started crying, the fur on my cheeks damp with tears. I wished I could delete messages. Erase them from the screen, from the server, from Peter's mind, if he'd already read them. I wished I could take it back and just be empty in my room, at my poster-covered walls, rather than empty on the internet at distant friends.

Greeted with silence, I tucked my muzzle down and covered the rest of my face with my hands and held my breath, willing time to stop, reverse its own flow, and drop me back at work.

When I looked up again, I was greeted not with a reply from Peter, nor even simple silence, but a few lines on the screen.

```
Peter_P teleports away.
MEETME: Peter_P would like you to join them at
        their current location.
MEETME: type "mjoin Peter_P" to join them.
```

For another minute, I stared at the screen, unable to comprehend what would lead him to want to talk about this further, in some quieter room.

"Ah, fuck it," I said aloud, typed mjoin peter_p, and whacked the enter key.

```
Peter_P hugs!
```

Peter_P says, "Tell me what's up?"

Piree hugs and sighs. "I dunno. Depressed, I guess. That time of the month."

Peter_P says, "Yeah..."

Peter_P says, "I know you're poking fun, but it does seem cyclical."

You say, "'it'?"

Peter_P says, "Depression, yeah."

Peter_P says, "In you, I mean. You seem to go through these cycles of really energetic and really depressed."

You say, "Yeah..."

You say, "That noticeable?"

Peter_P sticks his tongue out. "Don't take it the wrong way. It's not like super blatant or anything, just something I've noticed about you."

You say, "heh"

You say, "You pay that much attention to me, then?"

I grunted and spent another moment wishing I could take back what I'd just sent.

Peter_P says, "I guess :P"

You say, "Sorry, that came out snippy. I didn't mean it."

Peter_P shrugs. "I guess I do, though. I like you. I worry about you."

Piree hugs. "Thanks. That means a lot."

When I next looked at the clock, it was nearing two in the morning. I'd spent nearly five hours talking with Peter. I thanked him profusely for staying up so late with me—"No problem, I don't have work tomorrow"—and signed off for the night.

I went to bed...not exactly happy, but comforted. As I started nodding off, I realized that I'd disconnected in Peter's room, my character had fallen asleep there. A smile tugged at my lips. It felt right.

★

The beautiful is right at the margin of the terrifying.

And it *is* beautiful.

With the sun at my back, I trudge east. The din of the freeway long ago softened through waterfall and back into the sound of distant winds.

I feel those winds blow through me. Not just blow through my fur—the air itself was still—but through me, through my core. I feel hollow, empty. I feel like one of the pipes in an organ I got to tour some years back. I feel the wind blow through me, and I feel myself excited, humming. Hollow, but humming. Cold, but buzzing.

I realize my breath is coming hoarsely now. My steps are heavy and my feet hurt and I'm breathing hard. I've been stomping without realizing it.

I slow my pace and focus on walking like a normal dog. No sense in getting worn out early. I want to get away from town. I want to walk far enough away that the town of too many memories. Of so many visits with Peter, of jobs left behind, of feelings too strong to bear.

I walk east under some other authority's direction. I am not in control of my body anymore. I am not in control of my thoughts.

I have no thoughts.

I have no thoughts. Emotions well up, rage, and die within, ceaselessly and directionlessly.

I have no thoughts. I ride my emotions from one swell to the next, surfing along, feeling that I, too, will rage and die.

I have no thoughts.

I keep walking.

*

Much of my undergrad was borne out of depression. School was just a thing I did during the days, but my time spent in front of a keyboard was a part of myself. Each story, each post, each role-play session was a piece of myself. Each was a tiny rock to throw at this vasty nothingness. Justifying the things I liked, delineating the craziness of lives real and manufactured, gushing about worlds fantastic...they were all ways for me to pound my fists against nothing at all.

A scant two months into my second year at university, I crashed hard and tried to commit suicide, a private affair I never told anyone about, and after that, I just buried myself in it—in my computer and in the life lived there, the life I was soon sharing with Peter.

I found ways to write more whenever possible, just to try and fill that big, quiet nothing. I splashed around in great heaps of words, scrabbling at every pebble of a story I could find beneath the surface. I prowled through the tangled thicket of fiction and nonfiction, hunting for ideas to highlight. I took way too many metaphors way, way too far.

And you know what? It worked.

At least, after a fashion. I started to feel fulfillment. I started *filling* my weekends with writing. I got in trouble with Peter for idling out repeatedly during conversations, words flowing into the editor instead of between the two of us. I started to gain energy just from the act of *spending* energy on something I loved wholeheartedly.

In a flash of insight—or perhaps mania—I scheduled an appointment with someone in the arts department. Changing degrees and the course of my life was, it turns out, as simple as signing a sheet of paper and waiting a week for confirmation. The next semester, I would be able to start signing up for classes to work toward a degree in creative writing. It would likely extend my undergrad by a year, but thankfully, I'd gotten plenty of the core curriculum classes out of the way already.

One of the downsides of working on insight is, by the very definition, a lack of foresight. Telling my parents resulted in them immediately pulling financial support for my tuition.

"I'm not going to help buy you a useless future," dad growled. "I can't stop you from throwing away your life; you're a fucking adult. That won't be on me, though."

It was only by dint of luck that the current semester, plus my living situation for the remainder of the semester and summer was already paid for. That check had already been deposited.

The thing that sealed the deal for me was that I still enjoyed my time at school even when the next downswing struck later that semester. I'd already realized that decisions made when I felt good weren't always the right ones, but if they still felt right when I was depressed, I could be sure that they'd be more likely to stick.

Such had not been the case with comp sci, it seemed.

Depression was not solved by increasing quality of life. Its tenor changed, to be sure, but the dependable five month cycle continued throughout the years, souring summers and leaving me bedridden with "the flu" or "a cold" for days at a time.

I would spend the days under the covers with the second-hand laptop I got from the library surplus and, depending on the weather, either a glass of gin and ice or a hot cocoa spiked with peppermint schnapps, alternating between writing and programming, masturbating to old TS logs, and crying.

I would role play as my best, purest characters. Or perhaps, with Peter, I would role play as my better self. Someone happier than I was. Healthier, more responsive, more engaging.

I would go to bed feeling guilty for wearing such a mask, consoling myself in the fact that without it, I might wind up without him.

I would marvel the enormity of this empty space in which I inhabited.

I would marvel at the film-like quality to my life.

I would marvel at the diegesis of objects, sounds, tastes, smells.

I inhabited a spotlight shone on a flat gray ground.

I began relying on alcohol to feather the edge of it, making the boundary between myself and that emptiness softer, less cruelly sharp.

I used the pain of plucked fur or hot knife-tip against skin to send up magnesium flares, enough to briefly light up the world around me and offer a sense of clarity, however superficial. The mundane, everyday-ness of wound care would ground me for a week, two. Before long, my arms were ragged, scarred.

None of that made me any less of myself. They didn't sweep away Derek. It simply became a part of me while I wasn't watching. The pain, the gin, the days holed up in bed were a fine set of glasses for helping me see which things I was burning myself over were real, and which were just phantoms in that dreamscape.

And then, with clockwork predictability, it would lift. With a sharp coolness burning my nostrils, I'd rise before the sun and walk the neighborhood, find my way to The Book and The Bean, and see eyes other than my own.

With only a modicum of foresight or perhaps practiced nonchalance, I slipped from my undergraduate program to an MFA program in Moscow, Idaho, off in the far west of the state.

★

Memories, fragments, wordless things crowd me, wraiths tugging at my clothing and fur. I am caught up in these non-thoughts, these non-memories and non-words, buoyed up, borne aloft, buffeted.

My steps falter. I stumble and weave. I fall once, twice. Tired. Exhausted. Spent. Drained of life and purpose and intent.

Derek is gone. The collie is gone. There is only the *I*, the *me*, the barest speck of *self*.

★

"Oh god, it's so much easier to fly into Boise than Moscow or Sawtooth," Peter grunted, luggage clattering to the floor as we hauled it from the carousel.

I laughed. "The city does come with its benefits, yeah. Pretty good food, and it's big enough to get you to visit more."

"Yeah, I turn into a pumpkin if I leave the five boroughs at all."

"Well, it's not *that* big, and not nearly as tall, thankfully."

Peter smiled apologetically, tall ears splayed. "Sorry. Can't help my apartment's so high up."

Telescoping the handle out of one of the shepherd's two suitcases, I guided him away from the crowd and over to the rental car stations. "You're fine, love, promise. You turn into a pumpkin when you get out of the city, and I feel like any building higher than three stories is bound to come tumbling down."

"I know. Different strokes, I guess. I feel so exposed out here. It's all so flat, I feel like the tallest thing around."

"And I feel like a tiny speck in New York." I shrugged. "Despite growing up next to the mountains."

The rental car was a concession to life in the Midwest. It was all well and good to take public transit in a place like New York City, or even cabs, but even though public transit wasn't exactly terrible in Boise, it was much harder to get from the airport to my apartment here on public transit than it was out east. Besides, it would allow us the opportunity to hunt down good restaurants or hunt for good hiking east of the city.

We spent the drive back catching up. We talked plenty, both over text and phone, but for some reason, those first few hours after touchdown always felt like a period of reacquainting.

I told him of life in grad school, of looking at doctoral programs, of the way that it always felt like stumbling when I started teaching in the fall, before I'd fall back into the rhythm of it, no matter how many fall semesters I taught. He told me about his design work in the city, and though I'd heard plenty about it before, it was suddenly more engaging, if only for the fact that I could see his wild gestures when describing it out of the corner of my eye as I drove us home.

By the halfway point, we'd re-purposed the center console as platform to bear our clasped paws, and by the final mile, our paws had each wound up on the other's thigh.

The bags didn't even make it to the bedroom. Neither did most of our clothes, for that matter. They left a trail of evidence for some keen-eyed detective from the entryway to my bed, where the heady scent of sex hung thick in the air: a final clue for why two dogs were sprawled, panting, fur matted with semen and lube.

An hour's lazy conversation, a shared shower, and a glass of wine on the patio led us to the conclusion that it was far, far too nice out to bother with eating indoors, and so we walked to the convenience store for a simple dinner and struck out for the park.

"It's a different kind of height."

"Mm?"

"The mountains," Peter said.

We'd settled down on a pair of folding camp chairs in a small park and were sharing an inexpensive can of wine—though perhaps 'inexpensive' isn't a necessary prefix to 'can of wine', but they looked like sodas from a distance, so they worked well for picnics. Before us rose a slow slope, the neatly manicured grass of the park ending abruptly at the base of a dun-colored hill.

"That's hardly a mountain," I laughed.

"Yeah, but, like...in Sawtooth. Those were real mountains."

"Fair. What do you mean, different kind of height, though?"

Peter took a long sip from the can, and we sat in silence, waiting for the last of the sun to slip off the tip of Camel's Back. Once it had settled into the evening with the rest of us, he continued. "It's so haphazard. All the buildings in the city, they're all so regular, even when they're tall. I can stand by the base and look straight up and know—*know*—that I will see sky. I don't feel that way with mountains."

"I suppose I felt the opposite," I said after a pause. "I always felt like they were looming over me, like their whole weight would topple down on top of me if the wind blew wrong."

The other dog laughed. "I guess we're the same, then, for different reasons. I always felt like the mountains were going to come down on me. They sit there to the...well, to the east, here, but back in Sawtooth to the west, and they just–" he waved his paw vaguely at the hill before us. "–they just stand there. Wild and untamed. There's no order. You don't know what they're going to do. Not like in cities, where the buildings are...are manifestations of order. Order imposed on physical reality."

"You, my darling, are drunk," I said, and we both laughed again. "But I think I understand. You feel like the mountains could coming crashing down on you, because there's nothing to stop them from doing so."

"Mm."

"And I feel like there's nothing to stop the buildings from coming down on me because I know how bad we are at ordering our lives; how could we possibly be any better at ordering nature?"

Peter passed the can of wine to me to finish, waited for me to transfer it to my other paw, and then took my closer one in his. We sat, paw in paw, until evening settled into twilight.

That night, as we lay curled together, I wondered aloud for the millionth time what kept Peter with me. He drew so much strength from order, and I was such a train wreck.

"Sometimes I feel like you're the mountains. There's nothing to stop you from falling, because there's so little order in your life. Doesn't mean I don't love you."

I hesitated in the slow strokes of my fingers through his fur, frowning up into the darkness.

"I'm sorry, Piree," he mumbled, falling back to that comfortable name of years ago, a username turned pet name. "That maybe came out wrong. Maybe I'm still a bit drunk."

"No, you're probably right." I sighed, turning until I could tuck my muzzle beneath his. "I *would* have a hard time trusting order. I don't have any proof that it actually exists."

We slept.

★

Shivering in the March evening's chill, I come to a tee in the road. Staring out at the unbroken rolling plains beyond town, I linger. The sun sets, the moon rises. Stars fade into view, and still I stare at the low scrub.

The first true thought that enters my mind is of how small I am. I mentally try to estimate how many of myself stacked head to toe and packed in cords it would take to equal just one of those low hills, not to mention just one of the mountains of the Sawtooth range behind me. And how little all my problems must mean to that many people.

All that I love feels poisoned to me, tainted by the fact that I burned so hard in an attempt to light up all this nothing a little better. I feel forced to like these things because I'm trammeled by this indescribably empty space with them.

No, tell a lie. I did this. I tore Peter up and threw him away because he wasn't in there with me in the midst of that nothing. I was a coward: afraid to be alone, but more afraid to ask for help, so I removed my choice in the matter.

All these words, all this burning bright in an attempt to light up vast, crenelated spaces of nothing...perhaps it's just a hunt for a reason to incinerate myself.

★

These upswings, if that's what they are, have long since ceased to actually feel good. It's just depression at the speed of sound. Depression, but if you stop moving, you die.

And now that's where I am. That's *who* I am. That's all that's left. In the last week, all of that sludge of depression sloughed off and I was left jewel-hard and burning from within. All of that nothing had transmuted into hatred, utter revulsion for myself and everything good in my life.

I am not myself.

Burned too long, and all that's left is a charred scaffold of a personality.

I am not myself.

In the middle of class earlier today, I simply gave in. I must have stopped talking for a long moment, as a hesitant "Doctor MacIver...?" came from the middle of the room. As my only response, I stood up and walked silently from the room.

No, not 'I'. I was not the one doing these things, anymore. Someone else was. Derek MacIver was. I watched numbly as he paced out the door.

He didn't stop in the hallway.

He didn't stop at the door outside, nor at the quad.

He didn't stop until he made it home.

He didn't stop at his door. Not until he made it to the computer did he stop, and only then to lean over the keyboard words spilling directly onto the screen with no thought to back them up.

> You mail, "I honestly feel sorry for you. The
> only thing more pathetic than myself is
> anyone who would love me." to Peter_P.

After countless nightmares wherein I would somehow find the one single thing I could say to hurt someone—no, not hurt, crush; completely and utterly destroy—any revulsion of actually doing so was lost amid the flames of boundless loathing for this Derek, this hollow shell of a collie.

Then it was just a matter of him grabbing a few things and hopping on the bus.

I had no thoughts.

I had no thoughts.

I had no *I*.

*

The sound of a car door shutting brings me out of my reverie, if reverie it is, and I blink at my surroundings. I'm standing at the side of the road with the barbed wire of the fence clenched in my fists, a small, cheap two-door parked about twenty feet away. It's a small wonder I hadn't heard it before, nor even noticed the headlights casting my shadow before me. There's a dull pain in my hands. A far away pain. A someone-else pain.

Once the driver walking towards me resolves from a blurry black cutout against their headlights to the features of one of my students—a solidly built mountain lion, glasses, feminine features on a masculine face; the one who had called after me in class—I relax my grip on the fence. Without saying a word, the puma leads me over to the passenger door of the car and makes me sit in the seat. They tear strips from a towel in the back seat to wrap my bleeding pads.

My paws. My paws covered in lacerations and punctures from the barbed-wire fencing. They are not my paws. They are someone else's. They are somewhere else.

Am I me? Is Derek myself? Who lived this life? Who loved? Who destroyed? Great, choking sobs begin to muddle all the 'who's and obscure all the 'why's.

With my student's help, I use one of the strips to wipe the tears and snot from my face. The mountain lion shuts the door, pads back around the car, and turns it around on the narrow county road.

When we reach the university, the cat finally speaks, asking me where I live from there. I mumble my address, and another two minutes of silence follow before we pull up in front of the condos I live in.

Both of us get out of the car. They ask if I need help inside, if I need an ambulance. I shake my head, and the mountain lion gives me a hug.

It isn't a guy hug, isn't that chaste, dry form of affection I've never been able to understand, though it's far from any embrace I'd shared with Peter. There's more support, more emotion, more understanding in that hug than in any of the many words I've been capable of hearing over the past week, month, year, lifetime, and I have to try my hardest to make it back inside before bursting into tears once more.

Who, if I cried out, would hear me among the ranks of angels?
And even supposing one of them took me suddenly to their
*   breast,*
I would perish within their overpowering being,
For the beautiful is right at the margin of the terrifying, which
*   we can only just endure,*
And we marvel at it, because it holds back in serene disdain
*   and does not destroy us.*
Every angel is terrifying.

I have found my *I*.

I fumble the snub-nosed revolver from the waistband of my pants, swing open the loading gate, and, one by one, dump the rounds into my bandaged paw. Acting on serene autonomy, I lock the gun into its case once more, and tip the cartridges out of my paw and into the trash.

What Defines Us

Darren,
    Haven't heard from you in a while. Do you think I could come up and visit for xmas? Been a while since I've seen the little monsters. Let me know before prices go up.
    How are you? How is Leila?
    LYF
    Mom

★

Mom,
    I'm sorry I haven't gotten back to you recently. Things on our end have been awful, if I'm honest.
    Leila and I are thinking of splitting up.
    I don't know about Christmas. I hope you understand.
    LYFA
    Darren

★

Oh honey, I'm so so sorry. What happened? Was it about work again?

I still want to come out and see you. More now than I did before.

Can I do anything to help? Do you want to talk over the phone?

LYF

★

Mom,

Sorry, I guess my last email was pretty skimpy on the details. Sorry, don't really want to call about this, since things are tense around here, and I don't want to sneak off just to use the phone.

Yeah, the work thing got bad, then got a whole lot worse. I knew Leila was unhappy with it and all, but I don't think I realized how unhappy. I mean, I'm not happy with it, either, but obviously it's the life I live and have lived. I grew up with it, too, so it's in my blood. It's stressful, it's hard, but I guess I kinda like it. She wasn't happy hearing that.

Well anyway, dozens of arguments later, it comes out that she got fed up enough to start sneaking out and seeing others. Maybe if she'd been open about it or whatever, I would've been more able to work with it, but I think it just goes to show that neither of us are happy and neither of us can trust each other.

We tried doing the counseling thing at one point. We did couples therapy and it worked okay for a little while. Like, we got a chance to talk with someone who mediated a bit, and it was nice that she taught us how to talk better with each other. Or argue more kindly. Something like that.

We even brought Jer and Eileen to some, but I don't know, mom. I feel like I'm in a bad spot with that. I don't trust it. I feel like I should be the one to talk things through with the kids, not some very expensive stranger, you know? It makes me feel like I'm out of touch with how they feel about things, and like it would just sow distrust in them of us. Leila kind of agreed, but I don't know.

I'm lost, mom. What do I do? This is all so overwhelming...

LYFA

D

★

Darren,

It's not easy stuff to work through, I know. It sounds like you're doing a good job of things, and certainly like you're doing right by the kids.

You both knew that there would be a lot of compromise going into this relationship, but maybe you just didn't realize how much? I hope I'm not overstepping or anything, just that sometimes compromise works and sometimes it doesn't. That's just the way of things. You and I had to compromise on a lot, and it's worked out okay (I think!!), but Justin and I tried and never could get it to work.

As for what to do, just be honest. Painfully so, if need be. That said, you should be careful about Jeremy and Eileen. If you want to talk about all this and work on the divorce thing, *don't do it on your own*. Do so with Leila. The last thing you want is for L to think you're using them against her. I know you wouldn't, but still. Both of you talk with them together.

And don't be afraid to talk with them about the problems you and L are having. They're smart cats, they'll be able to understand, and may have good advice for you, too! Treat them like adults, and they won't treat you (either of you!!) like mysterious unapproachable aliens throwing their lives into chaos.

I know it's a pain, but call me if you need?

LYF

Mom

*

Mom,

Sorry for the delay. Things are up and down over here. We did as you said and have been talking things through with the kids, to mixed results. I can tell they're uncomfortable and unhappy about it all, but I feel like they're getting it, and having their say. And I feel more connected with them about it.

The downside is that it's splitting L and I's thoughts on the matter in a weird way. When we talk about things in front of the kids, it feels like we're saying one thing, but when we talk in private, it's something different. We both act so civil around them because we have to, that it's made our arguments in private more painful. We keep our civility, sort of, but in tone only. The things we say toward each other are civil, but they're biting and mean. Just quietly so. Things were sort of a maybe until we started doing this. Now it's feeling more like a definite.

It hurts so much, mom. I love Leila, and I love the kids. If this is the direction we're going in, I guess that's what needs to happen. It's awful, and we're all going to suffer. Jeremy and Eileen especially. But none of this work stuff is going to look good to a judge. The thought of losing them has me not eating, not sleeping.

I don't know what to do.

LYFA

★

I know, honey. I don't want to sound like a broken record, but I know it's not easy stuff. When things have broken down this completely, there is no outcome of this that is going to feel fair. Still, you love your children. It's plain to me, and I hope it's plain to Leila and any judge in the matter. You won't have them taken away from you. Just make sure you stay in their lives. Make sure you do what you can to help them WANT to stay in yours, too. (Not saying buy their affection, just show your love and appreciate (visibly) the love they show you.)
LYF

★

Yeah, the goal is not to be my dad here.
Sent from MobileMail.

★

Darren,
That's not fair to me *or* your dad at all.
Can we please call about this?
LYF

★

Darren? LYF

★

Darren, please.

Justin and I had our differences and we couldn't work them out. We tried. We never took you, but we went to counseling, too. I know it hurt you, but my goal was never NEVER for you to hate him. We shared our time with you as we did, for better or worse, and I tried to keep channels open. That's why I'm saying what I am. Help them want to be in your life.

LYF

*

That's just the thing, mom. You keep pushing me to him, but there's nothing there. Not saying your advice is bad, it's certainly good. It's advice I wish you could give dad. The guy hit me, though. I was never good enough for him. He was an abusive jerk and you know it. Why would I want to go and show him *any* positive attention?

Seriously, I've tried to handle this divorce shit and my relationship (hell, my fucking life) the *opposite* of how you handled things. You both provided me with so many bad examples of how things could go. And yet here I am, reliving the fucking past.

Sent from MobileMail.

*

Darren, honey, I'm so sorry.

Not a day goes by that I don't think about you. You're my baby, remember? Long as I live.

So please, please understand me when I say that I'm sorry. Both your dad and I handled that entire situation terribly. *Both your dad and I.* I messed up back then, and if I could go back and change things, I would. I don't know if that means staying with Justin longer so that I could protect you or getting the divorce sooner to get you away from him. I don't know how I can fix it now, other than to help you not *become him.* We're after the same thing, here. Neither of us want you to be him, to wind up in his shoes.

That's why I keep pushing you toward him, though. I know it had to have hurt him for you to cut him from your life. I can't imagine how much it would hurt if Jeremy and Eileen did that to you.

I can't speak to your relationship with Leila. You know that Justin and I were cordial to each other, but when things ended, they ended, and there was no going back. If you two can patch things up, then that would be great! If you can't, though, you're right: don't be like your dad and I.

Love you forever

Mom

*

I'm sorry, mom, you're right. I know things weren't great for you and dad either, and I know you're just trying to help. It's just hard. It hurts a lot, and it's making me really upset at the drop of a hat.

Love you for always

D

*

And as long as I live

My baby you'll be!

The problem with being a parent (and you'll understand this more and more as Jeremy and Eileen grow up) is that your children are both the better versions of yourself and also doomed to repeat so many of the mistakes you did. That's what it means to be a parent. That's what defines us.

You took a lot away from how things were when you grew up. Like you said, you took away the things that went wrong and want to do the opposite. You have my blessing on that! You make me endlessly proud when you do so.

But you also took away my work ethic. That's a good chunk of why Justin and I didn't last. Not the main reason, of course, but still, it was there. And now it's playing havoc in your life.

All we can do is try and do better.

LYF

Mom

*

I don't really know what to say. I didn't realize that was a problem you and dad had, too.

When you two were splitting, all I knew was that you were gone all day and some nights, but that dad was getting worse and worse. He'd get so. angry. and I'd just have to deal with it. He'd pull my tail if I started walking too fast. He'd pull my ear if I started walking too slow. He'd shake me by my scruff if I did anything wrong.

I know he got way better after, but it's hard to internalize that. It's hard not to want to NOT be him. I hope you'll understand that's why I don't trust going to visit him, even if he moved here to Sawtooth.

LYFA

*

Darren,

Justin was a mess during all of that. He did a lot of that to me, too. As I said, much as it stings on sort of a personal level, I'm 100% okay with you doing better than me.

LYF

⋆

He did that to you too, mom!?! Oh god, I'm so sorry...

LYFA

⋆

Well, sure, but he got as good as he gave, don't worry. Once things shook out, though, that all stopped, and we even went back to being friends, though we haven't been talking much since he moved. Every time I suggested you go see him, I told him to get in touch with you. I don't know if he ever contacted you.

If you want me to stop, though, I will.

Love you forever.

⋆

...Wait, really?

I don't actually know anymore if I want you to stop. Maybe you're right, or maybe it's too late for him and I. I'll have to think about it.

Things are still up and down, but have been a bit more up recently. I still think things are going to end in a divorce, but talking with the kids forcing us to be more civil has helped a lot, and we've started talking about an equitable split.

Jer and Eileen have started talking to us a bit more, too. They don't like the way things have gone obviously, but when we talk more about why things are happening and the more practical side, they've given us some pretty good ideas as for how things could work. I'm...not surprised, I guess, given our family, but Jer seems to be wary of me. I'll watch my temper, I guess, if I'm going to keep with my promise of doing better. I don't want him to grow up like me.

Anyway, thank you, mom. I know I got snippy, but you're right, and have helped more than you realize.

So, yeah, if you think you can make it out for Christmas, I think that'd do us all good.

Love you for always.

D

A Theory of Attachment

A cool, pale blue lightness sitting just behind her sternum, Sélène made what she promised herself would be a quick pass through the kitchen.

She brushed her fingers along the edges of cabinet doors. Each one was opened and inspected, leaving her standing on tiptoes to peer in those above the counters. Nothing but cups and glasses, plates and bowls, cutting boards and pots and pans and trays and dishes. All clean and neatly stacked.

Each cabinet was carefully left ajar. The vixen had perfected the art of finding the balance point that would leave them open before the weight of the door on the hinge would close them, without simply leaving them all the way open. The barest crack.

The fridge bore her inspection patiently, door held open as she inspected along each of the shelves, gently moving well organized bottles to check between each of them. The freezer was equally patient as the vixen lifted containers of leftovers and trays of uncooked meats. Doing her best to avoid glancing at the back walls of either, she pressed the doors shut to keep the fridge from endlessly breathing cold out into the kitchen. Just to be sure, she opened them again, savoring that clean snap of the magnetic seal pulling away from the body of the fridge, then gritting her teeth in frustration as closing the door offered no such tangible reward.

The oven yawned out to her, empty. The oven was easy, because it had a light that turned on while open, and off when closed. The fridge did, too, but the oven had its pristine glass door through which she could observe the light cycling. The stove had similar lights which, the associate at the hardware store assured here, were connected directly to the burners. Even so, she touched each cooktop surface gingerly to test for warmth, turned all the burners on, then off again.

And again.

On a whim, the drawers were next. Thankfully, most of those were empty, and the rest mostly so. The underside of the silverware tray was inspected with care.

That coolness in her chest ticked up in intensity, a little pang, as she held the drawer partly open. Anxiety into fear. A cool, blue, perfectly smooth and perfectly round fear just behind her breastbone, snaking tendrils out along her limbs.

Down on her knees with tail bristled out, Sélène eased open the cabinet door and peered up toward the underside of the drawer, ensuring that there was nothing between the drawer's underside and the cabinet, nothing behind the drawer, that the drawer's walls sides didn't reach the underside of the counter, that there was a gap.

The pang continued to grow with an implacable intensity, arteries as avenues to carry it throughout her body. Pressing visions of cramped quarters and unassailable darkness, of not enough space and not enough air, of the sheer uncaring of one's surroundings.

So she checked the rest of the drawers.

Finally, swallowing her fears as best she could, Sélène stood in the center of the kitchen. She fished her phone out of her pocket, and thumbed the screen on. Turning a slow circle, she took a panorama of the kitchen.

She waited for the panorama to stitch itself together, then pulled it up and inspected it carefully, scrolling along its length. Cabinet. Cabinet. Fridge. Cabinet. Doorway. The barest hint of a figure.

Her head jerked up and she let out a shriek at the sight of her husband standing at the entrance to the kitchen, tired smile on his muzzle. Her phone dropped from her paws and she clutched at her chest, that cool ache replaced with hot embarrassment.

Aiden stepped forward quickly and lifted up her phone careful to touch only the edges, and deposit it back into her paw. "Sorry, Sélène, I should've stepped in more. May I hug?"

Sélène laughed breathlessly, inspecting her phone and tucking it back into her pocket. "Yes, sorry! Of course!" She leaned into her husband's open arms, breathing that familiar scent. "Are you okay?"

The taller fox—much taller, which Sélène quite enjoyed—tucked his muzzle over her head and nodded against her. "I'm fine, it's alright," he murmured. "You going to head into work today, sweetheart? You only have one more from-home day left this week."

"I think so, yeah. Feeling pretty good today, actually." That cool ache sat in her chest, where it didn't grow any, yet somehow made it's presence all the more known. The cold of anxiety tickled along her ribs, threatening to make a liar of her.

She had to ask. She had to. Just ask. Just once. She just had to ask. Ask. "You sure you're alright?"

The pang subsided.

Aiden leaned back and nodded where she could see him, then leaned in again to touch his cheek to hers—the closest she could stand to affection around her face. "Fine, love. I'm doing okay."

Sélène returned the touch and nodded, silently promising that thin pang of fear that Aiden meant to say "I'm fine", rather than a grouchy "*fine*", that her husband was just tired, not tired of her.

"I'd like to head out soon, is that alright?"

"Mmhm, I just need to grab my bag. Need to pack."

Aiden nodded. "It's by the door. Check your phone, it's already packed."

Her ears twitched to attention, smile brightening. Sure enough, just before the pano of the kitchen was a photo of the inside of her shoulder bag. Laptop, all her pens, an empty book of blank paper she never could bring herself to write in, and an umbrella.

"Alright, just a quick look. Let's head out before I get lost again," she waved vaguely at the cabinets, ignoring the cool blue sensation of doubt traveling down her arms, little flares arcing out from the anxiety in her chest, sparking invisibly from her fingertips. She could *see* the cabinets were open. She didn't need to check. She didn't need to check. She could see. She didn't need to-

Aiden seemed to pick up on her hesitancy and set his paws on her shoulders, "Come on, bag's all packed, love."

Sure enough, it was packed.

★

The ride to work was about a four, she decided. She'd had better days, but this was far from her worst, even though her morning had been a seven, approaching an eight out of ten on her arbitrary scale.

Most of the time, she was able to look out the window at the passing traffic, and the rest of the time, she was able to distract herself with her phone. The app she used for her federated feeds gave a satisfying click every time she pulled down from the top to refresh it.

Aiden talked to her about his upcoming day throughout the drive in his calm, soothing voice. That was the second best thing she loved about him: his words seemed to instill a sense of the proper temperature. Not the cool-to-cold obsession, nor the heat of frustration or embarrassment.

He put up with her, too; that was the best thing about him.

That was one thing that always calmed her. All of the things that made her life difficult, all those obsessions and rituals, they all didn't feel like so much work when she thought about Aiden and the way he cared about her. She could ask him if he was alright a million times, and he would always say yes. If he was upset about work or money, he would say that he was okay, and then explain his frustrations.

Everyone else moved so much faster than he did, so haphazardly. There was so much noise and so much movement. So many ways for things to go wrong, so many missed opportunities to make sure someone else was okay.

She'd gotten her job to let her work from home three days a week just to make sure she could get enough of a break to be productive. It had taken a doctor's note, but it had worked, and she'd kept her job.

That note was humiliating.

The medical industry solemnly swore that Sélène Kelly was off her rocker, utterly crazy, completely bonkers, that madness rode her like so many ticks. All so she could get three days at home to stay productive.

The diagnosis had been fine. Her family dealt with her getting steadily worse over the years, and when they finally got her in, hearing "obsessive-compulsive disorder" confirmed that they were not crazy, she was. She'd resented them right up until her first dose of the emergency sublingual anxiolytic. It had made her sleepy, but it had made her mind quiet. It had quelled so many of those cold pangs of anxiety.

She remembered thinking before nodding off that night, "Fine, okay, it is just me." It had been depressing, but it knocked her resentment of her family down a few notches.

Aiden one-upped all of her family's care: he'd fallen in love with her, he said, whether or not she checked all the cabinets to ensure that no one was stuck, slowly starving to death. He'd gotten her more than just meds, he'd gotten her therapy. A doctor who was working with her on a steady program of exposure: *"Next time you're in the kitchen, walk in, take a glass from the cabinet, pour yourself a glass of water, and walk out. Think about how that feels."* Little steps, over and over. Her family tried to hide her—literally, at one point. Aiden tried to help her.

And he'd gotten her more than just meds and therapy, he'd gotten her him.

By the time they'd stopped at her office, just outside the front door, the day had been knocked down from a seven, to a four, to more like a two. A brush of cheeks, two I-love-yous, and one are-you-alright, and then she was off to work.

★

"You're picking, love."

Sélène jolted to awareness, realizing just how much she had zoned out. She pinned her ears back, massaging the fur on her wrist in an attempt to cover the frayed patch where she'd been digging with her claws, trying to root out a bump she'd thought she felt under her skin. "Uh, sorry, Aiden. Are you okay?"

The fox smiled and turned off the engine, pulling the parking break up with a series of sharp, satisfying clicks. He looked exhausted "I'm alright. Work was...it was a long day. Eight appointments, two meetings, no lunch. I'm starving, can we get inside and whip something up?" His expression of excitement was transparently false.

"Mmhm, I'll make us something quick," she said, giving him her best goofy grin in return. "Microwave. I promise."

Sélène felt lucky she was actually able to pull off a seamless dinner, even if it meant relying on microwaved leftovers. She loved to cook, but sometimes, reducing the friction her brain seemed intent on pushing into the act was what the night called for. Ovens and stoves are fraught with needs, dangers, anxieties. The more tired Aiden was, the less she wanted her personal idiosyncrasies to intrude on him, or on them.

They settled into their respective sides of the couch with their plates, and set the TV to droning. It was Sélène's night to choose, so the result was a documentary. Aiden had put his foot down early on and specified that they would alternate nights of choosing programs to watch. That had soon after been amended to specify no repetitions of a program or movie within a month's span, when Sélène watched the same documentary four times in two weeks. Old habits from university turned coping mechanisms.

Tonight was some investigative journalism piece about missing people. It wasn't particularly interesting to Sélène, but the narrator's voice was nice.

Sélène finished faster than Aiden, but she always did. All of her anxieties around correctness and proper fit and safety, and somehow none of them ever involved food. Chow's chow.

"Sweetheart," Aiden murmured, setting his plate to the side. "Can you pet?"

The vixen straightened up and set her phone to the side, nodding eagerly. "Of course. Are you alright?"

"Mmhm, I'm alright. Is it okay if I lay down?"

Sélène nodded and shifted from her half-curled position to a proper sit as Aiden shifted and turned, settling back to lay his head in her lap.

"It's exposure therapy, just like with the kitchen," her therapist had said. "All of these are just means of exposing yourself to the biggest stressors and triggers in a careful and controlled way."

Aiden had come in with her that day. For a while, they had had group sessions once a month with her usual therapist, "so that you can learn to be whole together." The phrase had made Sélène roll her eyes, but there was no denying the utility of the sessions.

"So she should just touch me?" Aiden had asked.

"If you two would like, yes. Just a simple touch, a way to interact with fur deliberately."

"Would you like that, Aiden?"

He had grinned at that, she remembered, and nodded eagerly. "I always loved that feeling as a kid, but thought it was childish to ask for it."

Her therapist had smiled and nodded encouragingly. *"Just pet-ting, then. No picking, no grooming, no inspecting. And no goals, this isn't a sexual exercise."*

There had been a tense silence at that. Her therapist had looked between them, then offered, *"That can be a separate exercise. For now, there should be no goal to the act other than exposure and being close to one another. It should be a comfortable way for you to work on your coping mechanisms around the picking."*

And so Sélène set to petting, brushing her claws lightly through Aiden's fur, combing lazy rows into it, fingertips tracing around the base of her husband's ears. Her day had gone well enough that there wasn't any tugs this way or that on her anxiety. No tugs this way or that on Aiden's fur.

The narrator's voice droned on through the second half of the documentary, and neither fox noticed when it stopped and looped back to the loading screen. The motions of the vixen's petting had become hypnotic for them both: Aiden had nodded off, and Sélène wasn't far behind.

★

When Sélène received her work-from-home permission letter, it had been a joy and a relief. Getting the letter had been humiliat-ing, as had the request from HR. They had been so positive about it, so supportive, and so clueless. Lots of "we just need to make sure" and "we want you to be safe, but also present".

She *was* present. She was just *too* present.

Work had known this when hiring her, too. She had made it clear in her cover letter when applying, and had repeated it (and repeated it, and repeated it) during the interview. Aiden had had to talk her through a night of anxious pacing and had even requested she turn her phone to net-only mode so that she wouldn't be so tempted to call and reassure her potential employers, yet again, that she had OCD but was willing to do everything she could.

"*We are happy to welcome you to the team with the position of junior editor*," the acceptance letter had said. "*We are eager to help you achieve all that you can in your work life. Please see HR about additional accommodations during orientation.*"

And they did try. She was the cubicle furthest from the kitchen. They special-ordered her a desk which was a simple, flat table with no pesky drawers or cabinets. They provided her with a laptop—paid for in installments direct from her paycheck—instead of a desktop. It came pre-loaded with all the stuff she'd need, as well as some stuff she didn't, but found useful anyway. The time-sensitive monitor dimming software was nice, so she left that on, and she used the timed-break software to dictate when she could check her feeds.

It just hadn't been quite enough. Nothing ever was, with OCD, perhaps by its very definition.

Her cubicle being so far away from it hadn't necessarily kept her from the work kitchen. There had been several instances of her getting caught prowling through the cupboards. Caught by coworkers she didn't know well enough to explain *why* she had to leave the cabinets open.

She got a get-well-soon card addressed to her husband after she called to check on Aiden on every break and several times besides. She had accepted the card as gracefully as she could, stammering out a lie about a death in the family.

The worst had been when HR had called her in one day for a meeting. It was a toss-up as to who was more anxious, her or the fretful ferret saying, *"This is totally confidential, but one of your coworkers has been concerned about the appearance of your fur, and has asked me to pass this on."* On the printout she was given were several domestic abuse hot-lines.

That's when she'd asked about working remote.

Friday was a work-from-home day. It was always a bit of a relief for both her and Aiden. It was time away from all of the awkwardly shaped stresses of the office for her, a time with the more familiarly shaped stresses of home. And it was a time for Aiden to relax, drive as he pleased, go eat out. He had once admitted that he would, on occasion, duck over to a nearby coworker's home to join him and his wife in cooking a gloriously uncomplicated meal.

When Sélène had first set up this arrangement with her employer, she had imagined that remote days would be far easier than working from the office.

She was half right. At first, it had been much easier. The fact of just how terrifying driving was—there was doubtless some helpful exercise her therapist would come up with—combined with the completely uncontrolled and uncontrollable nature of the office weighed her down and left her anxieties scrabbling for purchase.

Home was where all the particulars lived, however, and so home housed all of her particular anxieties. After a week of trying to work from the living room, Aiden helped her move her setup to the breakfast bar in the kitchen. It was a less-than-ideal solution, but, on bad days, she would at least be quick about checking the cabinets.

Home is where her grooming kit was—something Aiden made sure she never brought to the office. Picking and over-grooming was a problem, but one that could be solved eighty percent of the way by just not having access to grooming implements. Her claws were only so good, after all.

Home is also where it felt okay to check her feeds. She began using the ergonomics software that timed her breaks in earnest, putting her phone in the living room and only checking it when the software told her to put a break. Or at least trying to.

Some days, days like today, it felt like the only anxiety remote days solved was that which surrounded driving.

Sélène knew the uptick in anxiety was due to the upcoming Saturday. An anxiety that seemed to veer wildly between "very good" and "oh no".

Work was obscured by a constant cloud of half-formed fears. Her thoughts were obscured by subtle corruptions, with so much *un*-rightness, *un*-well-being. Her view was filled with cabinets thrown wide open, the oven door hanging slack in an unchanging look of shock, or perhaps condemnation. And still she felt that trapped feeling, that fear of being locked in total darkness, too cramped to move, air too thick to breathe.

When her break timer went off, she skittered through the kitchen, pausing only to make sure that the cabinets on the other side of the breakfast bar were still left open, and dashed out into the living room to grab at her phone. Anything to scratch one of those myriad itches. Anything for some breathing room.

By the time she had curled on the couch, she'd already gotten her phone unlocked and her feeds open. There was nothing before her but her phone and the cushions at the back of the couch, nothing behind her but an empty room. She'd curled with her head toward her end of the couch, since she knew she'd have to call Aiden if all she could smell was him at his end.

One news item. Fluff story about mod shops.

Two social updates. High school friend posting a selfie (not a good one, could see up his nose), and Malina talking about food.

Her tail, already bottle-brushed and full of nervous twitches, nearly jerked her off the couch in a rush of excitement. She cursed and scooted herself further onto the couch, slipping a paw back to brush along her tail, to calm the fur.

Sélène tapped 'favorite' on the post and flipped over to her messaging window with Malina.

> *2:03 PM Sélène*
> Hey you. What's cooking?

The vixen winced. That had a different meaning, didn't it? What's cooking, what's *cooking*. What's cooking? What *is* cooking? Hey, what's cookin', sexy?

She growled to herself and tamped down her clamoring anxieties. Malina was endlessly patient. Had been from day one. Last thing Sélène wanted to do was let her anxieties spill over onto the badger.

> *2:04 PM Malina*
> Casserole! I made some marshmallows yesterday, too.
> Alright if I bring those with tomorrow? I was going to surprise you, but figured I should probably ask.

Tension drained from her as the chill of stress melted into a pleasant embarrassment. A flush of warmth within her ears. A goofy smile. Where Aiden was calm, collected, and supportive, Malina was kind, warm, and earnest. Both did wonders to calm her.

241

2:04 PM Sélène

You make marshmallows?

2:04 PM Malina

Yup, they're really easy. Just sugar, corn syrup, gelatin, and whatever flavor you want

Sélène grinned to her phone. She had no idea why it was surprising to her that people, not just machines, made marshmallows. It fit Malina perfectly.

2:04 PM Sélène

That's cool. What flavor?

2:05 PM Malina

Lime. Sound good to you?

2:05 PM Sélène

Sounds excellent.

She paused, then tapped at the keyboard to add, *I'm really nervous, but really excited.*

2:05 PM Malina

Me too. I've been thinking about it all morning. I've never been on a date

Sélène's grin grew wider and the flush within her ears grew warmer.

2:05 PM Sélène

Wait, never?

2:06 PM Malina

Well, I mean I've been on dates, yeah, but never a DATE date. Like, one that was agreed upon as a date ahead of time

2:06 PM Sélène

Oh. Me neither, come to think of it. Aiden and I would go out and whatever, and then just suddenly -boom-, in a relationship. I don't think either of us said 'date'.

2:07 PM Malina

laughs yeah? I suppose that makes sense. You sure Aiden is okay with this?

2:07 PM Sélène

He says he is every time I've asked. He says it'll be good for me, but I worry.

2:08 PM Malina

I know. We'll keep talking about it, though

2:08 PM Sélène

Yeah.

A comfortable pause, and then a thrill of chill anxiety behind her breastbone, a splash of blue mood.

2:09 PM Sélène

You alright?

2:09 PM Malina

Doing great!

The chill faded again. There was a soft, pleasant chime from the kitchen. Sélène grumbled.

2:10 PM Sélène

Break time's up, I gotta get back to work. You working tonight?

2:10 PM Malina

Yeah. I traded shifts so I could get tomorrow off

2:10 PM Sélène

Good. You sure you don't want to go to Book and Bean for our date?

2:10 PM Malina

laughs QUITE sure. Last thing I want to do is go on a date where I work

2:11 PM Sélène

Fine, fine. Have fun, and I'll see you tomorrow.

2:11 PM Malina

Can't wait! ♡

The chime was growing louder and more insistent in the kitchen, but Sélène clutched her phone in her paw for a moment longer, smiling at that little heart at the end of Malina's last message.

⋆

The rest of the day had passed with relative ease. The conversation with Malina had broken a lot of cycling trains of thought. Not all of them, but enough that she didn't get interrupted by her compulsions. She was at the point where, as her therapist put it, she could acknowledge the obsession, recognize it, and...well, not let it go, not this time, but at least set it at the periphery where she could keep an eye on it..

All the same, Sélène found herself spending as much time listening intently for Aiden's car as she did working.

When she finally heard it, the relief was palpable.

Levering herself up from her stool at the breakfast bar, Sélène saved her work and swung the lid of the laptop shut, stood, and stretched. She padded toward the front hallway and waited for her husband.

Aiden perked his ears and smiled to be greeted at the door. "Hi sweetheart. Everything okay?"

"That's my line." The vixen grinned and leaned in for a hug. "And yeah, I'm doing okay. A bit stressed, I suppose. Are you alright?"

Slipping his arms around her, Aiden leaned into brush his cheek against his wife's. "Mm, very good. Good end to the week, glad to be home."

Aiden felt secure to her. Safe. A warm and solid presence for her to lean in against, different from Malina. Steadier, perhaps, more familiar; less exciting, but pleasantly so. "Glad you're home, too," she purred. "You sure you're alright?"

"Very much so. Alright if I come in and get changed?"

Sélène canted her ears back and laughed. "Uh, sorry. Suppose I'm a bit in the way, huh?" She tightened her hug for a moment, then ducked back into the kitchen, letting her husband pass.

By the time Aiden joined her in the kitchen, she already had a pot of water coming to a boil, and cubes of chicken sizzling in a pan. Chicken and pasta was simple enough, clean enough, to make it an easy meal for her to deal with when she was up to cooking. Despite the day being something of a mess when it came to stress, she was feeling good enough after talking with both Malina and Aiden that she figured she'd try to work on engaging with the kitchen.

"Smells good, sweetheart. Chicken?"

"Mmhm." She flipped each cube of chicken precisely before tipping the box of dried pasta into the water and giving it a stir. "Wanted to cook something for you tonight."

Aiden padded beside her, murmuring, "Thank you, dear, that means a lot. May I hug?"

Sélène splayed her ears, hesitating for a moment before shaking her head. "Um, let me get to a better point, then I can. You alright?"

The fox nodded and slipped around the corner to sit on one of the stools. "Alright. And yeah, I'm good. Feeling lovey, is all."

"Let me finish, then," Sélène grinned. "And then I'll get all lovey with you."

Aiden laughed and nodded, watching her cook.

Simple or not, the chicken and olive oil smelled good to Sélène. Nothing special, taste-wise, but the homeyness was attractive. Chicken and noodles, some oregano and rosemary, some salt and pepper, and a very generous grating of Parmesan over the top.

Once Sélène got the food dished, leftovers boxed, and pots into the sink, they migrated to the couch with their bowls of food and ate quickly and quietly, both apparently too hungry to talk. No TV, just some music, a playlist Aiden queued up.

"Alright," Sélène said, once Aiden had finished and set his bowl aside. "Lovey time."

The fox laughed. "Alright. A hug and some pets?"

Sélène nodded happily and leaned into Aiden for a comfortable hug, each turning toward the other on the couch. After some affectionate cheek-rubs, her husband shifted about until he was sitting cross-legged facing her, muzzle dipped down and ears perked. Sélène obliged and reached up to brush soft paw-pads over the ears.

"Mm. Thank you, love."

She nodded and stroked along Aiden's ears from bases to tips a few times, then set to sifting fur through her claws. Confronting the kitchen by cooking, confronting the picking by brushing through dry fox fur. For as twitchy as the morning was, she felt a little proud with her engagement with this evening.

Plus, Aiden's little happy purrs and content sighs made her feel accomplished.

"You excited about tomorrow, sweetheart?"

Sélène nodded and brushed her fingers back through Aiden's fur, ruffling it up before combing it straight again. "Anxious, but excited, yeah. You sure you're alright with it?"

Aiden nodded. "I'm sure. It'll be good for you. And Malina's nice."

A twinge of cool unquiet struggled against a warm flush within her ears, but she nodded all the same. "She is."

"I'd be surprised if you didn't think so," Aiden laughed, flicking his ears against Sélène's paws. "You're picking a bit, love. Would you like to talk about something else?"

Sélène tugged her paws back quickly from there they had dug through Aiden's fur. "Uh, sorry. No, this is okay. Are you alright?"

"Mmhm. Maybe just pet my ears?"

"Alright." Sélène went back to stroking the velvety triangles. "And yeah, I'm excited. Still a little surprised that you're alright with me going on a date with someone else, but happy all the same."

Aiden finished another one of those content sighs before replying. "I love you dearly, Sélène, but I know how much Malina means to you. She's good for you, she's fond of you, you're cute when you're together. It works."

Sélène kept her bashfulness to herself as best she could, and focused on the feel of her husband's soft fur.

★

The bus ride to the 13th Street Plaza was uneventful in all ways except for how much Sélène fretted about the date to come. She pulled out her phone, refreshed her feeds, put the phone away.

Ten seconds later, and her phone was already back in her paw. A swipe down on the page, that satisfying click, no new items. She put the phone away with a conscious effort. She had promised herself she wouldn't text Aiden more than once during the whole date, unless she needed or wanted a ride home. She desperately wanted to text him now, but was doing her best to save that option for later.

Malina greeted her at the stop. The badger looked kind and cozy and happy, enough that a good chunk of Sélène's anxiety was transmuted into proper excitement.

She bounced off the bus and straight into a hug, "Hi you!"

"You made it," Malina laughed. "Good to see you. Been all nervous here at the bus stop. 'What if she doesn't come?' I feel like a dorky teenager all over again."

Sélène grinned. "Yeah, I was all fidgety, too. You alright?"

"Mmhm. Excited, is all." Malina leaned back from the embrace and grinned. She held up a small paper bag. "I'm sorry to say that I ate a bunch of them earlier, but I brought some marshmallows for you."

"I've never had a homemade marshmallow," Sélène admitted, peeking into the bag, then reached in to grab one. "They're square! What's the white stuff?"

Malina reached in to grab one as well. "Cornstarch. Keeps them from sticking together."

Sélène sniffed at it carefully. It smelled sweet, with a hint of citrus and what she could only describe as chalk. She figured the last was probably from the cornstarch, so she took a cautious bite and chewed. It was...well, a marshmallow. But it was fresher than any she'd ever had, far more flavorful and less cloying. The lime was delightful, almost as an afterthought. A bit of brightness that added without overwhelming.

"'oh-ee thit!" She laughed with a puff of cornstarch and struggled to chew the rest of the marshmallow, swallowing to say more clearly, "Holy shit, Malina. That's good!"

Malina grinned as best she could around her own marshmallow, a dusting of cornstarch on her muzzle. One she was able, she laughed. "Glad you like, dear. Come on, let's walk a bit before real food. We can save the other two for dessert."

The 13th Street Plaza had begun some decades before when the courthouse lawn and the road in front of it had been redone to fix the water main. The city had decided that in order to keep the shops there open for business, they would turn the two blocks to either side of the courthouse into a pedestrian mall. It was an attempt at turning the utility fix into something that benefited the city.

It had worked, after a fashion. Due to the traffic problems, 12th and 14th had to be reworked down the line, but the plaza had become an institution. It was anchored on one end by a record and video store, and on the other by The Book and the Bean, a coffee shop in front that faded seamlessly into a bookstore in back and the second floor above it.

On a warm fall weekend like this, the street was full of folks of all sorts enjoying the evening: lounging on benches, poking in and out of shops, watching buskers and jugglers. Several of Sawtooth's homeless and itinerant population were parked, as usual, on the lawn of the courthouse. Come eight or nine, the security guards and police would start ushering them off, but until then, everyone seemed cozy just where they were.

Down the center of the plaza, Malina and Sélène strolled side by side, talking. Malina described her son and his successes, her old job at a CPA office and how it went from comfortable and familiar to awkward and, at times, frightening when a coworker disappeared. How she'd left for a simpler life to work at The Book and the Bean. About the split with her husband that followed. About her love of food and cooking.

Sélène mostly listened. The excitement and nervousness had settled down to the comfortable glow she felt with the badger, with the added gloss of giddiness that came with the capital-D Date. It was comfortable around Malina, there was little she wanted to add.

"Antica Roma sound good for dinner?"

Sélène nodded, "I've only been once. Sounds good to me."

Malina grinned and nodded, letting Sélène stand in front of the restaurant while she went inside to get their name on the list.

5:53 PM Sélène

Hi Aiden! You okay?

5:53 PM Aiden

Doing great, love. Everything going well with Malina?

5:53 PM Sélène

Really good. She's getting us on the list at Antica Roma, otherwise just talking.

5:54 PM Aiden

Good, sounds good to me. You two have fun!

5:54 PM Sélène

Will do. You alright?

5:54 PM Aiden

I'm good, sweetheart. Have a good evening!

"Half an hour!"

Sélène jolted and grinned sheepishly to the badger, pocketing her phone. "Oh! Okay, sounds good. You alright?"

Malina tilted her head. "I'm fine, don't worry about me. How about you? Hope I'm not stressing you out."

The vixen splayed her ears and shook her head. "I'm fine. Sorry." She bit her tongue a moment, holding back another are-you-alright. "I'm good."

They turned and continued on their slow stroll down the plaza. Antica Roma was directly in front of the courthouse. Cozy and pricey. Definitely date material.

"You sure you're alright, dear? You got quiet."

"Uh, sorry. I'm fine." She laughed breathlessly. "Sorry. Are you...uh, sorry."

Malina tilted her head and gave the fox a nudge with her elbow, her concerned smile inviting Sélène to continue.

"I was just going to ask if you were alright, but I'd already done that." She scuffed at the back of her neck with her paw. "That's...one of my things, I guess."

251

Malina's expression softened. "A compulsion?"

Sélène nodded and gave an apologetic shrug.

"Well, I'm just fine," the badger smiled, leaned in, and gave the fox a kiss to the cheek.

Sélène froze, fur bristling.

"Shit, I'm sorry if that was–"

"R-really nice." Sélène giggled, ears pinned back. That giddiness swelled within her. "That was really nice."

It was Sélène's turn to pick up the conversational lead as they continued to meander east. She talked about the various compulsions and the obsessions and anxieties that drove them, about her struggles with relationship-rightness and need to repeatedly ask Aiden—and, lately, Malina—if they were alright. She talked about her therapist and attachment styles and the exposure therapy that was part of her work. She talked about the problems with touches to her face.

Malina, for her part, listened attentively up until the end. "I'm sorry about the kiss, I didn't know."

Sélène shook her head insistently. "It really was nice, Malina. I just have a bit of trouble with it, is all. I...hmm. Here. Like this."

She skipped ahead a pace and turned so she could face Malina, took the badger's paws in her own, and leaned forward to brush her cheek in against Malina's own black-white-gray cheek, feeling the coarser fur against her own.

"That's, um–" she murmured, smiling bashfully. "That's my kiss."

Malina went from looking startled to grinning widely in a heartbeat, leaning in to give another rub of the cheek in return. "You are adorable, Sélène, you know that?"

The vixen huffed and stamped her foot, shaking her head.

Slipping one of her paws free, Malina started to walking again, Sélène falling into step beside her, ears hot with embarrassment and excitement.

★

Malina drove Sélène home after dinner.

Sélène hadn't know Malina had a car, much less were the badger lived. After dinner, they'd walked down 13th, past The Book and the Bean for a few blocks, and suddenly, they were standing in front of a small townhouse and Malina was unlocking a car.

"Easy commute to work." Sélène carefully clambered into the badger's sedan. Old, serviceable, very clean.

Malina laughed. "Yeah, I'm super close. I walk, but have the car for errands and such."

The ten-minute ride was mostly quiet, otherwise. They had been talking nearly non-stop for well on five hours now, and their silence was comfortable. Sélène's mind was quiet, glowing. She reveled in the silence.

By the time they pulled up in front of Sélène and Aiden's house, the vixen could feel just how much the night and all the anxiety that led up to it had taken out of her. It was a cozy sort of exhaustion, the satisfying kind.

She sat in quiet for a moment after Malina put the car in park, then sighed contentedly. "Thank you, Malina. Tonight was wonderful." She hesitated, then added, "Would you like to come in? Say hi to Aiden?"

The badger shook her head. "Not tonight. You look exhausted, and I have work in the morning." She shrugged, looking sheepish. "Besides, I worry that'd be a little weird. Next time, perhaps."

Sélène lay her ears back and nodded. "Okay. Are you alright?"

Malina laughed and nodded. "Wonderful, Sélène. Can I have another, er...kiss before you go?"

The fox nodded once more, ears tilted back as if to hide her embarrassment. She leaned in and brushed her cheek in against Malina's, enjoying the familiar-yet-new sensation of it.

"Hey," the badger murmured as they lingered close. "I have Wednesday off. Can I see you again after you get off work?"

Sélène leaned across the center console to hug awkwardly around Malina, hungry for a bit more contact before heading inside. "I'll ask Aiden, but I think so, yeah."

With one last cheek-rub, she unbuckled and slipped out of the car.

Aiden met her at the door, smiling. He held the screen door open so that he could let Sélène in and wave to Malina out in the car. "Have a good evening, sweetheart?"

Sélène bounced once or twice in a fit of residual excitement, "Very good! You okay, Aiden?"

Her husband let the screen door shut and ushered Sélène further into the house so he could close the door proper. "I'm fine, yeah. Look at *you*, though, you're glowing," he laughed. "May I hug?"

"Mmhm. Sorry, I can't help it," she purred, leaning into her husband's arms and rubbing her cheek up against his own. His fur was softer, warmer, more familiar than Malina's. She certainly *felt* as if she were glowing.

Aiden returned the affectionate nuzzle and murmured quietly,

"No need to apologize. I'm happy for you, sweetheart. Did you invite her in?"

Sélène nodded and relaxed against her husband's front, tucking her muzzle up under his after the 'kiss'. "I offered, but she said she has work in the morning." After a moment, she added, "She said she also would feel a little weird about it."

"Mm, okay," Aiden said. "Maybe it would have been awkward. Hopefully that's something that will change, though. Something we can work on."

"Do you feel weird about it?"

"About her coming in?"

"Yeah." Sélène shrugged. "Or about any of this, I guess."

"A little," Aiden said. He leaned back from Sélène enough to meet her gaze. "I'm happy for you, though, sweetheart. It will take some getting used to for all of us, is all."

"I think I understand. Are you alright?"

Aiden nodded. "I'm alright, love. It's good to see you happy. You look exhausted." He hesitated for a moment before asking, "Would you be up for chilling on the couch for a bit before bed, though? I want to hear about your date, if you'd like."

Sélène nodded and tightened her hug around Aiden briefly before relaxing. She padded quickly past the entrance to the kitchen so as to not get caught up in compulsions just yet, though she could feel the doubt and worry growing frosty within. She clambered up onto the couch and dug her phone out of her pocket instead. She'd checked her feeds in the car, so they should be empty, but the act of pulling down to refresh was a comforting thought.

Aiden laughed and followed after her, flopping back onto the couch. "So," he lilted. "How was your date?"

Sélène tilted her ears back in the warm flush of embarrassment. "It was...good." She laughed giddily and shrugged. "It was good. We walked along the plaza. Ducked in to say hi to her friends at Book and Bean, ate dinner at Antica Roma."

Aiden grinned, nodded, and made little urging gestures with his paws, as if drawing more story out of his wife.

"We talked a bit about her and where she is in life." Sélène fiddled with her phone, pulling to refresh over and over, just for the sound of the click. "And we talked about me, and the compulsions. Like why I ask if she's alright, or you're alright, and why it's hard to have my face touched."

"Oh?" Aiden perked up. "Did she kiss you, then?"

Sélène's ears went from being just tilted to fully pinned back. "W-well," she stammered. "She did. I um...I showed her what works instead of that."

Aiden nodded and opened his mouth to speak, before being cut off frantically by Sélène.

"Are you alright? Is that alright?"

Her husband held up his paws to forestall any further questions. "It's alright, I promise. I'm really happy for you." He laughed and added, "Sweetheart, you're adorable."

Sélène smiled nervously and bowed her head. "Uh, thank you."

"Of course, love." Aiden held his paws out, offering. Sélène relaxed, set her phone in her lap, and rested her paws in his.

"Are you sure you're alright, Aiden?"

The fox brushed his thumbs over the soft-furred backs of his wife's paws. "I think so, yeah."

Sélène winced, more at the words than the touch. " 'Think so'?"

"Mmhm. I'm really happy for you. I was just thinking," he trailed off, shrugged, and pushed ahead. "I was just thinking, the kiss is probably something only the two of us had ever done, until tonight."

Sélène shivered and nodded. Without any direction for her nervousness, without anything to obsess over other than her relationship-rightness with Aiden, she felt trapped, frozen in an icy block of anxiety. "Is that okay?"

Aiden nodded. "It is, sweetheart. Like I said, it's something for us to work on. It's new, not bad, and I'm trying to change to make it work."

The vixen nodded, struggling to find an outlet for that energy. She couldn't meet her husband's eyes, and was unwilling to lose the contact of his paws holding hers for anything so silly as grabbing her phone. Her tail was already bristled out between her and the arm of the couch.

"Hey. Sélène, look here," Aiden said. When she pointed her muzzle at him without making eye contact, he lifted her paws in his, and gave them a rub of his cheek, a 'kiss' to their backs. A gesture he'd never done before. "Look at me, sweetheart."

At that, she did make eye contact. She felt on the verge of tears, without fully understanding why. Aiden was so reassuring, so loving; and she was so terrified of losing him. Aiden was smiling so kindly, and she could barely keep from crying.

"May I hug?"

Sélène nodded, and let Aiden draw her into his arms. They brushed cheeks a few times, before she just wound up resting against him. She managed to keep from crying outright, but at the expense of some sniffles.

"Tell me something good about your evening," Aiden murmured, after Sélène had calmed down.

She thought for a moment. "I think...that I was able to open up, I guess. I can talk *about* stuff with people, but only really engage with you two." She hesitated, then added, "If that makes sense."

She felt Aiden nod above her. "Yeah. Talking can take a lot out of you, if you're not engaging."

"Mmhm."

"And did you come up with any plans for another date?"

"She suggested maybe Wednesday. She said she had it off."

"Go."

Sélène jolted at the word, and Aiden laughed. "I mean, go on the date. Not go away or anything."

"Really?"

Aiden nodded again. "Definitely. Go. I want you to experience more of that, and I want us both to get more comfortable with this. All three of us, I suppose."

"Okay." Sélène bit at the side of her tongue, realized what she was doing, and forced herself to stop. "And you're alright?"

"I'm alright, sweetheart."

★

Sunday was a calm leisurely day for the pair.

Aiden cooked brunch—Sélène was hopeless when it came to eggs—while Sélène picked out songs she thought were interesting and tried to explain why to Aiden. Later, they walked to the park at the end of the block and made their way through the Frisbee golf course. Neither played, but it was low-key exercise, and comforting for Sélène to walk each hole from start to finish.

Later, Aiden ran to get groceries while Sélène wrote on some of her personal projects.

That night, they watched two movies, having each picked one.

The sheer normalcy of the day helped to dampen Sélène's lingering anxiety, keeping the day from going above a four. She liked Malina a lot. Maybe even loved her, who knew. But the things that she shared with Aiden she could never share with the badger. She and Malina could watch movies, but it would never be the same as watching movies with Aiden.

Throughout the day, it never felt right to bring up in conversation, though. Neither she nor Aiden talked about the night before, nor the upcoming Wednesday. It didn't feel like a closed topic, so much as something that was comfortable to wait on.

It only came up again on Tuesday night, when it came to setting up logistics. It was Aiden that brought it up first.

"Do you know what you two are doing tomorrow night?"

Sélène looked up from her phone. She'd spaced out during whatever Aiden had picked to watch after dinner. Chatting with Malina, no less. "She suggested dinner at her place."

Aiden nodded. "Do you want to me to drop you off on the way home from work?"

"Oh! That would work." Sélène sat up. "Would that be okay?"

"Of course, sweetheart."

Sélène picked at the fur on her wrist. There was a slight bump just on the top of the bone, perhaps a small scar from picking earlier. She'd already worried a small bald-patch in the fur. "You sure that's alright?"

"Mmhm, I'm sure." Aiden held out one of his paws for hers.

She transferred her phone to the other and let her husband take her paw. She smiled bashfully, "Sorry, I was picking."

Aiden lifted her paw, turned her wrist upward, and leaned to brush his cheek over it. "A kiss to make it better."

Sélène giggled happily and moved her phone to the armrest of the couch so she could lean in closer, and return the kiss in turn, brushing her cheek in against his. "You're a dork."

He laughed and gave her paws a gentle squeeze in his own. "I love you too, sweetheart."

She squeezed his paws back before tugging free, grabbing her phone once more and squirming around to lean back against him. "Alright, let me tell Malina, then, before I lose my nerve."

Shifting to let her get more comfortable against him, Aiden rested his arm up along the back of the couch, making a show of watching the movie. Sélène was protective of her phone, but Aiden always went out of his way to show he wasn't shoulder-surfing.

Once she'd finished and gotten the okay from Malina and set her phone back down in her lap, Aiden tilted his muzzle enough to brush it against one of his wife's ears. "You've been doing really good the last few days, you know that?"

Sélène tensed at a frisson and flicked her ears against Aiden's muzzle. "Tickles," she mumbled, then nodded. "Yeah, it's been good."

"Any particular reason why?"

"I think–" Sélène hesitated while she dug for words. "I think just having a direction to put energy."

"Good, yeah." Aiden gave her ear another nuzzle before leaning down to put a kiss—a proper one, rather than a cheek-rub—atop her head.

Hunching her shoulders and splaying her ears to the sides, Sélène tucked herself in closer to her husband, paws folded together so she could pick at her wrist again.

"Sorry, sweetheart. Bit too much?" Aiden lifted his muzzle clear of the area to let Sélène scrub at the spot with her paw.

"Uh, a little." Realizing what she was doing, she reached up to tug Aiden's arm along the back of the sofa down along her front so that she could focus on petting rather than picking. "Sorry. It was still nice– sorry. Are you alright?"

Aiden let his arm be claimed, carefully snaking it partway around his Sélène in a sort of hug. "Mmhm, I'm fine."

The two sat quietly, letting the rest of the show play out until the credits.

"I love you, Aiden."

"Mm? I love you too, sweetheart."

"I think I forgot to say so earlier," Sélène murmured sleepily. "Thank you for putting up with your nutball wife."

Aiden turned enough to give her a fond cheek-rub. "Of course, love, that's my job. Let's get you to bed so you can be all rested for tomorrow."

★

Work often colors the perception of days of the week. Sélène, for instance, had three quarters of her meetings on Wednesdays. It was her day of drudgery. The one day she wasn't allowed to work from home. There was a project sync-up, an editorial staff meeting, a project lottery, and a one-on-one with her direct supervisor.

Best case, Wednesdays felt like less-productive workdays. Sélène would sit in her spot by the door and try to pay attention to the staff meeting. As junior editor, she wasn't eligible for the project lottery, but she might be working with someone who was.

She'd talk through progress on her own project with the team during the sync-up, then she and Jeff, her manager, would hash out the details. Jeff always seemed vaguely puzzled by Sélène, but she got her work done, at home and at the office, so he never complained.

Worst case, she'd be a jittery mess. She'd play with her phone, or pick at spots on her arms. She'd fret over Aiden. She'd fret over home. One week, she seriously considered buying a net enabled camera for the house so she could keep an eye on things, then had to run to the restroom and wash her face to clear thoughts cameras and stoves and cabinets.

This Wednesday was seemingly neither of these. It was apart from other Wednesdays in some intangible way.

She was going to have her husband drop her off at her girlfriend's house tonight.

She kept repeating that over and over inside her head, trying to make the shapes fit. *Work. Husband. Girlfriend. Husband...driving me to girlfriend. And it's a good thing? Very good.*

She'd never had a giddy Wednesday before.

"Sélène? You okay? 'Bout done here."

She snapped her head up, smiling apologetically to the coyote. She brushed her fur down on her wrist. "Sorry, Jeff."

"It's okay. Stressful day?"

"No." Sélène thought for a moment. "Well, yes, but not at work. Date tonight."

Jeff racked his notes against the desk. "That sounds good. Where are you and Aiden headed?"

Sélène halted halfway out of her chair.

Shit.

"Uh. We're..." She struggled to come up with something, feeling suddenly more on the spot than she probably was. All that she could think of was the truth. "We're going to someone's for dinner."

True enough.

"Oh, well, have a good one," Jeff said, smiling quizzically as Sélène skittered out of his office.

She managed to make it through the rest of the day without incident, but perhaps only by dint of her sticking to her cubicle as much as possible. She spent half her time there working, and the other half daydreaming and digging at the spot on her wrist. That little bump she'd found had been a focal point ever since, and she'd already picked it clean of fur. There had to be something there. Splinter, ingrown fur, something.

As early as she could manage without attracting attention, Sélène made her way out to the front of the building, camping on one of the benches normally used by smokers during their breaks.

Fall had treated Sawtooth well, this year. There had been a few chill days, but no freezes yet. It had remained unremarkably comfortable. The sort of weather you never think about. The sort of weather that was only ever "nice" in conversation.

It was nice, too, so Sélène sat and waited outside for Aiden. Enjoying the non-conditioned air, relative quiet, and natural light.

The sun warmed the dark fur of her paws as she brushed her claws through fur, half-conscious of searching for any other perceived imperfections. The rest of her dreamed of Aiden and Malina, and the different sensations of their cheeks against hers.

"Sweetheart?"

Sélène yelped and jumped to her feet. "Aiden! Sorry!"

The fox laughed and held out his arms to offer a hug. "It's okay! It's okay. Spacing out?"

"A little," Sélène gasped. She got her breathing under control and un-bushed her tail with a few brushes of her paws before leaning into Aiden's arms. She brushed her cheek up against his. "Sorry. You alright?"

"I'm alright," he said, tightening the hug for a moment. "How're you?"

Sélène relaxed against her husband a bit longer, enjoying the solidity of him. "I'm good. Weird day, spent most of it up in my head."

The fox nodded, gave her a squeeze, then guided her back to his car. "Good weird? Stressful weird? Your paws and arms are all ruffled."

"Good weird, mostly." Sélène brushed her paws down over her arms, realizing she'd gone after more than just that spot on her wrist without realizing it. "Better than I look, I guess. Are you alright?"

Aiden waited to respond until they'd both clambered into the car. "I'm alright. Long day, but a pretty good one. Going to meet up with Aaron from work, grab dinner with him and his wife while you're out. You excited?"

"Yeah. It's been going through my head all day. You sure you're okay driving me?"

"I already am," he laughed.

Sélène tilted her ears in a flush of embarrassment. "Right...but to Malina's?"

Aiden nodded.

"Alright." She picked at her thumb briefly, then forced herself to stop. "This feels a little goofy, I guess."

"What?" he laughed. "Driving my wife to a date with her girl-friend? I guess it is. It was on my mind all day, too. I'm still happy for you, though."

Smiling nervously, Sélène brushed her fingers along her arm, finding bits of fur she tugged out of order and straightening them out as best she could. She kept finding new bumps and spots begging to be picked. Eventually she just gave up. "I hope it goes well. Been looking forward to it."

"It will sweetheart, I'm sure of it."

"Just hoping I don't get all weird about her kitchen cabinets or whatever, is all."

"If so, do you think you could ask to put on a show or something?"

"Mmhm." Sélène grinned to her husband. "She's got your taste in movies."

"So, good movies, then?" Aiden laughed. "Maybe we could do a double date or something, sometime. A...one-and-a-half date."

The vixen grinned. "That might be fun. Is that something you'd be up for?"

Aiden hesitated. "Down the road, perhaps."

Sélène's smile faded. "Okay. You alright, Aiden?"

He nodded. "Yeah. Just hit by the realization of how strange and new this feels, still. I'm trying, though. Maybe we ought to all get together soon, just so we can...I don't know, be around each other. See how we work."

"That'd be good."

They drove in silence for another few minutes, until they made it onto east 13th street. Aiden rested his arm down on the center console, paw up, and murmured, "You're picking, dear. Want to hold my paw?"

Sélène squirmed and clenched her paws into fists, then relaxed them again and rested her paw in his. "Sorry, Aiden."

She still felt itchy those last few blocks, still felt as though her skin were imperfect beneath her fur. Dirty. She focused on just resting her paw in her husband's, on the feeling of his pads against hers. She imagined she could trace every line across his them, feel every perfection of his and each imperfection of hers.

Aiden smiled over to her, then nodded up the street. "This it, here?"

"Oh! Already." Sélène smiled. "Yeah, the one with the green car out front."

The car slid smoothly up to the sidewalk in front of the townhouse. Aiden had to reclaim his paw to shift into park, but quickly returned it. "Have a good evening, okay, sweetheart? Message if you need a ride back."

Sélène gave his paw a squeeze once she got it back, leaning over to brush cheeks with her husband. "Mm, alright. Can I leave my bag with you? Um, and are you okay?"

Aiden laughed and nodded. "I'm good. I'll get your bag home safe and sound. Now go, have a good time," he said, tugging his paw free so he could shoo his wife out of the car.

"Alright, alright." Sélène beamed, leaned in for one more cheek-rub, then slipped out onto the sidewalk. "Love you."

"Love you too, sweetheart."

The vixen closed the car door behind her and made her way up to the stoop. She knocked, and once Malina opened the door, waved back over her shoulder to her husband.

"Hey you." The badger grinned.

Sélène smiled back and leaned in to brush her cheek against Malina's. "Hi. Long time no see."

"It's been ages," Malina laughed, opening the door further. "Days, even. Come on in, dinner's already ready, so no need to prep anything."

She followed after Malina, slipping into the entryway, swishing her tail out of the way, and closing the door behind her.

Malina's place is bright and spacious. A simple place, clean and orderly, the room was larger than she would've expected, though perhaps that was due in part to the way the kitchen was an open corner of the room. Kitchen, dining room, and living room provided a veritable landscape of a room.

It was very Malina.

"Your place is beautiful."

Malina nodded. "I like this place. Cyril never did, so I lucked out on that end of things when we split. Come on in, though, make yourself comfortable.

Sélène followed the badger as she trundled in to the kitchen. The sight of all of those cabinets, clearly visible from anywhere in the great room, made Sélène's arms itch all over again. "Didn't realize how big this place was. Never seen a kitchen this exposed to the rest of the house."

"It's nice, isn't it?"

"Mm." So many cabinets. So many drawers.

Stop it, Sélène.

"I can duck in and out of the kitchen whenever I want," Malina said proudly. "Suits me, I guess."

The fox forced herself to stop gritting her teeth and smiled, "That it does. Smells nice in here, too."

"Chicken and pasta sound okay?"

"Sounds wonderful," Sélène laughed. "My favorite, actually. Good guess."

Malina tapped at her temple with a claw. "Smart folk, badgers. Read it in your future."

"Read?"

"Dumb joke. I do tarot readings on the side."

"Really?" Sélène blinked. "I mean, I guess it fits. Madame Malina with a wicked pack of cards."

"I'm no clairvoyant, more like something between a therapist and a mom." Malina laughed and shook her head, "I did make us food, though. Ready to eat now?"

The two ate at the dining room table, though the 'dining room' was simply a handy spot next to the kitchen.

After some waffling, Sélène took the seat facing away from the kitchen, though she regretted it soon after. It felt as though the cabinets were watching over her shoulder. Too much anxiety, too much blue.

Still, the food was very good, and not at all how she would've made chicken and noodles. Malina had cooked the chicken to be quite spicy in the barest hint of a sauce, and the noodles were tossed with peppers and vegetables. Looming kitchen or not, Sélène cleaned her plate. The badger was a wonderful cook.

They talked about their day, though Malina did most of the talking. All Sélène could manage was to say that she'd been nervous all day. Malina filled in for her, talking about deciding what to cook, running into people at the store, peeking in at The Book and The Bean to say hi.

From anyone else, Sélène would've glossed over all of this as polite chatter, but it was comforting, coming from the badger. Her voice was soothing, her words reassuring. She had a kind sense of humor, and could get Sélène laughing without anyone being the butt of a joke except perhaps herself.

The conversation flowed from the day to broader topics, and as Malina swept the dishes off to the sink, Sélène talked about her work, and what had gone into finding a job that would work with her as well as this one did. They wafted over to the couch—much to Sélène's relief—and slouched together. Sélène kept talking, about school and finding ways to live and work, and about meeting Aiden.

"You're a very lucky, fox, Sélène. You and Aiden fit together so well." The badger smiled kindly at the vixen's embarrassment before carrying on. "I mean this in the nicest way, but I think he needs someone to care for, and you need someone to care for you. It's a good fit."

"Thank you." She looked down at her paws and shrugged. "I guess if I'm honest, it wasn't until I admitted to myself that I couldn't do things alone that I started doing better. I never did well as a kid, and no one knew what to do about it, so they just left me alone."

" 'They'?"

Sélène gave a dismissive wave of her paw as though to brush away the memory of those closed-in spaces, of her sister closing the door, hiding her away beneath the drawers of silverware. "Mom and older sister. Mom was unpredictable, Marguerite was just mean."

"Yeesh, childhood's hard enough as is, without that." Perhaps sensing the tension in the fox, Malina shifted the subject. " 'Marguerite'? Is your family French?"

"Oh goodness no," Sélène laughed. "We're from here, via the east coast, and I think England before that. Mom was crazy, though, and really wanted to have been from France. 'Sélène' isn't even really a French name, not like 'Selena' or 'Celine'. My mom thought the extra accent made it sound more French, but now I just mean 'lunar'. She lived in a fantasy."

Malina gave the fox an appraising look. "You don't look much like a moon, dear."

"I'd hope not." Sélène grinned.

The badger slipped her arm around Sélène, gently tugging the fox toward her. Sélène squirmed to get her tail out of the way and let herself be guided until she was leaning back against Malina, and Malina back against the arm of the couch.

"You are looking kind of pocked and cratered, though," Malina murmured, brushing fingers along the scuffed up and pocked fur on Sélène's arm.

"Sorry. I was picking, I guess." Sélène massaged at a tuft of fur on the back of her paw self-consciously. The badger was comfortable and comforting, but that didn't stop the desire to dig at her fur.

"It's alright, dear. You don't need to apologize." The badger fussed a dull claw through another of those tufts, then paused. "I should have asked. Is this alright? Me touching where you were picking?"

"It's okay, yeah. If I try to do it now, though, I'll find what I was picking at and start doing it again." Sélène tilted her head enough to get a peripheral glance of Malina, a pale blue flare of anxiety tickling along her spine. "Sorry. I mean...sorry. Are you alright?"

Malina met Sélène's head-tilt with her own, brushing cheek to cheek. "Shh, I'm alright, dear. Let me take care of you," she murmured, setting about grooming along one of Sélène's forearms. She worried her claws through the fur around each spot, straightening it out to lay flat again.

The sensation of being fussed over and cared for made Sélène feel small, young. It was some combination of intimate and caring, that touched on both the parts of her that needed affection and the parts that needed attention. It calmed her and made her anxious at the same time.

"You're still all tense," Malina said. "You sure this is okay?"

The vixen nodded, "It's okay. I just...still kinda anxious, I think."

Those attentive paws continued their work of grooming down her arms as the badger brushed her cheek to Sélène's. "If you need to pick at something, you can pick at my fur."

Sélène buzzed past possible responses—"that's not how it works" and "it doesn't feel good, I don't want to do that to you" and "are you alright?"—and just did her best to settle against Malina and enjoy the touches. *It's exposure therapy, maybe,* she thought desperately. *I'm being present without engaging in the compulsion.*

"This is nice."

"To be touched? Or groomed?"

She shrugged. "Both, I guess."

Malina nodded and brushed her fingers down over the fox's left arm, having mostly sorted out the rough patches, and moved on to the right. "When I first met you, when you started coming to Book and Bean, I'd see you with your arms or neck like this, and I thought you were sick, like your fur was falling out."

"Thankfully not," Sélène giggled.

"And once I knew what was up, I guess I wanted to sit you down and help you groom."

"Like this?"

"Well, I figured it was more likely we'd sit at a table all professional like." Malina laughed. "That I get to do it with you in my arms is certainly beyond anything I imagined."

Sélène tilted her ears back, feeling a blush rise within them. She shifted herself more comfortably against Malina, thankful for a partner larger than herself, even if only by a few inches. "That's the nicest bit," she purred, brushing her free paw along the badger's arm.

Neither seemed keen to move even after all the grooming that could be done had been done. Malina hugged her arms comfortably around Sélène's middle, while Sélène brushed and petted through their fur, an echo of the grooming she'd just received. They shared brushes of the cheeks and soft, content noises and familiar scents.

"Should we start the movie?"

"Mm."

Neither moved from their spot on the couch. Neither moved at all, other than Sélène's claws tracing lazy lines through Malina's arm-fur and Malina's paw scrunching up a pawful of Sélène's shirt to brush her knuckles through belly-fur.

After a minute, they both laughed.

"Guess not, huh?" Malina said.

Sélène stretched a little at the tickle of claws in fur. "We seem to be doing okay without. You alright?"

Perhaps sensing Sélène's ticklishness, or perhaps for her own reasons, Malina ducked her paw beneath the shirt she'd scrunched up to pet through fur more directly. "I'm okay, dear. This alright?"

The vixen relaxed again, without the ticklishness keeping her tense. "Mmhm, mostly just around my face and arms that I pick."

"Not just where," Malina said, stroking through soft fur. "But me touching you like this. Petting. Is that okay?"

Sélène nodded, relaxing back against the badger and brushing her fingers through coarser black-white-gray fur. Her ears and cheeks were flushed warm, giddiness making her breathing pick up. "Very okay. It feels nice." She giggled quietly and added, "Feel anxious, still, but the good kind of anxious."

Malina laughed, "Isn't that just 'excited'?"

"Excited, yeah," Sélène said, after a moment's thought. "Excited and warm."

Rubbing her cheek to Sélène's, Malina broadened the reach of her touches, hiking Sélène's shirt up a little further to comb her fingers through more fur. "You are warm, at that. And soft. Is this okay?"

"Mmhm." Sélène felt as though she was thinking through warmed honey, her thoughts and feelings coming through softer, warmer, more rounded than they would have otherwise. The sensation of Malina's fingers brushing and stroking through the mussed up fur beneath her shirt added to this muzziness with each pass.

She stretched almost luxuriously, careful not to melt out of range of the badger's wide paws. It was unusual for her to relax under touch, rather than tense up. Even when the touch felt good, it usually brought with it tension, if not anxiety. She was keen to enjoy what she could.

"When we started to get closer," Malina murmured, muzzle resting against Sélène's cheek. "I would think a lot about how soft you must be."

Sélène perked an ear up. "Soft?"

Malina nodded, smoothing out the fur under her paw. "Even

when you were picking, your fur looked so much softer than mine. Or Cyril's, for that matter."

Sélène laughed.

"I'd think about that a lot. Just kind of daydream."

"And?"

Malina tilted her head. "And what?" she murmured, putting both paws to work petting over Sélène's belly and sides.

The fox squirmed at the touches, and Malina paused. "S'okay, little ticklish. Am I as soft as you daydreamed?"

The badger nodded and shifted her paws back toward Sélène's belly. "I think so, yeah. You're not pillowy soft or whatever, but your fur is way softer than mine."

Sélène brushed her own paw-pads along the backs of Malina's paws and up her forearms a ways. Her fur was far coarser than a fox's, but no less pleasant to touch. "You thought about that a lot, didn't you?"

Malina nodded again, whiskers brushing against Sélène's cheek. "I thought about *you* a lot, dear. I was sweet on you for a long time, there."

Tilting her head back, Sélène did her best to rub her cheek against Malina's, murmuring, "I'm pretty sure that went both ways."

She languidly lifted her arms to try and loop them loosely around the badger's shoulders. It was a bit too much of a stretch, but she made it far enough to comfortably reach Malina's nape, which she set about combing with her claws.

She could feel Malina shiver behind her in response to the touches, hear a growl and a chuff. She quickly lifted her paws. "Sorry. You alright?"

"Mmhm." Malina's arms tightened around Sélène, one paw slipping around the fox's waist and the other slipping up beneath her shirt, wandering perilously close to her chest. It was a kind grip, but a possessive one. "Bit of a tender spot, there."

Sélène held still in the badger's arms, tense and quiet. "In a good way?"

"In a good way."

Slowly relaxing once more, Sélène delicately set her paws back down on the badger's scruff, petting slowly through the fur. "Are you...uh, is this okay?"

The growl came out as more of a rumble this time. "This is okay. I'm alright, dear."

Sélène relaxed back against the badger, trying to get back to that warm, cotton-muffled space. It was easy to do. So easy to relax into comfort like this around Malina. So warm and so far removed from the chill anxiety of obsession.

It took another moment or two, but they both settled down again. Malina resumed her petting, ruffling, combing, and grooming with one paw on Sélène's belly and the other just above that, inching her shirt up higher and higher.

For her part, Sélène combed and stroked down over the scruff of the badger's neck, gently at first, and then a bit more firm, listening and responding to the pleased sounds.

They murmured quiet things to each other. An is-this-alright here and a you-can-do-that-more there. Through careful negotiations, their touches moved from comfortable to sensual, from aimless to focused. Each explored the ways in which the other moved, found ticklish spots and avoided them, found pleasurable spots and gravitated toward them.

Sélène learned that if she combed her claws from the base of Malina's skull down to the base of her neck, she could get a thrill out of the badger, a shudder and another of those chuffs. She used this sparingly, knowing full well that too much touch left one tingly.

She also learned that she arched up when Malina's paws brushed up over her chest, cupping a breast. She learned that Malina enjoyed such responsiveness, that the pads of the badger's paws were pleasantly coarse, that an embrace could be both tender and possessive. It all added to a pleasurable current of warmth flowing through her.

That current stole time from her. It took logic and caution. It lowered defenses and raised sensitivity. It was a smooth sense of pleasure that arced from behind her sternum to the center of her abdomen. Smooth and alluring, it made her want more, and the more she got the more she wanted. It was panic inverted. It was desire.

By the time the badger's other paw dipped down over her belly to tug at the drawstring to her pants, Sélène was lost to that current.

She gave herself up to Malina.

Malina, who was so comforting a presence, who had so sure a touch, who seemed to know just what Sélène needed.

Malina, who learned quickly how to draw a moan from Sélène, who knew to shift her focus before a touch got to be too much, who responded to Sélène as readily as Sélène responded to her.

Malina, who seemed to know just how intensely that desire moved within Sélène, who knew how to track it—its rise, its plateau, its crest—and who held Sélène tightly to her as the vixen cried out and shook when the desire crashed down into a sudden rush of pleasure.

And as the wave of warmth and ecstasy passed, Malina kept Sélène held comfortable and safe.

Sélène brought her arms down to simply hold onto Malina's arm. The warmth within her faded and was replaced by that cottony, honey-colored feeling magnified ten times over. She could feel a touch of anxiety, a touch of shame peeking in, but it was muffled, distant, barely visible behind the comfort and calm.

"Is this alright, love?" Malina's voice was soft, low. She sounded as though she were in the same comfortable dream as Sélène.

Sélène purred. "Wonderful."

The two sat in silence, Malina hugging around Sélène's middle and Sélène hugging Malina's arms to her front.

★

Sélène must have dozed off, or at least gotten close to it, as she jolted suddenly awake at the feeling of her phone buzzing against her thigh.

"You're vibrating," Malina mumbled, sounding about as sleepy as Sélène felt.

Squirming, the vixen struggled to free the phone from her pocket. She blinked and squinted as the screen swam into focus. "Nine thirty, yikes," she mumbled, and pawed at the message notification from Aiden.

9:32 PM Aiden

Having a good time, sweetheart?

Sélène furrowed her brow.

9:33 PM Sélène

Wonderful!

9:33 PM *Aiden*

Glad to hear! Would you like me to pick you up tonight, or will Malina drive?

"Shit."

Malina yawned. "Everything alright, dear?"

Logic seemed to be making its way back in fits and starts. Late. She needed to be back home tonight. Aiden had to come pick her up, or Malina had to drive her.

"Shit." She squirmed until she could sit up straight, tugging her tail around to her side. "Um. Sorry. Are you alright?"

The badger, nodded. "Sleepy, but alright. Is everything okay?"

"I need to be back home soon." She bit at the side of her tongue and winced. "Aiden is wondering whether he should drive or you."

Malina shrugged, yawned once more, and smiled to Sélène. "I can drive, if you give me a bit to stretch and wake up."

"Sorry, Malina. I hope it's not...I lost track of...are you alright?"

"I'm alright, love." The badger leaned in for a kiss, seemed to remember herself, and rubbed her cheek to Sélène's. "It's no trouble. Sorry I dozed off there. It got late, didn't it?"

Sélène settled down at the 'kiss', returning the cheek-rub and smiling bashfully. "A little, yeah. I think I dozed off, too."

Malina nodded. "Well, alright. I'll get ready. Do you want to take any of the chicken home with you?"

Stretching and twisting at the waist, Sélène winced at tense muscles and cool anxiety, then nodded. "If you'd like. It was wonderful, and I bet Aiden would like some." She hesitated a moment, before asking, "May I use your bathroom before we leave?"

"Mmhm, first door on the right, dear."

Sélène padded off and locked herself in the restroom, which was, thankfully, as spotless as the badger's kitchen. She had made the judgment between urgency and anxiety, factoring in the admonition to urinate after sex and the likelihood of cabinets, and...

She could feel herself starting to spiral, She felt ashamed. She felt sticky and unappealing and dirty. She felt like she'd intruded and had done something horrible.

She tamped it down as best she could. The night had been good. Spectacular, really. The last thing she needed was for it to be painted blue with worry.

All the same, she quietly eased open the cabinets under the sink, settling down on her knees to peer into the darkness.

On finishing up actually using the restroom, she tugged her phone out and swiped over to Aiden's messages.

9:37 PM Sélène
Malina will drive. Home in a bit.

9:37 PM Aiden
Okay, see you soon

Sélène padded back to the great room and smiled sheepishly to Malina. "Sorry. I'm about ready. Are you alright?"

Malina beamed. "Wonderful. Come on, dear, let's get you home."

★

The drive back was quick and quiet. Both Sélène and Malina seemed lost in their own thoughts, and while she couldn't speak to Malina's, Sélène's swirled in a figure eight around how nice the evening was and how she would even begin to talk about it with Aiden.

The ride wasn't nearly long enough to sort out either, and by the time they stopped in front of home, Sélène could feel the anxiety coming on in icy pangs. It made her chest tight and her fingers tingle.

"Tonight was wonderful, dear. Thanks for coming over," Malina rumbled. "I hope you enjoyed, too."

Sélène nodded. "Very much so. You sure you're alright?"

"I'm alright, dear, promise. Enjoy the rest of your night, and lets see about getting together soon. Friday or Saturday work for me."

The fox nodded again and picked at a spot on her wrist. "I'll ask Aiden. And you're sure–" She cut herself off and shook her head. "Sorry. Um, kiss before I head off?"

They brushed cheeks and smiled to each other, exchanging their goodbyes before Sélène slipped out of the car and padded up to the stoop, clutching her little container of leftovers.

As before, Aiden was waiting at the door with a smile. He waved to Malina and held the screen door open for his wife. Sélène ducked inside quickly. The night felt crisp and chilly. She wasn't sure how much of that was actually the case, though, and how much was just her anxiety robbing her warmth.

"Hi sweetheart. How was your–" Aiden paused in the act of leaning forward to brush cheeks with Sélène. His nose twitched and his whiskers bristled, ears laying flat. "Uh...date went well, I'm assuming?"

Sélène's own ears perked up, and then flattened back as she realized that her husband could smell her. He could smell Malina.

He could smell what they had done.

Her body tensed up as she tried to make herself smaller, tried to hide without moving. The chill blue of anxiety froze to a bright, frozen white of outright panic, and Sélène began shivering. "I'm s-sorry Aiden...I– W-we just..." She swallowed. "Are you alright?"

"I'm..." Aiden frowned, then shook his head. He straightened his back and squared his shoulders. "I'm okay, I think." He furrowed his brow, seemed to master some complex emotion, and said, "I know you're stressed, sweetheart, but can we talk?"

Sélène could hardly move, and certainly couldn't speak. So calm was Aiden usually, that this reaction felt like an slap to the face. Almost literally: her cheeks were burning, and she could barely get any air. She nodded as best she could.

Aiden's shoulders sagged and his expression softened. "Oh, love, I'm sorry. You look terrified." He frowned, "And you're barely breathing. Come on, let's go sit on the couch, and we can talk."

When Sélène didn't move, he gingerly took her by the elbow, guiding her over to her spot on the couch. Sélène sat on the edge of the cushions and set the container of leftovers on the table by the couch. Her muscles felt tight and ready to launch; this wasn't just panic, it was an adrenaline spike that robbed her of thought, corrupted vision and hearing and touch.

Aiden sat in his spot and looked down at his paws thoughtfully. After a moment, he spoke. "So, when we first started talking about this, we talked about sex right away, and I agreed that it'd be fine. We agreed, I mean."

Sélène stared at her paws as well, watching her pick at that spot on her wrist. She kept her ears pinned back. "I remember, yeah," she whispered.

"And I think–" He cut himself off and appeared to be turning the rest of the sentence over in his head. "I think I'm still okay with it."

Sélène nodded. Unable to shift her gaze, she could only see her husband out of the corner of her eye. " 'But'?"

Aiden sighed. " 'But', yeah. But I'm a little upset over how soon it happened, I guess."

"Second date?" Sélène murmured.

"I guess. Or maybe it'd be more accurate for me to say that I'm upset over how easy it seems to have been."

Sélène nodded. She kept watching herself pick and pick at that one spot. It seemed like it was happening to someone else. Or maybe that something was doing it to her, and she had no control over it. The madness rode her, and it hurt.

"We've not had the best of luck with sex," Aiden continued. "And I'm okay with that, I really am. It's pretty far down on the list of things I need out of our relationship."

A silence followed this (pick pick, each pick seemingly closer to excising some foreign object or dull-cornered sin), until Sélène nodded and said, "But it is there."

"Yeah. It is there." Aiden shifted on the couch, to face Sélène more directly (pick pick pick, each dig of her claws sending a bright spark of pain into her wrist). "And we agreed that you liked Malina for different reasons than me, and that you still loved me. And I know it's not a race, but I feel left behind all the same."

The last of Aiden's words came out in a rush, and Sélène could, through a haze of fear, see his muzzle drop after he finished. The conversation seemed to be taking a toll on him. "I'm sorry, Aiden–" (pick pick, pick pick, almost there, almost to tearing loose whatever was under her skin, whatever taint of evil) "I love you so much, and...and–"

"Sweetheart– oh jeez, hold on." Aiden scrambled up from the couch and dashed off to the kitchen.

Sélène sniffled, unable to see through the tears, but she heard Aiden trot back and felt the coarse texture of a paper towel press to her wrist.

"No. Hold still, Sélène," Aiden mumbled, tightening his grip as she tried to tug her paw back. "Here, wipe your other paw here–" he guided her paw to one bit of towel then handed her a separate one. "–and then you can wipe your face with this one."

Sélène struggled to follow the directions, some remote part of her confused as to the sudden halt in the conversation. She fumbled with a bit of paper towel Aiden put in her paw, lifting it to wipe at her eyes and nose.

"Oh, uh...shit." She whined quietly, more tears immediately filling her eyes. "I'm sorry, Aiden, I didn't mean...I mean, are you alright?"

Aiden folded his long legs and sat cross-legged before her, pressing a paper towel, wet with blood, to the spot on Sélène's wrist. "Hush, love, I'm alright. I know you didn't mean to."

She held the paper towel to her face and stifled a sob, struggled to keep from totally breaking down. "Im-important c-conversation and here I am making a mess."

Aiden laughed. "It's okay, sweetheart. Really. Lemme look."

She wiped her face again as Aiden dabbed at the stinging spot on her wrist before peeking under the paper towel. "Oh, that's not as bad as it looked. Must've just nicked something."

Sélène struggled to smile at her husband. "I'm sorry. Are you alright, Aiden?"

"Mmhm, I'm alright."

"I'm sorry." Sélène pawed at her face again with the paper towel. She had been picking on her right paw, too—she felt clumsy and awkward using the towel with her left. "I promise I'm not, uh...not trying to beg off or- or turn this into a pity party."

Aiden laughed. "I know, sweetheart."

"I, uh...are you sure you're alright?"

"I am." Aiden leaned forward and brushed his cheek over her wrist, paper towel and all. "Kiss to make it better."

It was Sélène's turn to laugh, though it sounded strangled to her ears.

"I'm sorry things got stressful there, but-" He shrugged. "I don't know. I love you, Sélène, and I trust you through all this. I just got a bit upset, I suppose, because it felt like I wasn't getting all of you."

Sélène nodded. "I'm sorry, Aiden. If you want, we can try and do more."

Aiden tilted his head. "I won't say no to that, of course, but I don't want to push you. I know sex can make you feel gross."

Wiping at her face, Sélène was a little surprised that she'd managed stopped crying. "Yeah, I'm sorry," she mumbled. "We can maybe work on that, though."

"I'd like that, sweetheart." The fox bowed his head for a moment. "Though I was also wondering if you had thoughts on if I branched out some, myself."

Sélène sat up straighter, turning over the idea in her mind. She knew she could not, in any circumstances, get by without Aiden. And yet she made a less than ideal partner in so many ways. Now, however, she was also getting help from Malina, so maybe she wouldn't need to lean so heavily on her husband for support. It only made sense.

It only made sense, that is, except for all of the ways it ground up against her problems with relationship-rightness.

For Aiden to be not getting all he needed from her made her feel like a failure. It was a horrific condemnation, and she could barely consider the full idea in her mind, only peek at it sidelong.

It made her feel monstrous and demanding, that she should seek love and support, and yet feel so bad letting Aiden do the same.

"Love?"

Sélène snapped to and shook her head to clear it. "Sorry, Aiden. Are you...uh, I mean, sorry." She closed her eyes and forced herself to collect her thoughts. "What were you thinking?"

Aiden shrugged and peeked under the makeshift bandage. What he saw must have looked alright, as he nodded and wadded up the paper towel. "I didn't have anything particularly in mind."

Sélène looked down at her wrist. It didn't look bad at all, but she'd need to wash and bandage it proper, so she wouldn't pick the scab, as she knew she would.

"Only, I've been talking with my coworker–"

"Aaron?" Sélène blinked in surprise.

"Mmhm. He's the one I go get lunch with some days. I've been talking with him, and he says he and his wife do okay...er, playing around with others to get what they need, and it got me thinking, is all."

Confused as she was, Sélène had to smile. A bashful Aiden was a rare sight.

"I guess that's what I was thinking of. You mean the world to me, sweetheart, and I don't think I could manage a–" He broke off, swallowed and shook his head. "Another relationship. I'm happy for you and Malina, but I don't think I could do the same."

This was a whole new take on it, then. Sélène struggled to make that fit in her picture of things, to see how life would be. Her and Aiden. Her and Malina. Aiden without anyone, but...something. But having sex with friends? Swinging?

She laughed, and Aiden tilted his ears back. "I'm sorry, Aiden. I just remembered the term 'swinger' and laughed, is all."

Aiden looked confused, then broke out in a grin. "It is pretty ridiculous."

"Is that sort of what you were thinking?"

He nodded. "Not a relationship, but...uh..."

"Sex?" Sélène immediately shook her head. "That sounds bad, sorry. Um...sexual fulfillment?"

Aiden nodded again, more emphatically. "Yes! That's a good way to put it."

Sélène shrugged and smiled. "I can go along with that, I think. Maybe something to try out, like us trying with me and Malina?"

"I suppose, yeah." He frowned. "Would you still be willing to work on our own sex life, too?"

"I would, yeah."

"I would really like that, sweetheart. The playing around thing is one thing, but I don't really want to use it to...I don't know. I don't want to use it instead of fixing our relationship"

Sélène winced and nodded. "I really am sorry, Aiden. I didn't mean to. I didn't mean to hurt you."

Aiden slipped his paws up into Sélène's. "I know you didn't, sweetheart. You're right that it did– that it does hurt, but I'm still not totally sure why. Maybe I just accepted things intellectually without understanding them. It's hard, Sélène."

Clutching at her husband's paws helped keep Sélène from picking, so she held on, even if she felt a little gross with what blood was left in her fur. "Hurting you is the last thing I want, Aiden."

"I know, love. I trust you fully, in that." He gave a lopsided grin and added, "I'm not actually sure you'd be *able* to lie or hurt me intentionally."

Sélène giggled and shook her head, "I have my tells, don't I?"

"Mmhm."

"So," she sighed. "I want to try and make things better. And I don't want to hurt you again."

Aiden nodded. "And I want to see you happy, too. I don't want you to stop seeing Malina or anything. I just–" He toyed with her fingers for a moment before apparently finding the right words. "I need to make this work in my head that you and Malina are more compatible than you and I, in some ways."

Sélène splayed her ears. It wasn't really something she could argue against. Whether or not the sex had been a fluke, it was true on a very base level. If Aiden was her rock, the steadying force in her life that kept her going, Malina seemed to be her blanket, her pillow, her means to relax and rest from too much energy.

"What should I do?"

Her husband frowned, looking down to her paws rather than up to her face. "That's a hard one, Sélène. I don't think either of us can make long term decisions with what little we know, now."

She nodded and squeezed his fingers in hers.

When he did finally look up to her, the pain and anxiety in his face startled her. "Can you give me some time though, sweetheart? It may not be fair of me to ask, but can you and Malina at least hold off on sex for a little bit? I'm trying, I'm–"

Unable to respond, Sélène slid off the couch and down onto her knees in front of where Aiden was sat on the floor. She tugged his paws toward her and guided his arms around her shoulders, before leaning in to hug around him in turn. The position was awkward and she felt surprisingly stiff from all the stress, but she wanted—needed to be closer.

Aiden seemed to need the closeness as much as she did, as the hug he gave her was tight and shaky.

It took what felt like several minutes before Sélène was able to speak, and then only hoarsely. "Oh, Aiden, of course, of course."

Loosening his grip, Aiden rubbed his cheek against Sélène's firmly. "I love you so much, sweetheart, and I want to be fair. I'm just having a hard time, is all."

Sélène nodded, adding another cheek-rub as she did so. "Do you want me to call things off with Malina?"

Aiden leaned back from the hug, letting Sélène sit back on the floor as well, though he kept her paws in his. "No, sweetheart. Not at all. Just slow down a bit, for me. Let me get used to this."

"Of course," she murmured. "The last thing I want to do is to hurt you."

"I know, love." He lifted her paws and brushed his cheek against them, then seemed to remember the wound on her wrist and smiled apologetically. "Sorry. Are you alright?"

"S'my line," she giggled. "It's alright. It stings, but isn't bad." She paused, then picked up the thread again. "Still, do you want me to hold off on any more dates with her for a while, too? Would that help any?"

Aiden shook his head. "No, that's alright. In fact, more would probably be better, so I can get used to things faster. Call it exposure therapy."

He looked exhausted. *She* was exhausted. Work, a date, sex, an argument, blood, love. Sélène felt like she lived in a soap opera. She winced as she struggled to stand, helping Aiden up shortly after. Then it was time for a proper hug, with no leaning forward or awkward angles. Aiden really was her pillar, her anchor.

"Malina wanted to meet up Friday or Saturday, would you like me to cancel?"

Aiden was quiet for a few seconds, then he smiled and brushed his cheek against hers in another soft kiss. "Do you think she'd be willing to have dinner over here?"

"The three of us?"

Aiden smiled and nodded. "The three of us."

"Are you sure?"

"I'd like that."

Acknowledgements

As with any written work, there are many to thank who helped along the way. Thanks to Rob Baird for the boundless optimism and flattering words, as well as the inspiration from his Cannon Shoals stories; to Zeta for all her heart; and to JC and Robin for their help on reading and editing. Thanks, also, to Thurston Howl Publications, Sofawolf Press, and Red Ferret Press for working with me on three of these stories. Thank you, of course, to the advance readers for their kind words.

And thanks, of course, to the polycule. Just as each story here explores a different theme meaningful to me, each of you fills a different role in my life and make me all the more complete.

The Fool — Copyright © 2017 Madison Scott-Clary
The Fool originally appeared as *The First Step* in *Arcana — A Tarot Anthology* edited by Madison Scott-Clary and published by Thurston Howl Publications.

Disappearance — Copyright © 2017 Madison Scott-Clary
Disappearance appeared in *Hot Dish Vol. 3* published by Sofawolf Press.

Fisher — Copyright © 2019 Madison Scott-Clary

Centerpiece — Copyright © 2016 Madison Scott-Clary
Centerpiece appeared in *Knotted — A BDSM Anthology Vol. 2* published by Red Ferret Press

You're Gone — Copyright © 2018 Madison Scott-Clary

Overclassification — Copyright © 2017 Madison Scott-Clary

Acts of intent — Copyright © 2017 Madison Scott-Clary

Every Angel is Terrifying — Copyright © 2019 Madison Scott-Clary

What Remains of Yourself — Copyright © 2017 Madison Scott-Clary

A Theory of Attachment — Copyright © 2017 Madison Scott-Clary

Madison Scott-Clary is a transgender writer, editor, and software engineer. She focuses on furry fiction and non-fiction, using that as a framework for exploring across genres. She has edited and written for [adjective][species] since 2011, and edited *Arcana: A Tarot Anthology* for Thurston Howl Publications in 2017. She is the editor-in-chief of Hybrid Ink, LLC, a small publisher focused on thoughtful fiction, exploratory poetry, and creative non-fiction. She lives in the Pacific Northwest with her cat and two dogs, as well as her husband, who is also a dog.

www.makyo.ink
www.hybrid.ink

CPSIA information can be obtained
at www.ICGtesting.com
Printed in the USA
FFHW010827111119
56023896-61936FF

9 781948 743099